Strawberry Mansion:

A Philadelphia Story

Strawberry Mansion:

A Philadelphia Story

Julia Press Simmons

www.urbanbooks.net

Urban Books, LLC
300 Farmingdale Road, N.Y.-Route 109
Farmingdale, NY 11735

Strawberry Mansion: A Philadelphia Story

ISBN 13: 978-1-64556-425-6
ISBN 10: 1-64556-425-8

First Trade Paperback Printing April 2023
Printed in the United States of America

10 9 8 7 6 5 4 3 2 1

*This is a work of fiction. Any references or similarities
to actual events, real people, living or dead, or to real
locales are intended to give the novel a sense of reality.
Any similarity in other names, characters, places, and
incidents is entirely coincidental.*

Distributed by Kensington Publishing Corp.
Submit Orders to:
Customer Service
400 Hahn Road
Westminster, MD 21157-4627
Phone: 1-800-733-3000
Fax: 1-800-659-2436

Strawberry Mansion:

A Philadelphia Story

by

Julia Press Simmons

Chapter 1

Tabitha

Tabitha lost her mind on a sunny Wednesday in May.

She was cooking breakfast, nothing special. Eric didn't like special. He liked bacon and eggs, toast and coffee—black. The salty and sultry scent of the bacon wafted through the air as her 3-year-old daughter, Erica, made a mess of her bedroom. Tabitha smiled at the thought of her daughter gleefully pulling out every toy she owned. Then her smile faded. She hoped Erica didn't make a big enough mess to spike her father's temper.

Tabitha sighed and wiped the sweat off her brow with the back of her hand. Walking to the back door, she cracked it open, hoping to let in a little air and a little heat out, but there was no breeze. The air outside was just as hot and thick as the air in the kitchen. "Summer's coming in hot and early," she mumbled as she picked up a piece of bacon and started to nibble. She resisted the urge to peek into the living room to see if Eric was still out there reading the paper and, instead, focused on the kitchen, making sure that everything was in its proper place before serving.

As Tabitha set the table, Erica ran into the kitchen dressed in a Cinderella Halloween costume she refused to take off at home. She'd been obsessed with Cinderella ever since her grandmother bought her the costume and videotape last October. Tabitha looked at the tattered gown and shook her head. "Mom said you would be over Cinderella by Christmas, and now it's almost June."

Erica twirled in the dress and then went into the cabinets near the stove, with her eyes on the pots and pans.

"Oh no, you don't, little girl." Tabitha pulled Erica out of the cabinets by her leg. "You know you can't bang on those pans when Daddy's here."

"But Daddy's leaving, Mama."

"He's not going anywhere, little girl." She smiled as she smoothed Erica's hair, which was quickly becoming little more than an Afro with barrettes.

"Uh-huh, Mama. He's putting on his coat." Erica pouted and skipped back into the living room.

Not again, she thought. Tabitha checked her watch. It was barely six o'clock, and he had Wednesdays off. She placed the dishes on the counter and followed Erica into the living room. *He hasn't been home for a whole week, and now he's leaving again?*

"Daddy, Daddy," Erica yelled as she ran up to Eric, pulling on his coattails. "If you're going to the store, Daddy, can you get me some potato chips, please, please, pretty please?"

"I'm not going to the store, baby girl," he said. He smiled down at her with his warm chestnut eyes. "What have you done to your hair? Your aunt Shanice fixed it so pretty yesterday." He touched one of her unruly ponytails and smiled again. "You better go clean your room before your mother has a fit." He swatted her bottom, and she ran into her room with a little yelp.

Tabitha took a deep breath and put on a big smile. She quickly scanned the room, making sure nothing was out of place. The last thing she wanted to do was make him mad. Satisfied with the house, she smoothed her hands down the length of her ratty old nightgown. She was suddenly too conscious of her appearance. Memories of him laughing about her with his friends sprang to mind. He said she was 19 years old, growing on 60, and had the sex appeal of a grandma in a nursing home. Tabitha wanted to dress up for him, but she didn't own any sexy clothes, and she was always so tired from chasing Erica around and keeping the house up the way he liked.

She fidgeted with her nightgown. *You could have made a little effort. Now look; he's leaving again,* she thought, *and when he goes, you have no idea when he'll return.*

"Where're you going, baby?"

"Out," he said, shifting the magazines around on the coffee table. "Tab, you seen my keys?"

"No," she lied, knowing she had hidden them the night before. She took another deep breath, walked up to him, and tried again. "Where are you going, baby?"

He rolled his eyes. "I said I'm going out. Are you fucking deaf?" He patted his shirt and pants pockets. "Where in the hell did I put my keys?" Eric passed by Tabitha to look on top of the dining room table. He gave off a whiff of alcohol.

The smell melted into Tabitha, almost intoxicating her. *Damn,* she thought. *I should have hidden that case of beer too.* Malt liquor brought out the demon in Eric. He could be reasoned with when he wasn't drinking, but after a few beers, you were better off dealing with the devil.

How did I get here? she thought, fear vibrating through her body. Whenever she was out, she noticed other people her age laughing and joking without a care in the world. They wore the latest fashions, and their hair was cut in the latest styles. She didn't know what it was like to live life as a 19-year-old. She became a mother at 16. She had no clue how to be a teenager at all. Her best friends,

Lisa and Shanice, still got to go to school and school dances. She never even got to go to her prom. Her mom made sure she received her GED, but it wasn't the same as experiencing a graduation ceremony. She didn't like school when she attended and never really participated in school functions, but that was before Eric put her in prison. Before she could snap her fingers or blink her eyes, she went from a high school student to a mother/fake housewife with a man who made every step she took a nervous one.

She saw her reflection in the mirror and quickly removed the scarf from her head. She knew Eric wasn't fond of headscarves, but she was self-conscious about her new haircut. Not everyone could look like Toni Braxton, but Eric wanted the haircut, and Tabitha would do anything to keep him happy—anything. *I don't even look like a teenager,* she thought, glancing at the mirror again and taking in the dull sadness and fear in her eyes. She didn't look old. Her smooth brown skin was tight and wrinkle-free, but she didn't look young either, and she never looked happy. *Walk lightly, Tabitha. Be easy. Don't make him mad.* She watched Eric warily as he stomped around their tiny apartment, looking for his keys.

Clearing her throat, Tabitha said, "Well, duh, I can see that you're going out. It doesn't take a rocket scientist to see that."

Eric ignored her and started digging between the couch cushions for his car keys.

She pulled playfully on his coattails, but she wasn't graced with a good-natured response, not even a smile. Eric's face crumpled into something demonic. The change in his mood was so sudden Tabitha didn't have time to react. Eric stood to his full height and punched her with such force that she flew back into the entertainment center. She crashed into the lamp and fell to the floor.

Eric's warm brown eyes turned black with rage as he repeatedly kicked her in the gut.

Tabitha's world erupted in pain. *No, oh God, no. I'm so sorry.* Fear kept her mouth closed tight.

Erica appeared in her doorway, screaming. Her eyes were wide and frightened. "Are you OK, Mama?"

It hurt Tabitha to breathe. "I'm OK, baby. Go back to your room."

Erica didn't budge. She just stood there and broke into tears.

"Go to your room!" Eric shouted. The child disappeared behind her door as Tabitha lay on the floor, surrounded by broken glass. Eric towered over her. "Look at you, you fat, ugly bitch. Who would want to stay here with you?" he laughed. He hocked spit into Tabitha's face and turned his back on her.

The world tilted. His laughter echoed through Tabitha's mind, transforming her fear into a wild rage. Something inside of her snapped. She looked at him and no longer saw the man she loved. Instead, she saw a monster who hurt her; all she wanted to do was end the pain. With a growl, she grabbed a shard of the broken lamp and lunged at him. She tripped over Erica's toy and missed her target—his stomach—but slashed a deep cut into his thigh.

Eric grabbed his leg and fell back onto the sofa. "What the fuck is the matter with you? Are you fucking nuts?"

He didn't look so sure of himself anymore. Tabitha stood over him, clutching the broken glass so tightly that it ripped into her hand. Blood soaked through his jeans and started to pool on the floor.

"Oh my God, oh my God, look at my leg, Tab. What the fuck is wrong with you? Put the glass down, Tab. Baby, just put the glass down."

She could not believe that he was afraid. She took a step toward him, threatening him with the shard of glass. He scrambled to get away from her, his blood soaking the sofa.

Tabitha took another swipe at him and laughed as he recoiled. She feared this man more than anything in the world. He beat her so severely and so regularly that fear was her constant companion. She believed him when he said he would kill her, but at this moment, she wasn't afraid—*he* was, and she found that hilarious.

She threw the broken lamp onto his lap and laughed again. The sound, nearly as demonic as Eric's actions, felt foreign yet calming to Tabitha—and she couldn't stop laughing if she wanted to. She laughed as she stuffed all she could inside Erica's Barbie book bag. She laughed as she picked up a wailing Erica and headed for the door. She laughed when he asked where *she* was going. Tabitha laughed while she and Erica walked ten blocks to her mama's house. Even as Erica walked alongside her and tugged her gown, asking, "Momma, are you OK? Momma, you're bleeding!" Tabitha laughed.

She had an exhausted Erica in her arms when she reached her mother's home. But Tabitha wasn't exhausted in the least. A fire raged inside her, something that licked along the goodness she tried to exude. When her mom opened the door, Tabitha laughed at the startled look on her face.

"Tabitha," her mother yelled, nearly hysterical, "what happened?" She grabbed Erica from her arms and ran her hand over every part of her granddaughter. "All this," she motioned her hands over the blood on both Erica and Tabitha, "all this is *yours?*"

Instead of responding, Tabitha continued laughing while she stepped inside the home, walked up the steps, and entered the room of her childhood.

It was then she saw her reflection in the mirror on the far wall. She didn't feel afraid, but there was still fear and deep sadness in her eyes. Her lips trembled, and then her eyes fell to the blood on her gown. She gagged, quickly ripped the nightgown over her head, and chucked it into the corner. She stared at the scattered scrapes and bruises on her body, hugged herself, and wept.

Lisa

Always, in the beginning, Lisa was aware of the dream. Her stomach flopped. A tight coil of fear wrapped itself around her heart. But the feeling of awareness vanished almost as quickly as it formed. She was consumed by the dream. She was imprisoned by the dream.

"There's never anything good on." Turning down the sound, she flipped through the channels at warp speed. Her son's cries cut through the air like a siren.

"That boy has a nice set of pipes." She smiled, stretched, and then headed to the kitchen to get him something to eat.

No bottles in the fridge. "That's funny," she mumbled to herself. "I know I put his formula in there." She checked the cabinets above the sink and the stove. No bottles. The baby's cries became more insistent.

"It's OK, li'l man. Mama's coming. Where in the blazes is his formula?" She chewed on her bottom lip and then bent over to look under the kitchen sink.

The baby belted out a piercing scream—then silence. She whirled around. Her head spun. Her mouth went dry, and goose bumps dotted her skin while the soft, delicate baby hair rose on the nape of her neck. She froze for a few seconds, listening for the slightest whimper from her child.

She heard nothing.

"My baby," she whispered. The silence was so loud. "My baby," she screamed. She took the stairs two at a time. A million thoughts raced through her head.

"My baby, my God, my baby. Please, please, let him be okay." She ran down the hall to her bedroom and paused when she came to the door. Lisa could not make herself go inside the room. His little crib was so very still.

Panic took her, making her move when fear tried to root her to the doorway. She walked toward the crib like a machine instead of a terrified young mother.

The crib was empty. "Jesus." She tore away the blankets. "My baby is gone." Her heart refused to believe it. She threw the stuffed bears out of the crib and flipped the mattress over as if her baby lay beneath it. Lisa stooped to check under the crib.

And then she froze.

She knew he was there before she heard him because she had to choke down the bile that rose in her throat whenever she was in her stepfather's presence. He smelled of cheap cologne and even cheaper cigars.

"Lisa, what in the hell are you doing down there?" he asked in that horrible singsong Southern voice.

"I'm looking for my baby." Her voice shook, but she willed it to be stronger. "He was crying." She grabbed his teddy bear and clutched it to her breast, breathing in the fresh and clean newborn scent. "Then he just stopped and—"

"Aaaand?" He interrupted in that country drawl that she hated. "Well, of course, he stopped crying, sugar. He's with his daddy!"

Lisa awoke in a tangle of sheets, slicked with sweat. Her alarm clock buzzed angrily on the nightstand beside the bed. She picked it up and kissed it lovingly before she hit the snooze button and put it back down.

"You never kiss me like that."

Lisa nearly jumped out of her skin. "Damn, Tony, you scared the hell out of me." He was sitting in the corner of her bedroom, smoking a cigarette. The smell of the Newport reminded her of her stepfather's cigar, and she had to swallow hard to keep from throwing up.

"You look like the hell was already scared out of you. Were you having that dream again?"

She snorted and sat up on the side of the bed. "It's more like a recurring nightmare."

"You want to tell me about it?"

"No. You want to tell me what you're doing here?"

He wiggled his eyebrows suggestively. "I was hoping to get lucky."

She laughed despite herself. "I guess this *is* your lucky day." She stretched, arching her back provocatively, and her thick black braids brushed against the small of her back with the motion. She looked over at him and sighed. The concern that she saw in his eyes tore at her heart. She tried to move further away from her dreams and focus her attention entirely on Tony, who looked so handsome in his gray warm-up suit. Then to sway him from the conversation of her dreams and to remove the concern from his eyes, she stood in front of him and said, "You could join me in the shower, you know." She left him standing there, sputtering, while she walked to the bathroom.

Letting her nightshirt fall in a heap in front of the sink, she looked in the mirror. She thought death itself was staring back at her instead of her reflection. Her skin was pasty and pale. Her eyes held deep, dark circles under puffy, swollen bags.

No 17-year-old girl should look so old, tired, and defeated, she thought. *Girl, you must have big, brassy balls to invite someone to shower with you when you look like a troll monster.*

Yawning, she grimaced at the smell of her morning breath, grabbed the mouthwash off the sink, and took a hefty swig.

Turning the shower on to hell, she grabbed her strawberry body wash and loofah, then rinsed her mouth before stepping into the spray. The hot water needled her skin. She clenched her teeth against the pain, stuck her head directly under the nozzle, and prayed that the hot water would burn away the aftereffects of her dream.

As always, thoughts of her stepfather left Lisa feeling filthy. Squeezing her eyes shut against the memory of his hands on her, she soaped up the loofah and began to scrub herself with a vengeance.

I can still smell him. She choked down the bile in her throat, envisioning his hand sliding up her thighs, his hot breath on her neck, and that country twang in her ears. She scrubbed furiously until she finally began to feel clean. Finally, she leaned against the shower wall, taking deep, rapid breaths.

Wrapping her hands around the base of her stomach, she allowed herself one shuddering sob for the child who once lived there. "I'm sorry, baby."

She didn't hear the shower door open.

"Lisa, baby," Tony whispered as he entered the shower. Seeing her standing there naked and soapy under the spray had him instantly erect. "Damn, you're beautiful," he crooned. Tony ran his hand up Lisa's arm and gently cupped her left breast.

"No!" She turned and swung wildly. Her right fist connected with his jaw with a loud crack. He took the punch with a grunt and barely had time to recover before she swung at him again.

"Don't fucking touch me, you pervert. Don't ever put your hands on me!"

"Lisa, stop. Damn." His head collided with the soap dish while trying to avoid a mean left swing. "Are you fucking serious? You *asked* me to shower with you, *remember?*" He tried to get his arms around her, but she was slick with soap. "Lisa, what is *wrong* with you?" He blocked a knee to the groin and managed to get a grip on her, but she was trembling with fury.

"Look at me," he yelled.

She kept her eyes closed as she struggled to get free.

"Damn it, Lisa; look at me." She could tell he was trying to keep his voice calm. "You *invited* me in the shower with you," he said slowly. He took a deep breath to settle himself. "Lisa," he said quietly, "look at me."

She opened her eyes slowly, realizing it was Tony, not her stepfather, who held her. She lowered her head and closed her eyes. Humiliation covered her as entirely as the water did. Sobs wracked her body as he gathered her close and whispered soothing words into her hair. She clung to him despite her initial embarrassment. He was strong and clean and *not* her stepfather.

The erection that was forgotten after her first punch landed started to rear its ugly head. *No,* Tony thought. He lifted Lisa higher so she wouldn't feel it. She was wet and clinging to him, and though his body was eager, he knew that sex was the last thing she needed right now. He sighed and stepped out of the shower. No matter how much he wanted to bury himself inside her, he knew he needed to be patient with her.

She stood still as he grabbed a towel and wrapped it around her. She said nothing as he lifted her from the shower and carried her to bed. Her thick wet braids slapped against his side. He took her towel off and tried to dry her braids before tucking her into the tangled sheets. Then he started back to the bathroom to get his clothes, but she grabbed his arm and clung to it as if her life depended on it. With another huge sigh, Tony slid into the bed beside her, doing his best to ignore that they were both still naked. He rocked her to sleep, praying that whatever chased her in her dreams would leave her be and let her rest.

Shanice

Chemistry blows royally.
Shanice sat at her favorite spot in the back of the class and lazily twirled bubble gum around her finger, ignoring Dr. Pitman's lecture. She hated her advanced classes. She was 14 years old in a sea of 16- and 17-year-old kids who ignored her. So she busied herself by staring out the window and daydreaming about what she would get into when she got home. The only thing good about advanced chemistry was the location. It was on the fourth floor on the northwest corner of the school, and she could see the rooftops of the row homes against a clear blue sky. From that vantage point, she could imagine she were anywhere looking out at any city in the U. S. of A. Shanice was currently imagining herself in downtown Miami.

Dr. Pitman struck his desk with his yardstick and snapped her back to reality.

Fat pig, Shanice thought. *Your butt is way too big to walk around and teach. Hell, it was probably molded to that damn swivel chair.* She had to laugh at the thought, which brought his beady little eyes zeroing in on her.

"Am I amusing you, Miss Thomas?" he asked, pushing his glasses up from the tip of his nose.

I can't believe he asked me that. Is he serious? He couldn't be, standing there looking like a walking egg with suspenders and bifocals. Yes, you certainly are *amusing me.*

"No, sir," Shanice responded. Then with perfect posture and a mock salute, she said, "I find your lectures to be utterly fascinating and intellectually stimulating."

"Utterly fascinating and intellectually stimulating? I see." Pitman smirked and sat back in his chair, which began to squeak as if it were crying for mercy. He took off his glasses, placed them on his desk, and folded his hands atop his ample belly. "Which part?"

"Which part of what?"

"Which part of my lecture did you find utterly fascinating?"

"Oh, you know, the shit about hydrogen and oxygen making water."

The class erupted in laughter just as the bell rang.

Saved by the bell.

She stuck her gum under her desk and picked up her book bag from the floor. She had a third-period date with Tonya's boyfriend, Troy, who was captain of the football team. Shanice shuffled to the doorway as fast as she could without knocking anyone over.

Dr. Pitman cleared his throat. "Oh, Miss Thomas."

Damn. She rolled her eyes and stood still while the rest of her class filed out around her.

"I would like a word with you, young lady."

She sucked her teeth and trudged toward his desk. "Look, I'm sorry for cursing, Dr. Pitman. It just slipped out."

"You know very well that I don't appreciate that type of language in my classroom. However, that is not what I wish to speak with you about."

He put on his glasses again and pulled his grade book from the desk drawer. He made a big to-do about reviewing her grades before bringing his beady eyes back up to hers.

"You are failing miserably, young lady." He leaned back in his chair and shook his head sadly. "I don't understand you, Shanice. You have an inquisitive and engaging mind. Why, just last year, you were an honor student at the top of the class."

Shanice's back stiffened. Her fingers tightened on her notebook, and her eyes narrowed. "Well, this is a whole new year, isn't it?" She didn't need a reminder of how good a student she used to be. Nothing was like it used to be. She was a good student because her mom was a good mom. Her mom used to help her and care about how well she did. Now, all her mom cared about was church, Jesus, and the Bible. Shanice wasn't part of the Holy Trinity, so how she did in school really didn't matter. *I don't really matter,* she thought bitterly.

He sighed and began to scribble on his notepad. Shanice rolled her eyes and stared at the clock. *Troy is going to be pissed.*

"I'm going to give you ten demerits for your behavior in my classroom."

The flash of anger was gone as quickly as it appeared. It was replaced by sulky teenage angst. "Aw, man . . . Dr. Pitman. That'll get me detention for a whole week."

"I know, and I think that is more than enough time to improve your attitude."

Shanice lingered in the hall until the last student disappeared. Then she made a beeline toward the girls' bathroom. Troy was staring out the window with his back stiff and arms crossed. He wore a red and gray UNLV T-shirt with black jeans and the new black high-top Fila sneakers, which cost about $150. One look at his tall, lean frame and broad shoulders, and she forgot all about detention and Dr. Pitman's judgmental, beady eyes.

The boy definitely has style. Damn. He's also definitely pissed—and definitely sexy. "Are you waiting for me, Troy?"

At that moment, his shoulders relaxed, but he did not respond or turn to face her.

"You're mad, aren't you?" she asked as she checked herself in the mirror. She wore a red baby T-shirt; a red-and-green plaid, pleated skirt; white thigh-high stockings; and black patent leather Mary Janes. She worked that schoolgirl fantasy to the fullest.

Digging into her book bag, she pulled out her vanilla body spray and spritzed herself generously. She wanted his stupid girlfriend to know who he was cutting class with. "It's OK to be mad at me, Troy. I am very late, and that's very inconsiderate."

She glanced at Troy from the corner of her eye, but he hadn't budged. He just stared out the window.

Shanice pulled her Pizzazz lip gloss out of her purse. She wanted her already pink and pouty lips to shine. Then she leaned into the mirror to check her cinnamon skin for blemishes. Reassured that not one pimple lurked, she let down her ponytail, so her thick, dark curls brushed her shoulders. After that, she leaned close to the mirror and wiped the smudge of mascara from under her eye, and Dr. Pitman's words returned to haunt her. *"You used to be an honor student . . ."* A memory of her mother's excited dance when she made the Dean's List for the first time popped into her head. *Ancient history,* she thought and swallowed the lump of resentment and regret that rose in her throat.

Her cell phone vibrated on her hip. Irritated by the interruption, she turned it off and hooked it to the top of her T-shirt. Then she shimmied out of her skirt and panties and faced Troy.

"So, you're not going to talk to me? You could at least look at me."

He turned slowly, and his eyes bulged out of his head. His angry scowl quickly turned into a lusty smirk after seeing her naked from the waist down.

Shanice sauntered up to him and placed her hands on his chest. She looked up at him from under her lashes and said, "I've been a bad girl, Troy, and I should be punished."

Mabel took her grandbaby up to her bedroom. She sat her on the bed and pulled a few plush toys out that Erica liked to bathe with. Her heart broke at the sadness on her little face.

"How about we get washed up, dressed, and have some of Grandma's special pancakes? Would you like that?"

Erica looked up at her grandmother with a small smile and nodded.

"Oh, we can agree better than that." Mabel swooped her granddaughter up in her arms and nuzzled her neck with sloppy kisses. She tickled her and bounced her up and down until the room filled with her squeals and laughter. Then she plopped her down on the bed and picked up her feet. "Maybe I should just cut these little feet off, and we can eat baby toes for breakfast," she said, tickling her feet.

"No, I want pancakes," Erica giggled, trying to free her feet.

Mabel bent over the bed. "You sure? These toes look mighty tasty."

"Pancakes, pancakes, pancakes," Erica shouted with laughter.

Mabel smiled at her granddaughter. "Okay, baby, pancakes it is." She turned on the TV and put the Cinderella movie on the VCR. "You stay here and be a big girl while I get your bath started."

Mabel walked down the hall to Tabitha's old bedroom, took a deep breath, knocked softly, and walked in.

Tabitha was lying across the bed sobbing.

Mabel sat beside her and stroked her hair. "Are you hurt?"

Tabitha shook her head.

"Can you tell me what's going on?"

Tabitha just pressed her head into the pillow and continued to weep.

"Okay, baby," she said, stroking her head. "I'm going to get Erica cleaned up and make some breakfast. I want to help you, baby, but I need you to tell me what's happening." She sat beside Tabitha for a few moments waiting for a response.

Tabitha stopped crying but remained silent.

Mabel sighed, kissed her on the forehead, and then quietly left the room. Once in the hallway, she paused at the door. *You may not talk to me, but I know who you will talk to,* she thought as she walked into the bathroom and filled up the tub. *There's more than one way to skin a cat.*

Chapter 2

Tabitha sobbed for what seemed an eternity. She cried for nearly an hour, then was positively all cried out. Finally, she forced herself to get out of bed and walked to the dresser to find something to wear.

She sighed and brushed her hair down. *I'm never going to get used to this short haircut.* Slipping effortlessly into her old T-shirt, she took a deep breath and prepared to wage war on her very old, very small jeans.

Her mother poked her head into the room just as she was about to beat the evil jeans into submission. The tiny button at the top of her jeans screamed to be set free. "Good God," she said as she strained to get into the jeans.

"Tabitha Pauline Williams, you know better than to take the Lord's name in vain in my house."

Tabitha jumped, spun around, and stumbled into the dresser. "Mama, you scared me."

"You *need* to be scared. I thought you had lost your mind with all that hollering, screaming, and carrying on. So I came to see if you were okay and to let you know that Lisa was on the phone."

"Lisa called? How did she know I was here?"

Mable walked over to Tabitha, gently cupped her chin, and smiled sadly. Her voice and whole demeanor softened. "She didn't, child. I called her. I thought you could use someone to talk to, and I know you will not tell me what's going on with you."

Tabitha's heart sank at the look of sorrow in her mother's eyes. "Aww, Ma, I will tell you everything that's going on. Just not yet." Her mother's face glimmered with relief as Tabitha drew her into a hug.

"Well, OK, baby," she said as she returned her daughter's embrace with a heartfelt sigh. "All in due time." She hugged her daughter tighter for a few moments and then released her. "Now, don't have the poor girl on hold forever. Come on down and get the phone."

"I'll take the call in your room if that's all right with you."

"Sure, it's okay, baby. Go right ahead." Her mother cupped her face again and gave her a quick kiss on the cheek. "You know I love you, right?"

Tabitha smiled and nodded. No matter how grown it was of her to go off with Eric and have a baby, she still loved feeling like her mother's baby girl. "Yes, Mama, I know you love me. I love you too."

Tabitha was an only child and never really had much of a family. Her father was never home, and her mother was either in the streets looking for him or at church praying for him. Lisa and Shanice were the closest she would ever get to having sisters. They were her real family, or at least she wished they were. It always amazed her that the three of them had become hard, fast, forever friends. They were all so different, but they were solid, and if she couldn't depend on anybody else, she could always depend on them. Although Tabitha was two years her senior, Lisa seemed older and wiser, and she took every word Lisa uttered as if it came from on high. Shanice was the youngest, and all Tabitha could do was pray for that poor child. On the other hand, Lisa was everything Tabitha wished she had the courage to be. Despite their differences, Tabitha loved both girls fiercely.

"Hello," she said breathlessly, half from her mad dash to the phone and half from the relief of hearing Lisa's voice.

"You are so scandalous," Lisa's perky voice chimed through the receiver.

Tabitha shook her head in disbelief. "I am *not* scandalous. I have *never* done anything that would be considered a scandal."

Lisa laughed so hard that she nearly dropped the phone. "Yes, you are, girl. You are scandalous as hell, and I ain't mad at you at all."

"What's so scandalous about me, huh?"

"Well, first off, you finally got some backbone and left Eric's punk ass."

"What makes you so sure I left him?"

"Aw, come on, Tab. Why else would you be there with the munchkin? And Aunt Mabel told me that you two were there since the crack of dawn."

"Okay, Columbo, all up in my business. For your information, I *did* leave Eric."

"Attagirl, Tab. I knew you had some steel in you. Did you hit him before ya left?"

"No, I didn't hit him."

"Well, did you kick him in the nuts?" Lisa asked, hoping Tabitha sought out some form of revenge.

"No, girl. You are crazy. I did *not* kick him in the nuts."

"Well, what *did* you do to him before you left him, Tab? Bake his ass a cake? That would be just like you. You're too sweet for your own damn good. I can just see you sittin' in your living room all prim and proper."

Lisa cleared her throat and made her best Tabitha impression. "Oh, my dear Eric. I know you hit me, cheated on me, and made my life a living hell, but I love you. And although I will leave you, here is a cake to say goodbye."

Tabitha stifled a giggle. "Are you finished?"

"No, I'm not finished. Girl, if I were you—"

"But you're *not* me."

"Yeah, yeah, yeah. I know, but if I *were* you, I would have set his bed on fire—with him in it." Lisa laughed, but it took her a minute to realize that Tabitha wasn't laughing. "Tab? Tab, are you still there? Come on, Tab. You know I was just teasing you, girl. I was just trying to make you laugh, that's all. Are you OK?"

There was a long pause, and then Tabitha took a shuddering breath. "Lisa, I stabbed him."

"You did what?"

"I . . . I stabbed him."

"Are you shitting me?"

"No, I'm not. Lisa, I . . . I . . . I—"

"When, where, and what happened? Is he OK?"

"I don't know." Tabitha moaned as she squeezed her eyes against the tears. She promised herself she would not cry. *Not one more tear, Tabitha; not one more.* She tried to remember what exactly happened, but it was all a blur. All she could see when she thought about that fight was her laughing—and him bleeding.

Lisa called Tabitha's name repeatedly, but she didn't hear it.

"I'm okay, Lisa."

"Bullshit. I'm coming to get you."

"Don't you have to go to school?"

"Well, Tony has already made me late for school, and I don't have to work until three o'clock. Besides, I know exactly what you need."

"What do I need?"

"Shit, girl, we need to go on a shopping spree. It ain't every day that your best friend stabs somebody."

"You are crazy. You know that?"

"Whatever, girl. You know you love me. I'll be there in twenty minutes. Kiss, kiss," she said and abruptly hung up the phone. She didn't want to give Tabitha a chance to object.

As soon as Lisa ended the call with Tabitha, the laughter and smiles vanished.

Closing her eyes and massaging her temples, Lisa thought, *This has been one hell of a morning.* She leaned against her bedroom wall, eyes still closed, and sighed. *While I'm running from nightmares and trying to whoop Tony's ass, my homegirl is running from an actual living nightmare where she may have murdered a man. I mean, damn, you should be able to remember where you stabbed somebody. That seems like some memorable shit.*

Lisa smiled despite her fear. *I didn't think my girl had it in her.*

She opened her eyes and slowly glanced around her room, which was a mess in every sense of the word. She picked up clothes scattered across the floor but paused when she saw one of Tony's T-shirts. She picked it up, brought it to her nose, and inhaled its scent.

God, Tony, why do you have to be such a prick?

He had left in a huff an hour earlier. She'd woken up snugly in his arms: peaceful, rested, and feeling more than a little frisky. However, he was not feeling it. He insisted that they talk, which was cool, but he wanted to talk about things that Lisa had no desire to discuss. To talk about it was to relive it. It would bring back the pain of it, the filth of it. And what if he felt like her mother? What if he thought she deserved it and asked for it? She didn't know what to do with that kind of pain, so she told him to leave. He reluctantly complied, which left them both frustrated.

Well, there's no point in brooding over that. Tony will live, but Eric may not. My girl stabbed his ass. Ooooh, I wish I could have been there. I wish I could have seen his face when the rabbit had the gun. She frowned, feeling a little bad about being excited about another person's pain. Then she shook it off. Eric was a piece of shit, and getting stabbed was no more than what he deserved.

She walked toward the phone and took a deep breath. She hated the next call she had to make because she couldn't really care less about what happened to Eric. She hated him and all men like him. In her opinion, men who put their hands on women deserved whatever they got. However, she pushed those thoughts to the back of her mind. She needed to see how Eric was doing—for Tabitha's sake. So, she steeled her resolve and called the bastard.

"Hello, can I speak to Eric?"

"Yo, who is this?"

"It's Lisa, Tabitha's friend. Is Eric available?"

"Hold on, shawty. Aye, yo, Eric. Hey, come get the damn phone, dawg."

"Who is it?" Eric asked in the background.

"It's Lisa."

"Who?"

"I said, Lisa. Damn, dawg. Come get the phone."

By that time, Lisa had already hung up. She only called to see how much damage Tabitha had inflicted, and from the sound of it, whatever Tabitha had done wasn't nearly enough. "The nigga sounds all right to me." Lisa grabbed her keys and purse off the dresser and set out to discover what exactly went down.

Shanice was bent over in the small, smelly girls' bathroom stall, reading the names scrawled on the yellow cinder blocks above the toilet. *You really picked a winner this time,* she thought darkly. *You need to start thinking things through because this ain't it.* She braced herself as Troy thrust his pelvis into her hips.

"Ouch. What are you trying to do, Troy? Drill me a new hole?"

"Naw, baby, I'm sorry. Just hold still. I'm almost there." He tightened his grip on her waist and awkwardly rubbed himself against her. "I'm so sorry."

Like hell you are. "Uh, I've been holding still for the last ten minutes."

"You're so fucking pretty." He leaned over to give her a sloppy kiss on the cheek. "Just a little tight, that's all. I'll get in. Just give me a minute."

Troy took a firm hold of her hips, and Shanice sucked her teeth and returned to her study of the wall. She tried to ignore the fact that her legs were beginning to cramp, and the musty bathroom smell seemed to be getting stronger. Troy wasn't exactly the Casanova she had envisioned, and she'd grown tired of this little episode. Just as she was about to tell him as much, they heard the door to the bathroom open. She turned toward Troy to tell him to get off, but he slipped one hand around her waist and the other over her mouth.

Fuming, she contemplated biting his pudgy fingers but changed her mind when she heard the neighboring stall door open and close. Her heart pounded against her chest as sweat trickled down her brow. Then Troy suddenly shoved her against the toilet.

Her knee hit the white porcelain hard, and she bit her bottom lip to keep from screaming.

"Tonya," he called out to the face peering down on them from the adjacent stall.

"Surprise, surprise," Tonya sneered, showing off a gleaming set of big silver braces. She had a fresh set of microbraids pulled up so tightly in a bun that small red bumps dotted her hairline from the tension. Her eyes narrowed and darted back and forth between Troy and Shanice. "A little bird said I would find my ex-boyfriend and the class whore together in the girls' bathroom. And I'll be damned if that bird wasn't tweeting the truth."

"Tonya, baby, I'm sorry—"

"Shut the fuck up, Troy, you limp-dick motherfucker. I was gonna break up with you anyway. You know, I would really like to have sex with a dude who knows what he is doing before the year is out."

Shanice couldn't help but laugh, which turned Tonya's fury to her.

"I don't know what you're laughing at, bitch. Ain't shit funny about trying to fuck somebody's boyfriend in a dirty-ass bathroom. What's the matter, huh? You can't find your own man?"

Shanice bristled. "Oh, I got your bitch right here."

"Oh, really?" Tonya beamed. "Nothing would suit me better than stumping a mud hole in your nasty ass, but I don't fight in school. And seeing how I threw your skirt and panties out the window, I don't think you will be able to meet me outside."

"Fuck," Shanice hollered. Her heart thumped against her chest as she pushed past a dumbfounded Troy, only to look out the window and see her panties and skirt sprawled upon the pavement. She turned around, ready to commit cold-blooded murder, but Tonya and Troy had already exited. Shanice ran into the last stall, locked the door, and flopped down on the toilet seat.

"Shit! Shit! Shit!" Tucking in her feet, she tried to think of a way to get her ass out of this one. She threw her head back and stared blankly at the ceiling, praying for divine inspiration. Five minutes later, without a sign from God, she put her feet on the floor, resigned herself to the fact that she was defeated, and would have to peek into the hallway to call for help.

"You really are a dumb ass sometimes," she said, finally remembering her cell phone was clipped to her T-shirt. She knew that Lisa would come to her rescue.

Chapter 3

Lisa drove like a bat out of hell, and Tabitha's worries were almost forgotten by the time they hit Cheltenham Mall.

"Girl, girl, girl," Tabitha said, clutching her chest.

"What?"

Tabitha looked at her like she had lost her mind. "What do you mean, what? You know you ran that light, right?"

Lisa laughed. "What red light? I did no such thing."

Tabitha gripped the dashboard while Lisa turned the corner like she wanted to flip the car over. "Red means stop."

Lisa sighed. "This is why you don't have a driver's license, honey. Red only means to stop when there are other cars and cops around." She pulled into the parking complex and slid into the first available space.

"Whatever, Lisa," Tabitha said as she grabbed her purse and exited the car. "I'm hungry. I should have grabbed a sandwich before we left."

"Well, we're here now. Let's head over to the food court."

Tabitha frowned. "Food court? Please. I don't have any food-court money."

"Girl, don't worry about that. I got you."

"But you know I don't like handouts."

Lisa sighed. Her head was hurting, and she really didn't feel like having this argument again. All she wanted to do was have a good time with her friend. "It's not a handout, girl. It's a gift."

Lisa walked to the Great Wok Chinese and American Food Kiosk in the middle of the food court before Tab could try to talk her out of it. She knew Tabitha hated borrowing money, even if it was just to be treated to lunch, but they deserved a good time. *We deserve to go to the mall and get some food and buy some shit just like everyone else,* she thought. Her head began to pound as she walked up to the counter and squinted up at the menu. *We shouldn't have to fight off perverted stepfathers and drunk-ass boyfriends.*

Lisa looked over her shoulder and pointed up at the menu. "What do you want?" she asked between clenched teeth.

Tabitha rolled her eyes. "I told you that I don't—" She paused when she saw the look on Lisa's face. She could tell by the tightness around her mouth and her squinting eyes that she was in pain. "What's wrong?" Tabitha asked, grabbing her by the wrist.

Lisa snatched her hand away. "Uh, besides the fact that you won't tell me what the fuck you want to eat?"

"Naw, Lisa. Tell me what's *really* wrong with you."

Tabitha stared at Lisa in that penetrating way that could bug anyone out. Lisa took a step back, embarrassed by the sudden scrutiny.

"I'm okay, Tab."

"Yeah, right. Sure, you're okay."

"Yes, I'm fine. So quit it," Lisa said and turned toward the counter, hoping that would end the conversation.

"Uh-huh. You're fine, just like I'm fine. However, I stabbed my boyfriend, and you're having nightmares, aren't you?"

Lisa whirled back around to face her friend. "Okay, honey. You want to do this? Then let's do this." She caught Tabitha's arm in an iron grip and dragged her into the restroom, banging through the door and scaring the shit out of the old lady washing her hands. Lisa stopped dead in her tracks and threw her hands in the air in exasperation.

"What the fuck do you want to know, Tabitha? Or better yet, what do you *think* you know already? "

The lady at the sink took one look at Lisa and Tabitha and high-tailed it out of the bathroom.

"Why do you always have to press, Tab? I told you that I was fine."

Tabitha crossed her arms, leaned against the wall, and stared at her best friend. She noted the dark circles under Lisa's eyes that she tried to cover with foundation. She reasoned that a gallon of Visine would not fix her eyes. They were bloodshot red from hours of crying and restlessness. "When did the nightmares start again?" Tabitha asked softly.

"I'm not having nightmares."

They both stood in silence and stared at each other. Lisa broke first, hanging her head low and walking toward the mirrors. "God, is it that obvious?" she asked, checking her reflection. "The dreams started up again last week or so, but I feel like I haven't slept in a month."

Tabitha stayed silent, afraid that if she said anything, Lisa would stop talking.

"It's always the same, you know? Either I'm pregnant, and he's there, or I've already had the baby, and he's there. The scary thing is that he's always there. I can't escape him. How do you escape a fucking dream?" As Lisa began to reveal her tortured soul, her pager vibrated. She pulled it from her belt, grateful for the distraction.

"Is it your job? Lord knows they act like they can't run the place without you."

"No, it's a message. Do you have your mom's cell phone with you?"

"I left it at home."

"Well, shit. Come on, let's find a pay phone."

After several failed attempts, the pair found a working phone by McDonald's on the other end of the court. Lisa called her message service, and Tabitha gazed longingly at a man eating a Big Mac.

I seriously need to get a handle on my pride, Tabitha thought. *My stomach is touching my back, I'm so hungry. I am two minutes away from snatching the rest of that man's burger and making a run for it.*

Lisa burst out laughing. She hung up the phone and held her hand out for more coins.

"What's so funny?"

"Shanice . . . Shanice is in school."

"Okay? Shanice is supposed to be in school," Tabitha said, confused.

"I know," Lisa said, taking a quarter from Tabitha and dropping it into the phone. She dialed Shanice's cell phone number and paused for a split second before blurting out, "How in the hell did you end up half-naked in the bathroom?" It took all of Lisa's spirit not to laugh in Shanice's ear. Her whole body shook with the effort. "What do you mean it could happen to anybody? That's not regular shit, Shanice. This is epic. You should be proud." She laughed so hard she had to grip the phone to keep her balance. "Okay, I'm sorry. No, I mean it. I am really sorry," she said between giggles. "We'll be right there."

After taking a minute to regain her composure, she took a deep breath and said, "Your friend is at school in the third-floor girls' bathroom, naked from the waist down."

Tabitha's eyes bulged out of their sockets. "What happened? Did she piss herself or something?"

"No." Lisa laughed hysterically. She took her purse from Tabitha and dug out a twenty-dollar bill. "Go get her some jeans from the Seven Dollar Store. I'll pull the car around."

"Will you just tell me what's going on? And you know Shanice wouldn't be caught dead in jeans from the dollar store."

"Just go get the jeans, Tab. Beggars can't be choosers. I'll tell you in the car."

It was 12:30 p.m., the first lunch period at Strawberry Mansion High School. Students slipped in and out of the building to go to the Chinese store across the street, and, as usual, the teaching assistants turned a blind eye. Although sneaking into the school hadn't been the fiasco she had mentally prepared herself for, Tabitha was still nervous as hell. She had to stuff her hands inside her pockets to keep them from trembling. She hadn't attended high school for two years and was paranoid that someone would recognize her and say she didn't belong.

Several emotions washed over Tabitha as she stared at the bulletin boards hanging outside each classroom. She really missed going to school, and she hated that Eric made her quit. He was convinced that she was messing around with a guy there because he couldn't imagine anyone honestly liking high school. Tabitha loved everything about school and always had. She was a bookworm, a whiz at math, and absolutely loved science and history. She used to dream about going away to college and getting an advanced degree.

Stopping in front of one of the classroom doors, she peered through the window at the lively debate inside.

"What are you doing?" Lisa asked from between clenched teeth. She grabbed Tabitha's hand and tugged her to the stairwell at the end of the hall.

They made it to the third-floor girls' bathroom with not as much as a batted eye in their direction. They found Shanice in the last stall, crying her eyes out. When Tabitha opened the stall door, Shanice flew into her arms. Lisa was laughing her ass off, but she sobered quickly when she saw how truly shaken her friend was.

"I thought you guys weren't coming," Shanice said, wiping away the tears. "What took you guys so long? Did you get me another skirt from Express?"

Lisa rolled her eyes and snorted. "Uh, what we got you was a pair of jeans from the Seven Dollar Store."

"Seven Dollar Store? I don't wear clothes from the Seven Dollar Store."

"Fine," Lisa said, turning toward Tabitha. "Let's get out of here. Little Miss Princess doesn't want these." She stuffed the jeans back into her purse and walked toward the door.

Shanice panicked and ripped Lisa's purse from her hand. "Psych, girl. You know I was just trippin'." She kicked off her shoes, shimmied into the pants, and then took her cell phone off her shirt and hooked it on the pocket. After that, she put her shoes back on, rubbed her hands together, and looked at her friends. "Okay, girls. Where are we going now?"

Lisa rolled her eyes at Shanice's assumption that she was invited along. "Me and Tab are going back to the mall, and you, little girl, are going back to class."

Shanice walked to the mirror and swooped her chocolate curls into a ponytail. "Like hell I am. You guys can't leave me here. I'll be up on murder charges because that little bitch had no right to throw my clothes out the window."

Tabitha leaned against the wall, shaking her head. "Do you kiss your mother with that mouth of yours?"

Shanice checked her reflection one last time and looked at Tabitha through the mirror. "Look, Mama," she said, "I know you got a baby and all, but I am *not* Erica. I'm grown."

A flash of anger rose in Tabitha for a moment, but it dissipated when Shanice worked her best puppy dog expression on Lisa. She knew Shanice was quick to say something and move on . . . as if it were nothing important, so she let it go. Shanice acted like a tough guy, but she was still a little girl. A little girl with a garbage mouth and no common sense.

"Come on," Shanice said to Lisa. "Please? You know I can't stay here. I'll just beat the living shit out of that girl."

"You were screwing with her boyfriend," Lisa said, shrugging off Shanice's reasoning. "I believe she had every right to throw your clothes out of the window."

"You're lucky she didn't throw *you* out of the window," Tabitha joked in agreement.

Shanice took a deep breath, prepared to do some serious begging, but Lisa cut her off and started walking out of the bathroom.

"Damn. Come on, girl. I don't have all day."

Shanice let out a huge sigh. "I was prepared to kiss your entire ass."

Tabitha smiled as they headed down the hall. The uneasiness she felt since entering the school was forgotten, especially since she found that sneaking out of the school was just as easy as sneaking in.

Shanice called shotgun as soon as their feet hit the pavement outside. She raced to the passenger side of Lisa's blue Cavalier, which was cool with Tabitha. As long as she wasn't riding the bus, Tabitha felt no need to complain.

Once inside, Shanice threw an empty McDonald's cup into the backseat, narrowly missing Tabitha's face.

"Hey, watch it," Tabitha yelled, mugging Shanice playfully in the back of her head.

"I'm sorry, Tab, but it's not my fault. Apparently, Lisa believes that if she cleans this piece of shit out, it just might break down."

Lisa put her key in the ignition and gave Shanice a flat look. "You could always walk, you know. Or better yet, you could take your raggedy ass back to class."

True to her role as peacemaker, Tabitha decided to end the argument before either of them could put any heat on it. "Ladies, please. We must always remember to be classy, not ashy."

"Look, Tab, it's not my fault that this little wench is always starting something," Lisa said. "She knows better than to call Betsy a piece of shit," she said referring to her beloved Chevrolet. She rubbed her hands across the dashboard lovingly. "It's okay, Betsy. That evil little girl didn't mean it."

Shanice laughed, and Tabitha mugged her in the head again.

"Oh, all right. I'm sorry, Betsy," Shanice said, trying to fake a hint of emotion for the car.

"That's better," Lisa said, pulling off fast enough to make the tires screech. After slow-rolling through a stop sign, she took to the road like she was driving the Daytona 500. The trio headed straight to Strawbridge's. Now, because of the whole Shanice fiasco, Lisa only had a couple of hours before going to work.

The store's formal wear department was bloated with prom paraphernalia, which was heaven on earth to them. Lisa had seen her dream dress about a week ago and hoped she would see it again. She stopped in front of a pale, bald mannequin atop a pedestal in a slinky black, spaghetti-strapped gown and carefully touched the hem of the dress.

"I would *definitely* stop traffic in this dress," she said.

Tabitha gazed up at the dress. "To heck with traffic, honey," she said softly. "You'll stop hearts in that dress."

"Aye, yo. Check this out," Shanice said as she stuck her head from behind a row of gowns. "All of these gowns are tied together by some type of cord."

Lisa just stared blankly at her friend. "Uh, the cord is there to keep sticky fingers—like yours—from stealing."

Shanice scoffed and said, "Well, they'll need more than some damn cord." She dived back into the racks of gowns.

Refusing to be sucked into Shanice's silliness, Lisa turned toward Tabitha. "I'm gonna go find someone to help me." She pointed a finger in Shanice's direction. "Uh, keep an eye on Little Crazy. I don't feel like getting kicked out of the mall today."

Shanice peered through the gowns. "Hey, I heard that."

Lisa tossed her braids over her shoulder and walked away. "You were *supposed* to."

Tabitha paid no attention to the pair because she knew pushing each other's buttons was their favorite pastime. She, instead, turned her focus toward the beautiful gowns before her. A strapless powder-blue dress with tiny pearls across the bodice demanded her attention.

It is so soft and pretty. She rubbed the fabric between her fingers, faintly touching the pearls. She checked the size and clutched what she mentally claimed as her gown to her chest. In the midst of it all, tears began to mist her eyes as she realized all the things she'd given up for Eric. She wished she could have turned back time and stayed in school, wishing vainly for a do-over so she could experience her own prom night, graduation, and College Day tours. She wasn't aware of how long she stood there clutching that gown until Lisa's persistent tap on the shoulder broke her daze.

Suddenly embarrassed, Tabitha dropped the gown and quickly scrubbed the tears from her eyes. "What's the matter? You need some help? Need me to zip you up?"

"No," Lisa said softly, bending over to pick up the blue gown. She handed the discarded gown back to Tabitha. "Why don't you try it on?"

Tabitha took the gown and hung it back up on the rack. "No, I don't feel like playing dress-up. Today is about you." She took a step back to get a good look at her and motioned for Lisa to spin around with her finger. Lisa was wearing the shit out of the black gown, absolutely stunning—except for her Fila sneakers that she opted out of removing before trying on the gown.

Tabitha sighed. "You look beautiful, girl."

"I do, don't I?" Lisa said as she twirled and admired herself in the mirror.

"Yeah, you really do," Shanice said, putting her arm around Tabitha.

Lisa tossed her braids over her shoulder and signaled for the salesgirl. "Okay, enough about me. You really need to try that dress on."

Tabitha shrugged off Shanice's arm and took two steps away from that dress. "Oh no, I don't feel like trying on a dress I can't afford."

Lisa ignored Tabitha's protest and asked the salesgirl to bring them a size ten to the fitting room.

"Why in the world would I try that dress on, Lisa? I don't have any money to buy it."

Almost annoyed at this point, Lisa said, "I know you don't have any money to buy the damn dress, Tabitha. That's why *I'm* buying it." Then she tugged Tabitha to the fitting room.

"She is buying the dress so that you can have something to wear to the prom, ya idiot," Shanice said, pushing Tabitha from behind. "And for that to happen, she will need to know if you can at least fit in the damn thing."

Tabitha gave up and let them drag her to the fitting room, seeing how she could not fight off both of them. However, a warm feeling of hope bloomed in her chest and spread quickly throughout her system. *This isn't really happening,* she thought as she let them pull her to the fitting room. Is this *really* happening? Her heart rate sped up, and her palms began to tingle and sweat. *They are messing with me. I know they are.* Goose bumps rose on her arms, and butterflies fluttered in her belly. She turned toward her best friend in wide-eyed disbelief.

"You want me to go to the prom with you, Lisa?" she asked, giving a small voice to her heart's desire.

"Yes, genius," Shanice said from behind. "You know, Tab, you're really dumb for a smart person."

When they entered the fitting room, the salesgirl unlocked one of the stall doors and handed them the gown. Considering that Tabitha wasn't going to do anything but stand there, Shanice began unfastening the buttons on her jeans. Lisa then grabbed the bottom of Tabitha's T-shirt and pulled it over her head in one smooth motion.

"What about Tony?"

"What about him? He's not my best friend, and I'm going to the prom with my best friend."

Shanice swore under her breath as she struggled to get Tabitha's jeans off her hips. "How in the hell did you get these on?"

Tabitha smiled down at her. "With prayer and a lot of motivated jumping and wiggling."

Lisa ordered Tabitha to lift her arms so she could slide the gown over her head, and Shanice untied her shoelaces to slide off her sneakers.

"Suck it in!" Lisa said, straining to zip the back of the dress. Lisa spun Tabitha toward the mirror so she could see her reflection.

All three of them gasped at the transformation.

Tabitha couldn't believe her eyes. *Beautiful. Simply beautiful.* She ran her hands down the sides of the soft fabric and turned from side to side, so she could get a clear view in the mirror and see herself from every angle. She laughed and twirled and embraced Shanice and Lisa in a bear hug. Shanice wiped tears from Tabitha's face but didn't even realize she was crying. "I didn't think this would ever happen to me," she said softly, her voice cracking. "I dreamed of this but never really thought it could happen."

"Must you cry all the time? Get a grip, girly," Shanice asked, feigning annoyance.

"Oh, shut up, Shanice. The girl can cry if she wants to," Lisa said as she wiped away her own tears.

"You guys are both saps," Shanice said, being the first to break from the hug. "Give me the car keys. I'll pull the car around while you guys buy the dresses."

"The keys are in my pocketbook—and be careful with my baby."

"I will. God, chill. You act like you drive a Cadillac instead of a rusty blue tin can."

Shanice left Tabitha and Lisa crying all over each other. She couldn't get out of the store fast enough. As usual, boosting made her paranoid, and she wanted to get out of there before anyone noticed her little five-finger discount.

Chapter 4

Shanice waited in the car with the stereo blasting. She was doing her best version of Dr. Dre's "Keep Their Heads Ringin'," singing loud, off-key, and substituting words she couldn't remember. The day started as a disaster but was really starting to look up. Oh, she was still going to whoop Tonya's ass for tossing her clothes, but that was a problem for another day. It had been so long since she saw Tabitha happy. She couldn't remember the last time she saw all of the girl's teeth in that wide, goofy smile. She crawled into the backseat when she spotted her friends exiting the department store. She was about to ask what took so long before spotting the shoe boxes.

"I should have known," she muttered, smiling.

Tabitha slid into the driver's seat while Lisa put the bags in the trunk.

"So, what now?" Shanice asked. "Where are we going?"

Lisa hopped into the passenger's side and said, "You're kidding me, right?" She looked at her watch and sucked her teeth. "You're going home, little girl. School's out, and your mother will be worried."

"Humph," Shanice said as she crossed her arms and pouted. "Jesus is the only one she's worried about."

"Don't tell me you got beef with Jesus. What did God do to you?" Lisa asked.

Shanice flipped Lisa the bird as Tabitha pulled out of the parking lot.

"I'm going to drop you off at home and Lisa off at work." Tabitha turned to Lisa and said, "I'll bring Betsy home in the morning after I finish running around."

Shanice's eyes widened, and her jaw dropped. "Hey, why don't *I* ever get to hold your car?" she asked.

"Because you don't have a driver's license," Lisa said.

Shanice dropped her arms and looked at Lisa like she was crazy. "Huh? Neither does Tab."

"I know, but Tabitha has common sense, and she is at least old enough to drive legally."

"Whatever. You're only a couple of years older than me. Just because you got a job, an apartment, and a car doesn't make you an adult."

"The hell it don't," Tabitha said while merging on the highway. "That whole sentence screams adult."

"Whatever." Shanice rolled her eyes and changed the subject. "Okay, grown-ups, what type of car are we taking to the prom?"

Tabitha eyed Shanice through the rearview mirror. "What do you mean by 'we'? Wait a minute . . . Hold up. What did you do?"

Shanice pulled out a pale-yellow gown, hanger and all, from her book bag.

Lisa leaned back and tried to snatch it from her. "You little thief."

Shanice laughed and quickly stuffed the gown back into her bag before Lisa could get a hold of it. She clutched imaginary pearls and gave them both an indignant look. "I know you guys didn't think you were going to the prom without me."

Tabitha pulled up in front of Shanice's apartment and watched her hop out of the backseat.

"Hey, I'm only getting two tickets for the prom," Lisa shouted.

"Oh, I'll get a ticket, darling. Don't you worry your pretty little head about that."

Lisa sighed. "What are we gonna do with her?"

Tabitha looked at Lisa like she were crazy. "You're asking *me?*"

Shanice entered the apartment as quietly as she could, tiptoeing up the stairs and taking special care to skip over the squeaky steps. Their apartment was tiny compared to Tabitha's apartment but a mansion compared to Lisa's place in the projects. It used to be a bright, happy place filled with color and R&B and hip-hop music. Now, it was a dreary cave. Her mother, Stacy, had painted the rainbow walls tan and thrown away most of their worldly possessions. She figured her mom was still asleep since she worked the graveyard shift. Shanice and her mother weren't getting along lately. Ever since her mother found Jesus, she had been holy rolling big-time, and Shanice didn't feel like confessing any sins.

Shanice stared at the picture of *The Last Supper* that hung over the TV, where the portrait of her grandmother used to be, and shook her head in disgust. She turned on the TV, turned the volume down, and went into the kitchen to get a bowl of cereal. However, she stopped cold when she saw her mother sitting at the kitchen table, sipping a cup of coffee, dressed in a tattered blue robe and bonnet. Stacy had aged about thirty years since she became born again. For a moment, Shanice felt like a small child caught with her hand in the cookie jar. But her mother didn't give her the "stop being naughty" look. Her mother was pissed.

"What in the world is wrong with you, child?"

"Nothing's the matter with me, Mom." She crossed the kitchen to hug her mother. "I thought you would still be sleeping, that's all."

Her mother did not return the embrace but, instead, got up and walked over to the sink to rinse out her coffee mug. Shanice swallowed the hurt from that rejection. She couldn't remember the last time her mother hugged her.

"How was school, Shanice? Oh, and before you even fix your mouth to tell a lie, I think you should know that I got a phone call from the school today. They said you attended one class and ditched every other class after that."

Shanice gave her best innocent face. "Mom, they must have made a mistake because I was in school the whole day, I swear."

Her mother leaned against the counter and threw her coffee mug into the sink, shattering it into pieces. "Damn it, that's it, Shanice. *I am tired.* I am sick and tired of this behavior. You don't go to school, and if you do go, you won't do anything while you're there. You don't do any homework, and heaven forbid you try to do any chores around here."

"But Mom—"

"But Mom, nothing. You lie, you steal, and you dress like a whore." Stacy picked up the shattered glass and threw it in the waste basket. "You are turning out just like your father despite my best efforts."

Tears streamed down Shanice's face. Every word from her mother's mouth felt like a blow, but her spine stiffened with the comment about her father. With all that she did wrong, she tried her best not to disrespect her mother, but enough was enough. She was weary of the holier-than-thou act.

"You think I'm just like my father? Whenever I do something remotely wrong, I'm just like my father. Well, I can't tell, seeing as how I never met the man—never so much as seen a picture of him. You know what? I don't even think *you* know who my father is. I was at school all day long, Mom. What do I have to do to get you to believe me?"

Her mother stormed toward her, getting in her face, but Shanice stood her ground. Her anger at her mother was at war with her fear of her.

Stacy pointed her finger in Shanice's face. "First of all, all you need to do to get me to believe you is tell the truth once in a while. Second, your father, rest his soul, is dead."

"That's not what Grandma said."

"Your grandmother was lying. How many times have I told you that? How often do I have to tell you that Satan is the father of all lies? Father God is our provider. Both you and your grandmother need to find Jesus."

"I didn't know that he was lost."

"You watch your mouth, girl. Don't be playing with Jesus."

Shanice balled her fists at her sides. "God this, God that." She backed away from her mother, knocking over one of the kitchen chairs. "Where is God, Mom, when the rent is due, huh? Where is your God when we get one shut-off notice after the next? Where is your precious Jesus when the lights go out, huh? Yeah, you don't mind all of my stealing when I'm flipping it to help pay some of the bills in this house, do you?"

Her mother charged and pushed Shanice against the counter.

"I've taken a lot from you, girl. I've put up with all the lies, thinking that this was some sort of rebellious phase you were going through, but I will not have you take God's name in vain in my house."

Eyes wild, Shanice saw red. Her fear of her mother was utterly swallowed up by the anger and loss she felt after her mom became born again. Her mother no longer wanted her, no longer loved her. Nothing Shanice could do was good enough for "Sister Stacy," and her heart broke with that realization.

"You used to love me, Mom." She thumped her chest with her fist. "You and me against the world." Tears rolled freely down her cheeks. "You used to sing 'Just the Two of Us.' You sang that to me every night. You remember that?"

"What are you talking about?" Stacy yelled, throwing her hands up in frustration. "I *do* love you." She took a step toward Shanice, but Shanice backed away.

"No," she sobbed. "If you loved me, I would feel it—but I don't. I haven't felt any love from you since your pastor dipped you in the water under the pulpit. You don't talk to me. You don't come to my school. You could care less if it ain't about the church or the Holy Bible. Do you know how that feels? Do you *know* how much it hurts to have your own mother choose the church over you?"

Stacy picked up the Bible from the table. "Shanice, *you* are the reason why I joined the church. I joined to learn how to be a better mother to you."

"Well, it's not working, Mommy. 'Cause I'm hurting. I'm always alone. You were a way better mother before God came into the picture."

Stacy sighed. "Baby, having a good relationship with Jesus is the only way to raise you right."

Shanice bristled. "Are you even *listening* to me?"

Stacy raised her hand in warning. "Watch your tone, little girl. I'm trying to explain how God—"

"Fuck God!" Shanice screamed.

She did not see the blow coming, but heat exploded in her chest as she reeled back into the counter. Her head hit the cabinet before she doubled over in pain. Shanice gasped for air and looked at her mother with hurt and disbelief. Her mother had never struck her before in her life.

Clutching her chest, she searched her mother's eyes for some sympathy, but all she found was fury. Her mother raised her hand as if to strike her again, but all she did was point her finger in warning.

"Choose ye this day whom you will serve, Shanice. Because in this house, we serve the Lord."

"Well, I guess I shouldn't live here then," she said, breaking into tears. She shoved past her mother and fled the apartment.

Weeping, her mother dropped to her knees and prayed. Eventually standing, Stacy paced the kitchen floor. "You hit your child, Stacy. You ain't never hit your baby girl." Guilt twisted her stomach up into knots. She stopped pacing and rubbed her belly to ease the tension. *Could she be telling the truth?* she thought. *Oh, I don't know. If that girl's mouth is moving, she is lying.* She looked at the picture hanging on the refrigerator door. Shanice was picking daisies at Fairmount Park. She had to be about 6 or 7 in that picture. Back when she was so sweet and happy, back when they were the best friends. She picked up the phone to call the dean. Maybe Shanice was telling the truth.

"God, I don't know what to do with that girl," she whispered. "Please tell me what to do."

Chapter 5

Tabitha was floating. After she dropped Lisa off at work, she drove home with the windows down and the music blaring. She slurped on the last bit of her vanilla shake, wanting to savor every last drop of the sweet, thick frostiness.

I'm going to the prom, she thought. Tears of joy sprang to her eyes, and a smile threatened to split her face in two. She hurriedly wiped her eyes. She couldn't remember the last time she was this happy. Adjusting the rearview mirror, she smiled at her reflection. "You're going to the fucking *prom,*" she screamed when she turned on Lehigh Avenue. *This is how it feels to be a teenager.* "Oh my God, I can't wait. I *cannot wait.* I'm going to act a fool too. I'm going to dance, drink, and flirt. I'm going to do it the way it's supposed to be done."

Her favorite song came on the radio, and she took it as a sign that she deserved to be happy. "*How mannny waaaays I looove youuuu. Let me count the waaaays,*" She passionately sang along to Toni Braxton's soulful love song. Stopping at a red light with both hands gripping the steering wheel, she reared her head back and crooned.

"Sing it, girl," said the lady in the car across from hers. And she did just that. She sang her heart out the entire drive home. She pulled up to her mother's house and hurriedly rolled up all the windows. Tabitha could not wait to tell her mom about the prom and show off her new gown. She grabbed the dress and shoe bags, dou-bled-checked the doors to make sure they were locked, and rushed up the front steps.

Excited, she fumbled with the door keys before re-membering that she didn't have a key. She rang the doorbell, laughing at herself . . . but her breath caught, and she nearly passed out when the door swung open . . . revealing a smiling Eric. Tabitha's mood went from light to alert within seconds.

He was dressed in all black from head to toe, wearing a New York fitted cap, Nike T-shirt, Lee jeans, and fresh Air Force Ones.

That all looks new, Tabitha thought, fighting to keep a sneer of disgust from her face. He always looked like new money in name-brand clothes, while she and Erica had to rely on clothes her mom could get from the Goodwill thrift store. *I definitely didn't stab him deep enough.*

"What are you doing here?" she asked, clenching her fist on her shopping bags to keep her hands from trembling.

Eric raised an eyebrow at her harsh, cold tone but said nothing. Instead, he backed up a few paces, opened the door wider, and gestured for her to come inside. Tabitha just stared at him, afraid to flee yet too terrified to go in.

"Are you gonna just stand there and take up space?" He smiled, and his eyes lit up the way they always did when he could tell she was afraid. Knowing his methods, she stiffened her back, and she entered her mother's house without sparing him a glance. She may have been scared out of her mind, but she'd be damned if she let him know. Besides, if she remembered correctly, *he* was the one cowering from *her* the last time they were together.

He leaned against the entranceway and asked, "Were you expecting to see somebody else, Tabby doll?"

"No. Why are you here?"

"A guy can't come around to see his baby girl?" He smiled and stepped closer to Tabitha, fingering the bags in her hands. "Did you hit the lottery?"

Tabitha snatched the bags from his grasp, and his eyes darkened. He moved in to take the bags away from her but was distracted by Erica running down the stairs.

"Mama, Mama, you're home." She obviously had been playing dress-up because her new and very colorful outfit wasn't what had been laid out for her that morning.

"Lookit, Mama. Lookit." Erica dragged a half-dressed doll down the stairs, knocking the poor thing's head on every step down.

"Mama, Daddy bought me a new dolly, and her name is Rebecca."

Tabitha smiled, taking the doll with her free hand. "She's very pretty, Erica, but I thought you named your Cabbage Patch doll Rebecca."

"Yeah, but her name is Rebecca too." Erica held out her hand for her doll, but Tabitha gave her the prom dress and shoes instead.

"Take this upstairs to your grandma for me."

"Okay," she said with her snaggletoothed smile gleaming. With the bags in hand, she headed for the stairs. By the fourth step, Erica looked over her shoulder and said, "It's heavy, Mama."

"I know, honey, but you're a big girl, right?"

Erica beamed a smile at her mother. "That's right. I'm a big girl."

Tabitha's pulse raced as she prayed that Erica would get the dress out of sight before Eric could take it from her. However, Eric's attention had shifted back to her. He had forgotten about the bags.

He took a step toward Tabitha, and she took one back. He slid his hand lightly up her arm, which sent chills up her spine. She hated the way her body responded to his touch.

"What are you doing here, Eric?"

"I miss you, Tabby doll."

"You don't miss me."

He raised his hand to gently stroke her neck.

"No, don't . . ."

Eric saw the way her eyes reeled with pleasure from his touch. Encouraged, he moved in closer. She tried to retreat, but there was no more room. She was pinned between Eric and the wall.

"I miss you so much, baby. I'm sorry I hurt you," he whispered near her ear.

He was too close, *much* too close. His breath warmed her down to her toes. She thought she would melt but brought her hands to his chest in a weak attempt to prevent him from coming closer.

"You said you weren't going to hit me anymore, Eric. You promised."

"I'm sorry," he said, kissing her neck lightly. "I'm so sorry."

She pushed him back so she could look into his eyes. "You promised."

"I'm sorry, Tabitha. You know I don't mean to hurt you." His eyes misted as if he were about to cry, and she might have been moved by his tears if she hadn't seen it all before . . . but she had. It was the same routine, and it had quickly become played out. He would whoop her ass and then become all teary-eyed and remorseful.

I'm sorry, Tabitha. I didn't mean to hurt you, Tabitha. The script replayed over and over in her head. She had heard this routine so many times that she could predict his next line. *You know that my temper gets the best of me sometimes.* He went to kiss her, but she turned away.

A teardrop hit her hand, forcing her to look up at him. He was crying. He was really pulling out all the stops.

Eric gently placed his hands on her cheek, making no attempt to wipe his tears.

"You know my temper gets the best of me sometimes."

Tabitha laughed. "That was right on cue." She clapped her hands. "It was really a marvelous performance, Eric. You deserve an Oscar."

His eyes hardened, and he grabbed her arms, shaking her violently.

"Okay, Tab. Cut the shit. This is what you want, isn't it? You obviously like it when I lose control. I'm not the only bad guy here. You *did* stab me, *right?*" He shook her again, this time slamming her against the wall. "*Right?*"

"Right." She sobbed. The little bit of courage she felt moments before had dissipated.

Regaining control, Eric changed his voice to a sickly sweet tone. "Now, come on, Tab. You know I don't want to hurt you. Don't make me hurt you. Go ahead and get Erica's and your stuff and let's go."

"Mama, why are you crying?" Neither of them had heard Erica come back downstairs.

Tabitha looked down at her daughter's beautiful wide eyes and rediscovered her backbone. She looked Eric in the eyes, raised her chin, and said through clenched teeth, "I am not going *anywhere* with you."

Surprised by her tone, he released his grasp on her arms. "What the fuck did you say?"

"You heard me. I'm not going anywhere with you."

"Don't fight!" Erica screamed as she dropped her doll and tried to wedge herself between them. "Don't fight."

Eric raised his hand and firmly curled his fingers around Tabitha's throat. He nudged his crying daughter out of the way and placed his leg between Tabitha's thighs.

"You ungrateful little bitch. What the fuck you mean you are not going?"

Tabitha started to choke and sputter. She clawed at Eric's hands with her own, but they wouldn't budge.

He placed his mouth to her ear. "I could kill you, you know that? I can end you right the fuck here. If you don't want to live with me, you don't want to live at all."

"Daddy, no! You're hurting Mama! Grandma! Grandma!"

They could hear the upstairs bedroom door open.

"What in heaven's name is that baby hollering about?" Tabitha's mother asked.

Eric quickly let Tabitha go, and she grabbed her throat, gasping for air. He turned from Tabitha and scooped Erica up in his arms. He rocked her and stroked her hair, but it did nothing to quiet her.

Eric looked toward the stairs. "She's OK, Ms. Mabel. She just wanted me to pick her up, that's all. It's OK, honey." He rocked Erica back and forth, playing the role of the loving father. "Don't cry. Daddy's here. Don't you wanna come back home with Daddy?"

"Can Rebecca come?" she asked, looking up at her dad with wide, hopeful eyes.

"She sure can, sugar."

"Can Mama come too?"

He smirked. "That's up to your mommy."

Eric looked over at Tabitha, who was still nursing her neck.

"Mama," Erica said, "are you coming?"

Tabitha could not think clearly, so thankful she was for the return of air burning down her throat.

Mabel came down the stairs, stopped in the middle of the stairwell, and stared at her daughter.

"What in the world is going on down here?"

Eric walked over to Tabitha and took her hand. "Nothing is going on, Ms. Mabel. We were just leaving. Aren't we, Tabitha?" He dug his fingernails into the palm of her hand.

Her mother saw her only child's teary, swollen eyes and went to stand protectively in front of her. She snatched Tabitha's hand from his. "She doesn't have to go anywhere with you if she doesn't want to. I don't know what goes on in y'all's apartment, but I can tell you what will *not* go on in here."

"Fine," Eric sneered. "That's just fine. In that case, I'll just be taking my daughter home."

"No," Tabitha croaked. "You can't take my baby."

Eric laughed. "What do you mean? She *my* baby too. I can take her wherever I want, whenever I want." He walked toward the door and then looked back over his shoulder. "Are you coming?"

Tabitha's heart sank to her stomach. How silly she felt for thinking she could ever be free of him. She looked at her daughter's smiling face, nodded yes, and edged past her mother.

Mabel caught Tabitha by the arm as she walked past. "You don't have to go with him, baby."

Eric headed out the door toward his car and screamed, "Are you coming?"

Tabitha turned toward her mother and tried to reassure her. "It's okay, Mama. We'll be fine, and I'll call you as soon as we get there."

"Honey, that boy isn't going to keep your daughter. He's just doing this to get you to go with him."

"Come on," Eric shouted from outside. Tabitha jumped and headed to the door.

"You don't have to go, baby. If he doesn't come back with Erica tomorrow, we can go to the police."

"Tabitha," Eric screamed.

Tabitha smiled sadly at her mom and kissed her quickly on the cheek. "The police never helped me. I love you, Mom. I'll call you when I get home." She dropped her head and walked out the door, gently closing it behind her.

Mabel clasped her hands in frustration. She fought the urge to cry. "Tears ain't gonna help the situation, Mabel," she said softly while squeezing her eyes shut. Tears never helped anyone at any time. She took a deep breath to settle herself. "That child is not going to listen to you." She walked up the stairs and down the hall to her bedroom, making a beeline straight to her Bible.

She picked it up and clutched it to her chest. "Dear Lord, please release my child from this bondage." The fear and sorrow in her daughter's eyes broke her heart. A lump rose in her throat, and she swallowed hard to fight off the tears again. She started to open the good book to find some guidance in the scripture but put it back on the dresser abruptly when Tabitha's friends came to mind. She pointed up to the sky. "You're right, Jesus. She won't listen to me, but she *will* listen to them."

Mabel glanced at all the laundry strewn across her bed and sighed. She had been preparing to fold the clothes and tuck them away when that hateful boy entered her home. Pulling an old leather notebook from her nightstand, she flipped through it, looking for Lisa's cell phone number. Then she sat on the side of the bed and sighed heavily once she found it.

"Father, please forgive me if I'm doing the wrong thing," she muttered while carefully punching in the numbers.

The call went directly to voicemail.

Mabel squeezed her eyes shut, took a deep breath, and then called Lisa's house phone. She knew that number by heart.

"Hello." Gloria picked up the phone on the first ring.

Mabel's hand began to tremble, but she cleared her throat and sat up straight. "Hello," she said softly, "is Lisa available?"

"Mabel?" Gloria asked. She immediately held the portable phone away from her face so she could get a look at the caller ID display. She rolled her eyes in disgust. "What in the world is your fake-ass Mother Theresa-Bible-thumping ass doing calling my house? Shit, I really need to change my damn number."

Mabel did her best to keep her voice calm and even. "I'm sorry to disturb you, Gloria, but I really need to speak with Lisa."

"Lisa doesn't live here anymore, so I would appreciate it if you would refrain from dialing this number."

Mabel gasped. "What do you mean she doesn't live there anymore? Where does she live?"

Gloria chuckled at the shock in the older woman's voice. "How the hell am I supposed to know where she lives? You'd have better luck asking your daughter because *I* don't have a fucking clue."

"How could you let this happen? The child is only 17 years old. That's way too young to be out in the wicked world by herself."

Gloria couldn't believe what she was hearing. *This bitch*, she thought, clearing her throat. "You know, I'm having a hard time believing you think 17 is too young because *your* righteous husband didn't think so."

Mabel sucked in a shallow breath but said nothing.

Gloria let the silence drag on a bit until she was sure that the memory of what Deacon Frank liked to do to little girls rooted itself in both of their brains. "Yeah, your late husband thought 17 was old enough for a lot of things . . . didn't he?"

"I refuse to speak ill of the dead," Mabel said, barely louder than a whisper.

Gloria barked out a bitter laugh. "Well, I refuse to explain why Lisa's little fast ass doesn't live here anymore. So, it seems that neither of us has anything more to say." She slammed the phone on to the receiver so hard that it bounced on the floor.

Mabel sat there and listened to the dial tone, trying to erase the horrible memories of her husband from her mind. "Lord Jesus, that is an evil woman," she whispered while placing the phone and her address book on the nightstand. She glanced at her clock radio and remembered that Lisa had a job. "She works at the McDonald's near the college." She picked up the phone and dialed 411.

Chapter 6

It was five o'clock, and Lisa had only been at work for two hours, but it felt like eight. Rush hour had people pouring into McDonald's like a flood. And to make matters worse, she had to work the drive-thru window because three of her girls had called out with three weak-ass excuses twenty minutes before their shifts. The good feeling she always got from shopping was gone—well, maybe not entirely. She smiled, remembering the look on Tabitha's face when she twirled around in her new gown. Her smile fell when she thought about Eric. *That asshole needs to count his fucking days. I will stab his ass again if he thinks he's going to end prom night for my girl,* she thought. Lisa pushed her visor back to massage the headache booming above her ears.

"Shit. Wanda should have been here by now." Wanda was the manager. Her job description included coming in, clocking in, and rolling right back out the door. That girl stole more company money than the tax man, but Lisa didn't mind—live and let live was her motto. All she cared about was Wanda bringing her wide ass through the door so she could at least get out of the damn drive-thru window. Wanda may milk the clock like nobody's business, but for the short time she'd been in her position, she ran a tight ship, which meant she could get Andre off the damn phone and at this window before she went ape shit.

"Welcome to McDonald's. Can I take your order?"

"Yes, can I get two vanilla sundaes and two chocolate ice cream cones?"

"Hold on one moment, ma'am. Let me check if the ice cream machine is working," Lisa said while taking off her headset. She walked toward the small office in the back. "Aye, yo, Andre, did they fix the ice cream machine?"

Andre covered the phone receiver, cocked his head to the side, and pursed his lips. "What do you think?"

Lisa rolled her eyes and walked back to the drive-thru window. Slipping her headset back on, she sighed. "I'm sorry, ma'am, but the ice cream machine isn't working. We do have milkshakes, though. Can I get you those instead?"

"No, that's okay. I'll try another McDonald's," the customer said while pulling out of the driveway.

Lisa glanced at Carla, watching her struggle to take an elderly lady's order. Poor thing's line threatened to leave the store and wrap around the block. Carla looked like she was on the verge of a mental breakdown. The poor girl was sweating, shifting from side to side, and cracking her knuckles repeatedly.

Oh yeah, Lisa thought, *homegirl is about to lose it.* She sighed and told the next hungry customer she would be there in a minute. Then she took off her headset and went to rescue Carla. Tapping Carla on the shoulder and gently nudging her to the side, she stood in front of the register. "How can I help you, ma'am?" Despite her irritation, she smiled because the old woman was so cute. Dressed in a blue paisley housecoat adorned with small yellow and white flowers, she looked just like the lady who played in *Driving Miss Daisy.*

"There are so many choices," she said excitedly. "I just don't know where to begin. I came here for a milkshake because I hadn't had one in years."

"Well, you should order one before you croak," said one of the young boys standing at the back of the line. His friend started cracking up, but Lisa was just thankful the lady didn't hear them.

"I'll tell you what," she said, smiling at Miss. Daisy. "How about I give you a small milkshake, and then you can stand to the side and figure out if you want anything else. Carla here will serve you when you're ready."

"Oh, you're so kind. I think I'll do just that," she said while moving to the side.

Crisis avoided.

Shanice sashayed into McDonald's, full of attitude. She pushed and elbowed her way through the crowd of businessmen, all prim and proper in their three-piece suits, and secretaries in their straight skirts, flesh-toned stockings, and walking sneakers. They were all waiting impatiently for their next fix of a cheeseburger or happy-hour shot of milkshake.

She couldn't see how people could wolf down this crap. McDonald's food gave her the runs for real. As she went farther into the restaurant, the crowd changed drastically from corporate to family. There were your proud papas and your run-down baby mamas with their screaming kids. One of those mamas was breastfeeding her brat out in the open for the world to see. *Jesus, lady, get a room!* She looked away, and her eyes landed on what looked like a mother and tween daughter standing in the corner behind Ronald McDonald playing pattycake. They seemed so happy. *I remember when my mom treated me that way, looked at me that way, loved me that way,* Shanice thought as the pain of longing and regret filled her chest.

She pushed those feelings aside, shrugged off her jacket, and threw it into an empty booth. She wore black jeans and a plain black T-shirt tied in the back to expose her new belly ring. As soon as she started making her way up to the front of the store, she received catcalls from buster-ass young boys, to which she paid zero attention. She was almost to the counter when a fine-ass guy caught her eye.

He had to be about six feet tall, dressed in a navy blue sweatsuit. It wasn't tight, but it hung on his muscular form just right. *Damn! I would screw him oh, so hard that he would think my name was Oh God.*

She licked her lips and wondered if he was thinking what she was thinking. She was close enough to him to smell his cologne. *Brotha even smells tasty.* She smiled at him, letting her dimples work their magic.

Shanice bags another one, she thought. Inching past him with a soft "excuse me" in her best naughty-girl voice, she could see her legs wrapped around his torso, and her face flushed with the image. Rubbing her ass against him as she passed, she confirmed her suspicion: Papi was as hard as a brick—for real—and he was *definitely* working with something.

She abandoned her attempts to get closer to the counter because she had apparently found what she was looking for. In one smooth motion, she turned, extended her hand, and said, "I'm Shanice."

"Bobby." He hesitated for a moment before returning pleasantries. However, before their handshake could connect, his hand was smacked aside by a short, fat, ugly woman.

She sneered and shoved her hand in Shanice's face, showing off what had to be the world's tiniest diamond.

"Who he is, is married to *me,* and *I'm* expecting his baby."

Which explains the fatness, Shanice thought, sneering at the woman. "Well, damn. Can Bobby speak for himself?"

"That's *Mr.* Bobby to you, you little slut. I saw you rub yourself against him. How old are you, 12 or 13? Don't you have no home training?"

"What the fuck did you call me?"

Lisa came to the counter just in time, seeing as Shanice's mouth was about to write a check that her ass could not cash. She grabbed Shanice by her shirt and hauled her behind the counter.

"You better get your girl before I stomp the shit out of her ass." The woman was pressing her pregnant belly against the counter, flailing her arms like someone straight out of a mental institution. Her weak-ass husband wasn't doing anything to help the situation. Instead, his punk ass was hiding behind Ronald McDonald.

Pussy, Lisa thought, turning her attention back to Shanice, who was still lunging at the woman. *Dumb-dumb can't even tell when she's about to get her ass whooped.* Lisa dug her nails into Shanice's arm and led her to the back office.

"Ouch," Shanice screamed. "What's *wrong* with you?"

"No, what the fuck is wrong with *you?* Why in the hell are you up here startin' shit at my job?"

"I ain't do nothing to that ugly bitch."

"*Really,* Shanice? Do you call grinding up on her man *nothing?* I don't call that nothing, and apparently, she doesn't either."

"Oh, you gonna believe her over me? I thought you was my girl." Shanice jumped up and reached for the doorknob, but Lisa wedged her foot against the door.

"Where do you think you're going?"

"I'm outta here. I don't have to take this shit."

Lisa shoved Shanice into the swivel chair in front of the desk. "You're not going anywhere until you tell me *what* is wrong with you."

"There is *nothing* wrong with me."

"The hell there isn't. There is *always* something wrong with you when you go on full ho mode."

Shanice kicked the wastebasket over.

"Nice," Lisa said, picking up the toppled-over wastebasket and putting the trash back inside. "Now, what the hell is wrong with you? Are you going to tell me, or do you want me to let Ugmo out there beat the hell out of you?"

Shanice rolled her eyes but couldn't keep a small smile from tugging at the corner of her lips. "What the fuck is ho mode?"

"Oh, you know what it is. It's that thing you do whenever something is bothering you."

"I don't do shit."

Lisa smirked. "You turn into a fucking nympho whenever something is bothering you."

Shanice laughed. "Yeah, sex *does* make everything better." With a slight pause, she continued, "My mom kicked me out."

"Your mom did *what?*"

"She kicked me the fuck out. You heard me."

Lisa's jaw dropped open. "Why? What happened?" Her eyes narrowed. "What did you do?"

"We fought because she didn't believe me when I told her I was in school all day today."

"But you weren't."

"That's not the point. The point is that she didn't believe me. Somebody called her from the school and told her that I went to the first period and ditched the rest of the day."

Lisa stood in silence and stared at her friend like she was crazy.

Shanice sucked her teeth and crossed her arms across her chest. "I mean, I know that's what I did, but I told her that I didn't. And she didn't believe me."

"But you were lying."

"Yeah, but how did she know that?"

"Uh, because the school called her."

"Well, anyway. We had this big, knockdown, drag-out fight. She hit me, then told me to get out so—"

"So what now?"

"So . . ."

Lisa said nothing.

"Look, I need a place to stay for a while."

Without hesitation, Lisa fished inside her pocket for her keys and tossed them to Shanice. "I'll be home a little late tonight. I have to go check on Tabitha."

"What's wrong with Tab?"

"Aunt Mabel called me just before your little show and told me that Tab and the munchkin moved back with Eric, and she couldn't stop them. So she asked if I could drop by after work to make sure everything is okay."

"Do you need me to come with you?"

"Naw, I'll be fine. Just go home and get some rest, little girl. You do have school tomorrow, you know?"

"Uh, Lisa, for real, you're only two years older than me."

"Well then, that must mean *I'm* in charge. Now, run along and don't wait up."

"You suck."

"I love you too."

Chapter 7

Tabitha sat in the bathtub and simply held herself. She felt as if she were dead, but her body refused to accept it. She wasn't crying. She had no more tears. Rubbing her fingers, looking like prunes over her knees, she glanced through the bedroom door over at the gift Eric had bought for her: A black silk nightgown slung across the bed with a single red rose on top.

She gagged and looked away. The water had turned ice cold, but still, she sat. Getting out of the water meant putting on that nightgown, and putting on that nightgown meant Eric's hands on her. She shivered at the thought. Having his hands on her was something she couldn't bear.

"Why am I back here?" she asked herself for the thousandth time. The scene at her mother's house played on a continuous loop. She should have never left. She should have snatched her baby from his arms. She should have had a backbone. Her hands started to tremble. She raised them from the water and gently touched her neck. Eric's words echoed in her thoughts. *If you don't live with me, you won't live at all.*

"And that's the answer to the question, Tabitha." *If you didn't come here, he said he would kill you,* she thought, sinking back into the water. *He said he would kill you, and you believe him.*

She continued to recline in the cold water and listen to Erica's endless chatter coming from the living room. She closed her eyes and thought it would only be a matter of time before he grew tired of Erica and sent her to bed.

Attempting to change her mind-set, Tabitha thought about her appointment with the counselor at Thornton College. She left the application at her mom's. Now she just had to figure out how she would leave the house tomorrow.

"Don't you think you should get out of there before you shrivel up like a prune?"

The sound of Eric's voice struck like a blow to the gut. She jerked violently, splashing water on the floor. Eric's eyes squinted, and his hands curled into fists.

Tabitha froze and braced herself for the blow that was sure to follow. *Stupid, stupid, stupid!*

Eric stepped toward the bathtub and grabbed two towels from the rack, placing one on the wet floor and stretching the other out in front of him. Tabitha opened her eyes, surprised at Eric's restraint. His temper was white-hot, and punishment for her stupidity was usually quick and brutal. She stood, stepped out of the tub, and into the towel. He dried Tabitha slowly, his eyes filled with desire. Her stomach knotted as he ordered her to turn around so he could dry her back.

He fumbled with his zipper, and she sucked in one ragged breath, sick at the thought of what would come. Before she could exhale, he bent her over the tub and rammed himself inside her. He fisted his hands in her hair to hold her steady. The pain was blinding, but there was no shock. She was so accustomed to this form of punishment that she had to remember to scream. If she didn't, it would be worse. He yanked her hair out by the roots, and her mind threatened to go with it. Then he quickened his pace. Tabitha's stomach dropped down to her knees when she remembered that her diaphragm was not in place. Eric groaned, released her hair, and grabbed her waist.

Oh, please. Oh God. Oh, please, not inside of me. I can't get pregnant. I will not get pregnant!

"I want to go to school," she whispered.

"What did you say?"

"I want you to cum in my face, daddy," she corrected.

"What?" he repeated, keeping his strokes even and hard.

"I want you to cum in my face, daddy." She licked her lips like he taught her and watched as his eyes rolled to the back of his head. He pulled out of her, gripped himself with one hand, and grabbed her hair. Yanking her onto the floor in front of him, he released on her face. Afterward, he bent down to kiss her hair, whispering for her to clean herself up.

"Put on your nightgown and meet me in the living room. I've rented us some movies."

Tabitha sat there with her eyes and mouth shut tightly against his seed on her face. She reached blindly for a towel and gently wiped her face. She felt dirty and looked longingly at the tub but turned to the sink as a substitute. She washed her face and put Vaseline on the sore spots on her scalp. Finished, she took a glob of Vaseline and placed it between her legs, wincing from the pain. She limped toward the bed, tossed the rose on the floor, and slipped into the nightgown.

When she peeked into the living room, Eric was on the couch with the remote in his hand. She walked behind the couch toward Erica's room, but Eric grabbed her wrist and pulled her around the couch and onto his lap.

"Where are you going?"

"I'm just going to check on Erica."

"She's sleeping."

"Oh," Tabitha said, disappointed that she couldn't steal away a moment—anything to prevent spending time with him. "What are we watching?"

"*House Party.*"

"Oh, that's my favorite," she lied. She was more into *Star Wars*. Fighting to hide her discomfort, Tabitha kept her eyes glued to the TV. She knew how much he loved to see her squirm. Then suddenly, the doorbell rang, and Eric eased Tabitha off his lap.

"Go put on your robe. That must be James." He switched off the movie and grabbed the Sega Genesis 2 from the entertainment center. "He said he might stop by to play the game."

Well, so much for watching movies. She closed the bedroom door and slipped into bed.

Eric answered the door . . . and froze. Lisa stood on the stoop, leaning against the railing.

"What the hell do you want?"

"Well, I didn't come here to see you. Where's Tab?"

"She is in the bedroom sleeping."

Lisa tossed her braids over her shoulder and headed to the bedroom, but he grabbed her arm.

"I *said* she was sleeping."

Lisa turned slowly, looked down at Eric's hand, and then fearlessly into his eyes. "Eric, the next time you put your hands on me will be the last time you put your hands on anything." She yanked her arm free and stormed into the bedroom. When Eric started to follow her, she slammed the door in his face.

"Oh, turn around, Tab. I know you are not asleep, so cut the shit."

Tab stayed on her side, ashamed to face her.

Lisa sighed, sat beside her on the bed, and smoothed Tab's hair. "Did he hurt you?"

"No." Tabitha sobbed. She sat up slowly, her eyes glazed with tears. Lisa pulled Tab to her and rocked her gently. She was dying to know why Tabitha returned to this jerk, but she kept her questions to herself. She gently pulled Tab from her chest to inspect her for bruising, but Tab brushed her away. Then Tabitha sat up and brought her knees into her chest.

"He didn't hit me, Lisa. He just fucked me hard."

Lisa's heart dived into her stomach. "Did he wear a condom?"

"No, but he didn't come inside me."

Lisa felt sick but fought to keep those feelings concealed. Finally, she jumped up and grabbed Tabitha. "Come on, Tab. Get some clothes on. We're leaving."

"Lisa, no. He'll take her. He won't let me leave with her. He'll take her," she whispered furiously. *And he'll kill me,* she thought to herself. She wouldn't dare say that part. She grabbed Lisa's hand and stared into her eyes, pleading silently with her.

It broke Lisa's heart to see her friend so terrified, but she knew the feeling. Tabitha was crying hysterically and clinging to Lisa as if her life depended on it.

"What's going on in there?" Eric shouted from the living room.

"Fuck off," Lisa shouted in return, bringing her focus back to Tabitha. "Are you still going to apply to school in the morning?"

"I'm going to try."

"Good," Lisa said, heading for the door. "After we do that, we'll see my mom and talk to someone about getting sole custody of the munchkin."

Tabitha shook her head in disbelief. She knew how much Lisa disliked being around her mother. "Lisa, we don't have to do that—"

"Meet me at eight o'clock and try to get some sleep."

Chapter 8

Shanice awakened to the sounds of Frankie Beverly and Maze crooning, "Solid as a Rock." She wondered if she could convince her mother to make some blueberry pancakes. She looked up at the popcorn ceiling, the orange-painted walls, and tan and brown curtains, and remembered she wasn't home and seriously doubted that she could get Lisa to cook for her.

She frowned at the walls. *Mom used to be colorful,* she thought. She stuck her thumb in her mouth and began pulling and rolling up the bottom of her tee shirt. *She used to blast music and dance around the house. She used to make her face up and wear the prettiest clothes.* Shanice popped her thumb out of her mouth and clutched her imaginary pearls. "Oh no, Sister Stacy don't behave that way. Sister Stacy has given herself to the Lord and now believes that having a good time leads you straight to hell."

Suddenly cranky, she shouted, "Why in the hell are you blasting that crap, Lisa? You're 17, not 71."

Lisa came dancing out of her bedroom dressed in a navy-blue pantsuit.

"Jeez, girl," Shanice said, sitting up to get a better look at her outfit. "Whose funeral are you going to?"

Lisa crossed her arms and leaned against the door. "I'll be going to your funeral if you don't get your raggedy ass up and dressed for school."

Shanice rolled her eyes, grabbed the remote off the end table, and switched on the TV. "I don't feel like going to school today."

Lisa walked over and snatched the remote from her. "Well then, I guess you feel like going home because everyone that stays up in here goes to school. My house is not a hangout, Shanice. I don't lie around, so you won't lie around either."

"All right, all right. I get it. We're going to school."

"*We're* not going anywhere. *You're* going to school. I'm going to help Tab register at the community college," Lisa said while checking her outfit in the standing mirror that Tabitha found at Goodwill.

Shanice's back stiffened. "Well, I'm going with you guys."

"No, you're not," Lisa said impatiently. "*You* are going to school. *We're* going to my mom's office for advice on child custody."

"Oh," Shanice said. She knew how hard it was for Lisa to be around her mother. "Well, I guess I'll be a good little girl and run along to school." Shanice smiled with all dimples and innocence. She decided to cut Lisa some slack.

"You make me sick, little girl . . . sick and tired. Your mother deserves a medal."

They heard a car pull up, and Lisa checked her watch. "Damn, that must be Tab." She grabbed her purse off the table and headed for the door. "You can put on something of mine to wear to school, but keep your raggedy ass out of my Donna Karan."

Shanice gave Lisa a mock salute. "Yes, sir."

Shanice walked into homeroom decked out in a fitted black Donna Karan T-shirt and matching jeans. She spotted Raymond's sexy ass posted up in the back of the class, clowning around with his friends, and took the empty seat next to his.

"Hey, Ray-Ray."

He ignored her and continued talking to his friend, Kyle, like she wasn't even there. "Yo, dawg, did you see the part where he came bustin' out of the room all wrapped up in plastic? That was some funny shit."

Shanice felt a slight pang in her chest and an uneasy feeling in her belly, but she did her best to ignore the hurt.

Kyle deliberately leaned over Shanice's shoulder to stress Raymond's diss. "Naw, dawg, did you see the part where he threw the dog out of the window?"

Oh no, he didn't. Shanice thought, finding anger to be a much more useful emotion. Leaning forward, she threw her hand up in Kyle's face. "Excuse you. Damn." She turned back to Raymond and said, "Ray, why are you trying to ignore me?"

He stopped smiling and turned to face her. "I'm ignoring you 'cause I don't have no love for no hoes."

Shanice's stomach clenched into a tight knot.

"Damn, that was cold!" Kyle said loud enough to draw everyone's eyes to the back of the class. "Did that hurt? That *had* to hurt."

She put her hand back in Kyle's face, but he swatted it away. "Oh, so now I'm a ho? When did I become a ho, Raymond?"

"I don't know, Shanice. You tell me. When exactly did you become a ho?"

Shanice rolled her eyes and walked to the front of the classroom.

"Bye, ho," Kyle said.

"Fuck you," she replied, not bothering to look back at them.

In every class, Shanice experienced more of the same. The boys she used to hang out with were now all dissing her, and the girls giggled behind her back. She glanced at the clock on the wall. It was almost noon. The early lunch period was almost over. Pretty soon, the bell would ring, signaling the start of the second lunch period, and she could get the hell out of the school and clear her head.

She had just about all she could take when someone yelled, "Hey, Shanice, meet me in the bathroom. I want to see you pop that thing!"

She lost it. Banging through the stairwell doors, she flew down the stairs toward the basement cafeteria. There, she threw her book bag on the floor and scanned the crowd. Her breath came hard and fast as fury welled up inside her. *How dare that bigmouthed bitch.* She stalked the cafeteria looking for Tonya and found her sitting at the last table by the soda machines, surrounded by her little nerdy-ass friends.

"Hey, Tonya, why in the hell are you talking about me behind my back?"

Before she could answer, Shanice grabbed Tonya's chocolate milk and dumped it over her head.

"Oh my God, my hair," Tonya screamed while frantically patting at the fresh finger waves her mother had set the night before.

Next, Shanice threw the empty carton in her face.

"You little bitch," Tonya said, her anger flaring.

"Oh, I got your bitch." Then Shanice punched Tonya in the face. Tonya stumbled into the crowd that had quickly formed around the girls. Shanice was right behind her, grabbing her by the hair and flinging her onto the floor. She put her knee on Tonya's chest to pin her down, then whaled on her, punching her repeatedly in her face, bloodying her nose, and cutting her lip.

The crowd closed in to form a ring of screaming teenagers chanting, "Fight, fight, fight!"

Tonya clawed at Shanice's shirt, ripping it halfway down the front. Braless, Shanice's exposed breasts spilled out of the shirt to the crowd's delight. It took four teachers to shove through the crowd and pull the girls apart.

"Get off me! Get the fuck off me! Shit," Shanice screamed. She bucked and flailed her arms, but Mr. Jenkins had an ironclad grip on her waist. "I fucking hate her! Let me go. I'm going to kill her. You hear that, you bigmouthed bitch? If he lets me go, I will stomp you to death."

Mr. Jenkins swore under his breath as he tried to pin down her arms without touching her breasts so Mr. Thompson could cover her up with his jacket. Then realizing that calming her down in the cafeteria was a losing battle, he grabbed the jacket from Mr. Thompson, lifted Shanice, and carried her out into the stairwell.

"Jesus, kid, your shirt is ripped. Calm down and put this on," he said as he threw the jacket toward her but carefully kept his eyes on the floor.

"I don't care. I hate her. I hate her. She talks too damn much. She gonna learn to keep my name out of her damn mouth. You can believe that." Shanice slid her arms into the jacket and paced the floor. "Oh, she got the wrong one," she said between clenched teeth. "She got the wrong one today." Her heart was racing, and her head started to hurt as the images came to mind of the boys who she thought were her friends ignoring her or making fun of her. She thought about all the girls giggling and whispering behind her back, and the pain and embarrassment started to overtake her anger. Suddenly, she flopped down on the steps, covered her face, and started crying. "I want my mom. I want everything to be exactly like it was before."

Mr. Jenkins walked over to the steps, bent over, and awkwardly patted her back, attempting to support her, actually preferring the curses to the tears. Then furious with herself for crying, she wiped her eyes, pulled the lapels tightly across her chest, and quickly folded her arms to keep the oversized suit jacket closed.

Mrs. Waters, her math teacher, entered the stairwell, and Mr. Jenkins breathed a sigh of relief. She stooped in front of Shanice and cupped her chin. "Are you okay?"

"I'm fine," Shanice replied, jerking her face away.

"Very well, then. Come with me. We're going to the nurse's office first. After that, we're going to see the dean."

"I'm fine, really, Mrs. Waters." She could think of a thousand places she would rather be instead of the dean's office.

"Yes, I heard you the first time, dear."

And just like that, her anger and hurt feelings dissolved into fear. She hung her head as she followed Mrs. Waters to the nurse's office. *Maybe I didn't think this fighting thing through,* she thought.

Chapter 9

"My God, Tab. People are walking faster than us." Lisa grabbed her purse from the backseat and pulled down the visor mirror to check her makeup.

"Who's driving here?" Tabitha was doing 30 in a 25-mile-per-hour zone. She was surprised she wasn't pulled over for speeding. She checked her mirrors, put on her signal, and extended her hand out the window before merging into the left lane. She smiled at Lisa. "Not everyone drives like they are auditioning for NASCAR, sis."

Lisa prayed for patience because she knew Tabitha wouldn't speed up no matter how much she pushed. Besides, the tight ball of fear forming in the pit of her stomach provided a distraction. It grew bigger with each passing moment.

Lisa hadn't spoken with her mother in months, and their last conversation didn't go well. She called her mother last night and left a message about Tabitha and her dropping by on her answering machine. Although she put on a brave front for Tabitha's sake, she was terrified.

Calm down, girl. Shit, she thought as she applied more lip gloss. *It's not like you're going to see Carl Lee. Hell, y'all not even going to your old house. You definitely got this. All you have to focus on right now is getting Tabitha registered in school. Let's take this thing one step at a time. Get your head in the game. Neither Gloria nor Carl Lee is at Thornton Community College.*

Tabitha turned into the garage, retrieved her ticket, and crawled up the spiral ramp toward a parking space. She pulled up and prepared to back into an available spot near the elevator when a black convertible Mustang cut her off. Tabitha barely had enough time to slam on the brakes to avoid smacking into it.

"Holy shit," Tabitha shrieked.

"What the fuck?" Lisa yelled. She hopped out of the car before Tabitha could stop her.

Tabitha sighed, parked the car, and turned off the ignition. She knew Lisa's temper, and she wanted to avoid any confrontations. *Unfortunately, it's too late for that,* she thought. Sighing heavily again, she stepped out of the car and looked at Lisa.

Lisa had one hand on her hip and the other wildly gesturing. Although Tabitha couldn't hear over the Mustang's blaring stereo system, it was apparent Lisa was hollering. Tabitha knew there was no need even to try to calm her down, so she leaned against the car and waited.

"Turn that shit the fuck down. You saw us about to park in this space. Why the fuck do you have to be so ignorant?"

There were two guys in the car: the driver, a nice-looking, dark-skinned brotha with braids and a goatee, and the passenger, a light-skinned fella with hazel eyes and a close-cut fade. The driver smiled at Lisa and turned the music down, but his friend was not as amused.

"Calm down, ma. Damn," the passenger said. "This parking spot don't have your name on it."

"I'm not your ma, asshole, and I'm not talking to you." Lisa directed her steel-like gaze toward the driver, who was getting out of the car and heading toward Tabitha.

"What's your name, shawty?"

Startled by the attention, Tabitha took a step away from the car and smoothed down her skirt. "M-m-my name?"

"You do have a name, don't you?"

Damn, he is tall. "Yeah, I have a name. Everybody has a name."

He continued to smile at her, which made her very nervous. She smoothed her skirt again and dropped her car keys. She bent down to pick them up, but he was quicker at the draw. He scooped them up but would not hand them to her.

Tabitha's eyebrows knitted together. "Give me my keys."

"Not until you tell me your name."

Tabitha glanced over at Lisa, who was still involved in a heated debate with Hazel Eyes. "My name is Tabitha. Now, please, hand me my keys."

He dropped the keys into her hand and smiled. "Now, was that so hard? My name is Darren."

"That's wonderful." She turned and opened the car door, embarrassed down to her toes. "I'll be sure to alert the media." He made her nervous, looking at her like she was a five-course meal.

He grabbed the door and opened it for her. "Well, Tabitha, I think you're beautiful."

Beautiful? His compliment made her pause. She looked into his eyes, waiting for the punch line. No one had ever called her beautiful before.

Lisa walked over to the car, still determined to get her point across to Darren's friend. "You were raised wrong, and that's your whole problem. You don't have no damn home training. Now, come on, Tabitha. We have shit to do. We don't have time to play with little-ass boys."

Tabitha, however, was stuck, rooted to that spot by a simple compliment.

"Tabitha, come on. What in the hell is wrong with you? Let's go."

Lisa's demands finally snapped Tabitha out of her mini trance, and she slid into the driver's seat, never taking her eyes off Darren.

He closed the door for her and kept his hands on the open window. "So, could I get your phone number, Ms. Tabitha?"

Lisa leaned across Tabitha to remove his hands from the window. "What you can get is lost," she said icily. "Come on, Tabitha. Your appointment is at nine o'clock."

Tabitha tore her eyes away from Darren's and started her slow ascent up the ramp to find another parking spot. She tilted the rearview mirror just a little bit to get a glimpse of her reflection. *He said I was beautiful,* she thought. Looking away from the mirror, she scanned the lot for available space. *Eric never called me beautiful. I mean, he might say I look good once in a while, but he was usually staring at my ass in jeans or my breasts in a tight T-shirt. I don't think he ever looked me in the face and said I was beautiful. That's fucked up.*

While Tabitha pulled into an available slot, Lisa was still mumbling about stupid men wasting their time. Tabitha blocked her out and tried to remember a single time that Eric gave her a compliment that had nothing to do with her body. Thoughts of Eric quickly turned dark. Tabitha shook her head no. *I'm not going to let that nigga steal this moment from me,* she thought, turning the car off and handing the keys to Lisa.

"Girl, forget about them. I'm not about to let anybody mess this up for me, nor should you. We are going to college together like we always dreamed we would."

Lisa laughed. "Well, this isn't exactly Hillman College on *A Different World.*"

Tabitha smiled brightly. "To me, it is," She cleared her throat and hopped out of the car, singing the theme song of their favorite show. *"Here's our chance to make it if we focus on our goal. You can dish it, we can take it (hey!). Just remember that you've been told."* She walked around the car and stuck her imaginary microphone in Lisa's face.

Lisa laughed and took the pretend mic, and they finished the chorus together. *"It's a different world (it's a different world). It's a different world (it's a different world) than where ya come from. (Ooh ooh oooh) than where ya come from!"*

Laughing, they walked into the main hall of Thornton Community College arm in arm.

Lisa sat silently as Tabitha and her counselor explored options at Thornton. She watched as Tabitha picked her major and her core classes. She looked around the man's gray cubicle. It was filled with family photos at various vacation places. The pictures would have fascinated her on any other day, and she would have taken some time to grill him about each location. Lisa longed to travel, but she could only think about seeing her mother and reliving those awful feelings of hurt and betrayal.

Gloria had refused to believe Lisa's "ridiculous accusations" against her stepfather. She maintained that *her* Carl Lee wouldn't hurt a fly, let alone rape a little girl—and that was that. Lisa never mentioned the subject to her mother again, and her mother's disbelief allowed *her* Carl Lee to get bolder. He knew there would be no retribution for his crimes, so he began to rape her even while her mother was home. Her house had become a horrible, dark place, and Lisa could have sworn that her mother heard them sometimes. She did her best to signal to her mother. She screamed and fought, but Carl Lee was so strong, and he seemed to like it more when she resisted, so Lisa learned to fight less . . . and less.

Despite all her stepfather's abuse, the pregnancy was the last straw. When she found out she was pregnant, Lisa came home from school and confronted Carl Lee, who was sprawled in front of the TV, as usual. He didn't even look at her. He just drank his beer and flipped through the channels.

The next day, $350 was on her dresser with a phone number to an abortion clinic. Lisa called Tabitha and then the clinic to make an appointment.

She felt dead inside. Lisa couldn't bear the thought of Carl Lee's baby living inside her, but she hadn't bargained about not being able to live with the abortion.

"Hello! Earth to Lisa. Is anybody home?" Tabitha asked, waving her hand in front of Lisa's face. "Do you want to eat lunch on campus or at the Spaghetti Warehouse?"

"What? Oh, I don't care. We can eat anywhere."

"Well, good," Tabitha said, grabbing her arm and tugging her from the counselor's office. "I want to eat here. I want to see as much of this place as I can."

Tabitha walked around, gawking at the campus. Lisa tried to snap out of her funk and share in Tabitha's excitement.

"So, do you want to go by the bookstore after we eat? We can see if the books for your classes are available."

"We can do that?"

Lisa laughed at how far Tabitha's jaw dropped.

"I mean, how will they know what books I'll need? Are you *sure* we can do that? The hell with eating. Let's go to the bookstore now."

Tabitha's eyes popped out of her head, and Lisa giggled at the look on her face. At that moment, Lisa decided to put all thoughts of her stepfather out of her mind. Her girl was going to college. Nothing—and no one—could put a damper on that.

***

Shanice was drained. The adrenaline rush she got from the fight was gone entirely. The nurse looked her over and found nothing but her pride was bruised. She was given another T-shirt from the lost and found and retrieved her book bag and jacket from the cafeteria. Stuffing the ripped Donna Karen shirt in her bag, she had no idea how to explain the shirt to Lisa. Embarrassed by tears that refused to stop falling, she followed the nonteaching assistant, Mrs. Harriet, down the hall to the dean's office. Mrs. Harriet was as wide as a linebacker with a stomach that damn near touched her knees. All the kids secretly called her Butt-gut.

"You quiet now, huh? What happened to all the cursin' and spittin' you was doing in the nurse's office?"

Shanice kept her mouth shut and focused her attention on the floor. An hour ago, she could only think about having her mom with her. But that was her old mother. Her old mother would have turned this place out. She would have cursed them out for even stopping the fight, let alone blaming her daughter. Her old mother wouldn't have cared that Shanice started the fight because her old mother was always on her side. This new version of her mother, this Sister Stacy, wasn't finna do nothing but pray.

Mrs. Harriet shook her head. "What? Cat got your tongue? Why are you girls always fightin' over these good-for-nothin' boys? I never see the boys fightin' over y'all silly behinds."

She opened the door to the dean's office and motioned for Shanice to go inside.

"If you ask me, they should just go ahead and kick your uppity butt out."

Shanice stepped inside the dean's office and turned to face Mrs. Harriet. "No one asked you, Butt-gut." She slammed the door in Harriet's face. Then she turned and, upon seeing her mother, stopped cold. The ice she saw in her mother's eyes broke her heart. Ms. Stacy took one disapproving sweeping gaze at her daughter's appearance and immediately turned her attention back to the dean in disgust.

"Have a seat, Shanice," Dean Johnson said. "I was just telling Ms. Stacy about the little 'incident' in the cafeteria this afternoon. Would you like to tell me your side of the story?"

Shanice said nothing. She kept her eyes locked on the floor as the tears rolled down her cheeks.

"This is your third altercation this year. We were considering expelling you from this institution; however, out of great respect for Ms. Stacy . . ."

Who the hell is we? Out of great lust for my mother would be closer to the truth. She stopped listening. She remembered the sound of her mom's headboard knocking against the wall when dear ol' Dean Johnson would make house calls. She stole a glance at her mother and was sickened by her matronly outfit. *She looks like a fucking nun.*

". . . so we have decided that a three-day suspension and a psych evaluation would be punishment enough. Here is a list of child psychologists. I will, of course, need proof that Shanice has been seen by one of the psychologists on this list before she is readmitted to school."

When her mother stood, Shanice did the same and followed her quietly out of the dean's office, out of the school, and into the parking lot.

"I just don't know what to do with you," her mother said as she unlocked the car doors. "Where in the world did you stay at last night? Huh? You were probably out with some no-good nigga. Did he buy you those clothes? Does he know you're a little-ass girl? How old did you tell the man you were?"

Shanice leaned her head against the car window and willed herself to stop crying. It didn't work. "Why do you care?"

"Please, that's about the dumbest question: Why do I care? You *can't* be serious. I *am* your mother, Shanice, and I love you. I may not like your behavior, but I do love you, and you know that."

Shanice wiped her eyes as fresh sobs tore through her.

"Are you OK?" her mother asked, concern lacing every word. "Did that girl hurt you?"

"You . . . d-don't . . . love . . . m-me. Y-you . . . love . . . y-your . . . B-B-Bible. Y-you . . . don't even . . . know me, Mom."

Her mother looked at Shanice, pulled out a Kleenex from her purse, and gave it to her. "Oh, I know you, little girl. I know you better than you know yourself. I am you. You walk around with your chest puffed up and your behind tooted out, just like I did. You think the sun rises and sets between your legs, just like I did. Well, baby girl, you need to wake up. Don't nobody owe you anything, and the only thing you're gonna catch with your ass hanging out is flies. Grown men aren't interested in little girls, and despite what you may believe, you are *still* a little girl, running around here playing at being a woman. Well, grown women don't roll around on the floor ripping each other's clothes off."

Fat tears dropped on the steering wheel. "I've walked down the road you're treadin' on, and I'm here to tell you that it's hard. Life is hard, Shanice. It takes and takes and takes. Before you know it, you're used up and alone."

"But you're not alone, Mom. I can help you. We could help each other, just like we used to."

"And how could you help me, huh? You have no idea what life is all about." Her mother wiped away her tears. "You're just a baby, Shanice. What do you know about pain?"

She pulled the car over and pulled out her Bible from the glove compartment. "I'll show you why I love Jesus." She flipped it open and began to thumb through the pages.

Shanice unhooked her seat belt and hopped out of the car. "Fine then. You don't want me? I don't want you. Keep your Bible and your Jesus. I'm out of here."

Her mother poked her head out of the window and yelled, "You see, Shanice, that's *exactly* what I'm talking about. I *didn't* say I don't want you."

Shanice took off running.

Stacy drove after Shanice, but the girl was fast as she ran down a series of narrow alleys. Stacy circled a few blocks before pulling over and slamming her hands on the steering wheel in frustration.

"Jesus," she hollered, "how am I supposed to help her if she won't even listen to me, Lord? How?" She bent over to pick up her Bible from the floor of the car and gently dusted off the cover before placing the Good Book back into the glove compartment.

How was she supposed to get the girl to go and see a psychiatrist when she couldn't get her to sit in a car for five minutes?

"You are not going back to the school to see that man. It's sinful and shameful, and plain old stupid," she said. Then closing her eyes, she leaned back against the headrest. "Yes, you are returning to the school, and you will humble yourself and ask a man you know cares for his assistance. Pride cometh before the fall." She sighed and pulled away from the curb. She needed some help with her baby.

Stacy said a short prayer for strength and guidance and then walked back into the main office with her head held high. She walked over to the new receptionist. "Is it possible for me to speak with Dean Johnson again?"

The older woman looked up at Stacy and smiled. "Oh, I believe he is in with a student. They will only be about ten minutes if you don't mind waiting."

Stacy shrugged. "That's fine."

The receptionist smiled and pointed to the far wall. "You can have a seat over there, and he'll be right out."

Stacy sat down, crossed her legs, and placed her purse on her lap. She was about to make an earnest silent prayer when the senior secretary came out of the principal's office.

"Hey there, Stacy. Twice in one day—I think I should play the lottery," Jessie said, coming around the counter to hug Stacy.

Stacy smiled and returned the hug with enthusiasm. Jessie was an usher at Stacy's church, and that was one of her favorite lines.

"What brings you back in?"

"I need to speak with Dean Johnson again."

Jessie frowned. "So why are you sitting out here?"

"The receptionist told me he's in with a student."

Jessie smiled. "Girl, he is always with a student. I don't think anything serious is going on in there." Then, sitting behind the desk, she added, "Go ahead and poke your head in."

"Thank you, girl. I'll see you on Sunday, right?" Stacy said, walking past her desk.

"Sure will," the receptionist replied, not taking her eyes off her computer screen.

Stacy knocked twice and then quickly opened the door and stuck her head in the room. "I'm sorry to bother you, Gregory." She looked at the student and shook her head. "I mean Dean Johnson. I can come back another time."

"Don't be silly, Ms. Stacy, come right in," Dean Johnson said while waving her inside.

Stacy entered his office and saw a young man dressed in a suit, trying to tie his tie while pacing the office in frustration.

"Are you sure I'm not imposing?"

"No, you're fine. Young Troy here needed help learning to tie a tie for his first job interview." He looked at the young man. "It seems he also needs to learn not to let inanimate objects frustrate him."

Chuckling softly, he waved the boy over. "Come here. Let me show you."

Troy tugged the tie hard enough to jerk his head to the side.

The dean frowned. "Here, give me that." He grabbed the tie, smoothed it out, and placed it back around Troy's neck. "You must learn to be patient before you decapitate yourself. It takes time to learn how to do new things. Remember when I showed you how to make that swim move on the football field to get past the line faster? That took a couple of tries to get it right, and this is no different." He tied his tie slowly a couple of times, repeating the steps.

"Now, go repeat it a few times in the bathroom while I talk to this parent," he said while holding the door open for Troy. "If you can't get it, don't get upset. Come back so I can help you."

He closed the door, walked up to Stacy, and tried to kiss her on the lips.

She turned her head, and his lips landed on her cheek.

"Oh, it's not one of *those* meetings," he said, walking to the front of his desk and sitting on the edge of it.

Stacy didn't say anything for a while. She just walked around the office, looking at all his trophies from his old pro football days.

She smiled slightly and turned to face him. "I still don't see why you made all that money and decided to retire and work for a high school. Strawberry Mansion, no less. You could have gone to one of those uppity colleges like Harvard or Yale."

"I know you didn't come here to grill me about my career choices. You came here to talk about your daughter," Gregory said, throwing a balled-up piece of paper at Stacy.

"Stop it, you hooligan," she said, smiling wider. "Yes, I can feel Shanice slipping down a dangerous path, which I am all too familiar with. It's cold and lonely out there. I can't get her to talk to me. So how am I going to get her to see a shrink?" She sat in a chair in front of him.

"Are you coming to me as the dean of her school or as . . . more?" he asked, sitting behind his desk.

"What do you mean, *more?*"

"You know *exactly* what I mean."

"Are you willing to come to church with me and foster our relationship the godly way?" Stacy asked, furling her eyebrows up and waiting for the answer she already had.

"Come on, Stacy, why . . .?" Gregory threw his hands up in frustration.

"As the dean of her school then," she said, cutting him off with a stern face. "I like you, Greg, I mean, I really like you, but I have to be an example to my baby girl. So I don't know what to tell you if you can't understand that."

"I really like you too, Stacy, and things were going well between us, so that's why I don't understand." He bent over to stare directly into her eyes.

"Okay, I guess you deserve more of an explanation than what I gave, so let me lay it out for you. What we had was good, real good, but it was purely physical. When I gave my life to God, things changed inside of me. I want more. I know I deserve more. Look, I made so many mistakes growing up, and that's why the next man in my life must be a man of God first, a worthy father of my stubborn child, and a righteous leader for my household." Stacy exhaled. "But for now, I need help with Shanice. You gave me a list of psychiatrists, but I have no clue how to get her to go. I honestly don't even know where she is right now."

"I can help you, but it will take a whole lot of work to pull your child up from her pool of anger, hurt, and despair. Shanice and I have sat in my office many days because she just wasn't listening to her teachers." Dean Johnson reached into his file cabinet and pulled out a disciplinary file with Shanice's name. It was much larger than the others on his desk. "I haven't called you about everything in this file, and we don't have time to go over it today, but I want you to see how thick it is. So I'm going to keep it short and sweet—your child needs therapy. Unfortunately, there isn't a magic solution for what she is going through."

Stacy rolled her eyes. "That's it? That's *all* you got for me? All those tackles must've left you brain-dead, Gregory. I know where she needs to go. I just don't have a clue about how to get her there."

Troy banged on the door like he was the police with a warrant.

"I did it, Dean Johnson. I did it by myself," Troy shouted through the door.

"Good, now take that confidence with you on your interview."

"I will," the boy shouted, running down the hall. "Thank you."

Gregory smiled at the door and then turned his attention back to Stacy. "Your daughter is acting out because this is her rebellious stage. She'll turn around if you can just let her breathe a little and ease up on the church stuff. She just needs you to be there for her."

"Humph," Stacy said, sitting up in the chair. She opened her mouth to speak, but the dean raised his hand to cut her off.

"You must let people come to the Lord by their own free will. You can't browbeat them or offer them ultimatums like you just did me. A couple of years ago, you and Stacy lived very different lives, and although you were unhappy, she was not. To her, it may feel like your newfound religious ways are designed to punish her. She feels alone and rejected, and she's acting out." He leaned over and took Stacy's hand. "Let her breathe a little. Give her a tiny bit of space, and I will come over this evening to help you talk to each other." He tugged on her hands playfully. "From what I see, she's not the only person who is hard of hearing."

Stacy narrowed her eyes and tried to pull her hands away, but he tightened his grip.

"I'm not trying to come over for any funny business. I'm coming as a friend who cares for you both, and I will keep coming for as long as you need me to, with no strings attached."

Stacy closed her eyes to center herself. "Okay, I would like that. I'll even make some dinner."

"Yes, food. *That's* what I'm talking about." He tried to pull her close, but she held her ground and looked him dead in the eye. "This isn't a date or an invitation for more. This is about my baby, Greg. This is me, calling on the village. No more, no less."

Chapter 10

Lisa pressed her hand against her churning stomach as they arrived at her mother's job. Emotions were running through her too fast for her to name—memories of her mother's distrust and disapproval. Gloria never viewed Lisa as a daughter. But once she turned 12 and hit puberty, she became competition. *Calm down, girl,* she thought, chiding herself. *Carl Lee isn't going to be here, so there isn't any reason for Mom to act out.* She swallowed hard. *Besides, this isn't about you or him. This is about Tabitha and the munchkin. So you can stand your mother for a little while just to make sure that they're going to be safe.*

"Are you okay?" Tabitha asked. She didn't like the look on Lisa's face. "You're scared, aren't you? I told you that we didn't have to do this. We can find someone else to help us."

Lisa took a deep breath and stared up at her mother's building. The sixty-story building was all concrete outside with rows and rows of blacked-out windows. There was nothing special about it, nothing odd or off-putting about the structure . . . but it terrified her, nonetheless. She looked at the front door and shuddered. *Might as well be walking into the gates of hell,* she thought. Then she swallowed hard and looked at Tabitha. "Who exactly can we get to help us, huh? Who do you think will take *us* seriously?"

Tabitha shrugged. "I don't know about this, Lisa. All I know is that you look like stir-fried shit. We could always just look in the phone book, you know." She grabbed Lisa's hand and gasped. "You're trembling. Come on, let's get out of here." Tabitha put the key back in the ignition. "This was a bad idea, to begin with. I don't know why I went along with it."

Lisa unfastened her seat belt and hopped out of the car. "This is *not* a bad idea, Tab. I don't have bad ideas. Come on, girl. We're doing this."

The pair walked inside and saw Mrs. Gloria behind a huge cherry wood desk. She was talking to a rugged-looking man in a business suit. Lisa's heels clicked loudly on the marble floors. Wiping her sweaty palms on her slacks, she watched as her mom smiled at the man and directed him toward the elevator. *This woman can be sweet to everyone but her own child,* Lisa thought.

Mrs. Gloria's eyes frosted over when they met with Lisa's. She shot up from the chair like a rocket, smoothed out the wrinkles in her green and white polka-dot dress, and tried to fix her hair as she practically ran toward her estranged daughter and said, "What do you think you're doing here?"

"Hi, Mom. How are you?"

Mrs. Gloria grabbed Lisa by the arm and ushered her into the mailroom. Her face contorted into a vicious snarl, marring her natural beauty. "You think you're really smart coming here, don't you? Well, I won't have my dirty laundry dragged out at my job. I have worked too hard and too long to build up a good reputation here, and I refuse to let you ruin it."

"What are you talking about, Mom? Didn't you get my message? We are here because Tabitha needs some legal advice." Lisa snatched back her arm and tried to regain her composure.

Mrs. Gloria extended her neck out the door to make sure the lobby was still empty before continuing. "You expect me to believe that bullshit? Legal advice, my ass. You're here to spread all your nasty-ass lies about Carl Lee."

I knew this was a bad idea, Tabitha thought, trying to stay relatively unnoticed in the background of Lisa and Mrs. Gloria's dramatic episode. She wanted to leave but knew that wasn't an option when she saw Lisa's back stiffen at the mention of her stepfather.

"I don't give a damn about Carl Lee or you, for that matter," Lisa hissed. "You two deserve each other. I came here because I needed your help. That's all. You're supposed to be able to go to your mother for help. The only mistake I made is believing that you could ever really be a mother or know how to help someone outside of your precious Carl Lee. Come on, Tab. We don't need her. We can find a lawyer on our own. This place is crawling with them." With that, she turned on her heels, walked back out into the reception area, and headed for the elevators.

Mrs. Gloria grabbed Lisa and yanked her back inside the mailroom. "Listen to me, you little fucking slut. This is *my* job you're playing around with. I don't give a shit about what you tell your little girlfriends or think about my husband, but you better head out the front door and never step foot in this office again."

She pushed Lisa into the wall and emphasized each word by jabbing her fingers into Lisa's shoulders. Tears slid down Lisa's face, and Tabitha couldn't take any more. The image of Mrs. Gloria intimidating Lisa painfully reminded her of herself and Eric. She wedged her body between Lisa and her mother and pushed Mrs. Gloria into the corner.

"Get your hands off her, you grimy bitch. She came here to help me. What the fuck is wrong with you? You're her mother, you sick, twisted hag. You're *supposed* to protect her."

Mrs. Gloria braced herself out of the corner, stormed toward Lisa, and said, "She is *not* my daughter. She ain't shit to me."

Mrs. Gloria looked dead into Lisa's eyes and spat in her face. Then without warning, Tabitha slapped Lisa's mother with all her might.

She stumbled back, holding her face. "Get out of here!"

Tabitha pulled Lisa toward the door. "Go back to the child molester you call your husband, bitch."

"If you don't leave, I'll have security throw you out," Mrs. Gloria growled, but Tabitha and Lisa were already gone.

Lisa flew to the car, cursing herself for being so naive. "I'm sorry, Tab," she said between sobs. "I should have listened to you. I just thought she would help you. She always helps everyone but me."

"You don't have anything to apologize about," Tabitha said, pulling her into a fierce hug. "You didn't do anything wrong."

"I should have listened to you," Lisa said softly while clinging to her friend. "I remember hearing how she helped people at her job. She always bragged about the law firm and how she brought people to them who couldn't afford to pay, and they still helped them. I didn't think she would get so angry. I mean, I get it. It's not like we have a fucking loving relationship or anything. But I was hoping . . ." Her voice cracked in pain. She sucked in air, trying to stop crying, but she couldn't help it. "Why does she hate me?"

"Shhhh," Tabitha said, stroking her hair. "It's okay."

Sobs thundered through Lisa's body. *No, it's not,* she thought. *Things will never be okay between me and my mom. Never.*

***

Shanice ran until she felt a pain in her side and her lungs burned. Leaning up against an abandoned building, she fought for each breath. The temperature had spiked and sweat slicked her hair to her neck. Panting, she rested her hands on her knees.

Fuck you, Mom. If you don't need me, I definitely don't *need you.*

A breeze lifted her hair from her shoulders. Shanice turned into it, stretching her arms up in the air so the wind could dry up some of the sweat. Then relaxed by the calmness of the wind, she did a slow spin, cooling off her entire body. As she came out of her stretch, an elderly woman leered at Shanice and shook her head in disgust.

"What's the matter, lady? You never saw somebody cooling off before?" Shanice flipped the old woman the bird and walked down the pathway toward Lisa's apartment building.

She loved the housing project that Lisa stayed in. There was always something going on, and she never felt alone. Shanice stopped in front of Lisa's complex and inhaled the heavy, sweet smell of weed in the air.

I know those bitches aren't getting high without me. Digging into her tight-ass jeans pockets was an exercise in futility. *Fuck! I must've left Lisa's spare key in my mom's car.* She shrugged. "I guess it's gone forever now."

Irritated with herself, she pressed the doorbell. "Lisa, aye, yo, Lisa."

Tony leaned his head out of Lisa's bedroom window. "Shawty, get the hell off the bell. What's wrong with you?"

"There's nothing wrong with me, Tony the Tiger. Let me up. I forgot my key."

"A'ight, hold up. Nate is coming down to let you in."

Nate and Bunkie were sitting on the sofa playing Madden. They were dressed in the hood standard: white

T-shirts, blue jeans, and sand-colored Tims. Tony sat on the recliner, rolling up a blunt.

Bunkie and Nate were brothers and were frequently mistaken for twins. Their coffee complexions and ebony eyes often warranted a double take. However, their hair was what distinguished them. Nate kept his shoulder-length braids beneath a do-rag, and Bunkie rocked a close fade under a fitted cap.

Damn, they are fine as hell. "Wassup, fellas?"

They barely spared Shanice a glance, which annoyed the hell out of her. She walked in front of the TV. "I *said,* wassup, fellas?"

Tony dumped the tobacco into the trash, replaced it with marijuana, and pulled a lighter out of his pocket. "Aw, man, what you doin', yo?"

"I *said,* wassup?"

"And we heard you. Now, move your bony butt from in front of the TV. We tryin'a play the game."

"My butt isn't bony." She turned around so that he could see the truth of the situation.

"Shawty do got a phat ass, though," Bunkie commented.

Tony puffed on the blunt and passed it to Nate. "Yeah, but shawty is a little-ass girl. Why aren't you in school, Shanice?"

"You ain't my daddy, Tony."

Bunkie held out his hand, waiting for the blunt rotation. "I *could* be your daddy, baby."

"Shut the fuck up, Bunkie. I told you that she's a little girl, man. What is wrong with you?"

"Whatever," she said as she rolled her eyes at Tony. Then she turned to face Bunkie. "Let me hit that, yo."

Bunkie passed her the blunt, but Tony snatched it before she could get a hit. "What's wrong with you, Bunkie? Damn."

Tony took two puffs and passed it to Nate. "You are not getting high with us, little girl. You shouldn't even be here. Lisa isn't here. Your ass should be at school."

Shanice got up and stretched a little, letting Bunkie get a peek at the goods. Then Tony's pager went off, and he went into the kitchen to use the phone.

Shanice smirked at him. "Who's that, Tony? Your Colombian connection?" She turned to Bunky and motioned for him to pass her the blunt.

Tony flipped her the bird and turned his back. Shanice again motioned for Bunkie to pass her the blunt. He paused as if considering.

"Come on, man," she whispered furiously. He passed it to her.

Tony slammed the receiver down after watching his boy pass the blunt to Shanice. "Yo, what's wrong with you, man? I told you not to give her any. I don't get high with kids." He snatched the blunt from Shanice, but not before she got a chance to take a few puffs.

Damn. That shit is fire. I can feel it all the way down to my toes.

Tony rubbed the blunt out on the sole of his Tims and put it behind his ear.

"Aye, yo, what you doin', man? We in the middle of a cipher," Bunkie said.

Nate started to giggle, and Tony headed for the door. "I have to make a run to my moms' house, and I don't want y'all getting Shanice all high while I'm gone."

"I know how to take care of myself, Tony."

"Uh-huh, sure you do."

Nate reached into his pocket for a bill and handed it to Tony. "Bring back some OE."

"A'ight."

"Grab some chips and shit too, man," Bunkie chimed in.

Tony opened the door, turned to Shanice, and waved his finger as a parent chastising a child. "Behave yourself."

She gave him a fake smile, and he shook his head and slammed the door. Bunkie then walked over and peeked out the window. Satisfied, he pulled a fat-ass jay out of a pack of Newports.

"*That's* what I'm talking about," Shanice said. She walked to the stereo and put in Biggie's *Ready to Die* CD. Bunkie sparked up the joint and passed it to her. She took a long drag. The shit felt like love. *My day is finally starting to turn around,* she thought.

"You foul, dawg," Nate said. "Don't say nothing when Tony bitch slaps you, man."

"I ain't afraid of Tony."

"Uh-huh, sure."

Shanice started to roll her hips to the music, letting her braless boobs bounce. *I want to be fucked, for real.*

Bunkie sat down and patted his lap. Shanice took a puff and sat down. The weed was doing wonders for her mood, and she soon forgot about everything . . . Tonya, the fight, her mom. She wasn't even pressed about Lisa's ripped shirt anymore. All she could feel was the boom of the speakers, the weed burning its way through her system, and Bunky's dick getting hard under her ass.

Gloria rearranged the supplies on her desk a half-dozen times. Finally, she made sure the pen on the logbook had ink, the stapler had staples, and every pencil on her desk was sharpened to a fine point. "I can't believe that little bitch brought her raggedy-ass friend to my job to assault me. I thought Tabitha spent her time getting her ass whooped by her little boyfriend." She reached up to touch her cheekbone gently and winced at the pain. "I guess the ho learned a few tricks from him."

She had almost calmed down . . . until security came by to check on her. Someone reported the tussle as they were leaving at the guard station in the parking lot, and he just wanted to stop by and make sure that everything was okay.

"I'm fine, Fred, honestly," she said, forcing a smile. She waved her hands at the door. "A couple of teenagers came by and tried to make a scene. I chased them off, though."

A small, old Asian man shuffled in the front door and headed straight to the desk. "Excuse me, sir, ma'am," he said, nodding his head to them both, "could you tell me where I can find this office?" He handed an envelope to the security officer, who shrugged and passed it to Gloria.

Gloria took the envelope and smiled. "Yes, their office is on the third floor. Just go to your right when you get off the elevator."

He took the envelope and frowned at her. "Ma'am, are you okay? Your nose is bleeding."

Gloria looked down at her desk and blinked at the droplets of blood she saw there. She touched her nose and winced at the pain. "Excuse me," she said, grabbing her purse and running to the bathroom. She looked back at the security guard.

"Don't worry," he said while walking around her desk and taking a seat. "I'll take care of things out here. You just take care of yourself."

Rushing through the doors, she put her purse on the counter and turned the hot water on while inspecting herself in the mirror. "Oh my God," she said while looking at the bruise forming at her cheekbone to the bridge of her nose. "I should beat her ass." She pulled a paper towel from the dispenser, ran it under the hot water, and wiped the dried-up blood off her lip, chin, and cleavage.

Taking a deep breath, she closed her eyes and counted to ten. *I can cover up the bruise,* she thought, calming herself, *and my nose is not broken.*

Drying her face, she pulled her makeup from her purse and started going to work on the bruise with concealer. She thought about the blood as she made tender passes along her nose. *Shit, it probably didn't help to snort all that blow after those bitches left.* She listened to Lisa's message several times. She knew that Tabitha was getting abused and was afraid to leave Eric because he threatened to take her daughter. But she didn't take the message seriously, and she definitely didn't think they were actually going to show up at her job. What were the odds of two of the bitches she hated most in the world calling on her on the same day about the same shit?

That little cunt doesn't seem like she's in danger to me. She seems to be more than able to take care of herself. And why would Lisa think I would do anything to help her or Mabel's demon spawn? I got half a mind to go over to her apartment and help Eric whoop her ass.

She leaned toward the mirror to inspect her work. *Not half bad,* she thought. You could barely see the bruise, and there wasn't a trace of blood. She put her compact and foundation back in her purse and saw there was still some blow left in the baggie. She took it out and then rooted around her bag for a straw. She bent over and looked under the stalls, making sure nobody was silently struggling to take a shit. Then satisfied that she was alone, she locked the bathroom door and quickly took two good hits directly from the bag.

"Ummmm," she moaned as the drug coursed through her system. She leaned against the counter as her heart rate began to speed up, and the familiar sense of euphoria spread over her body like the warmest hug. Then blood dripped from her nose, and she sighed. Grabbing a paper towel from the dispenser, she placed it against her face and held her head back.

Memories of the hurt look in Lisa's tear-streaked eyes began to haunt her. "She isn't so innocent," she mumbled as a bit of anger sliced through the drug's haze. "Just like I wasn't innocent with Mr. Frank. I knew I wanted him. So I flirted with him and dressed up for him." She did a little cha-cha and spun around, laughing and pointing a finger at her reflection. "You thought he was going to take you dancing. You thought you would get a few kisses, but he showed you, didn't he? He ripped your dress and panties off in the back of that truck. You didn't think it would hurt so bad, but it was what you asked for. Same thing with Lisa. I know she asked for it because I asked for it. So, what am I supposed to do, huh? Just throw away my husband because that little girl can't keep her legs closed. Fuck out of here."

Chapter 11

Tabitha flew down the parkway, one hand gripping the steering wheel and the other braced on Lisa's shoulder.

"She hates me, Tab." Lisa sobbed. "I'm her daughter, and she hates me." Lisa doubled over in the car seat and clutched her stomach. Tabitha's sorrow turned into fury as she did her best to maneuver through rush-hour traffic. An old Buick suddenly cut her off. She tried to brake but was going too fast. Attempting to avoid the Buick, she skidded into the next lane and nearly sideswiped a truck.

Drivers' horns blared, and Lisa's moans grew louder.

"She hates me. She hates me."

Tabitha was forced to let go of Lisa and put a tighter grip on the steering wheel. She punched 70 miles per hour as they headed for the river.

"Sit up, Lisa. Don't you waste one more tear on Gloria, you hear me? Not one more tear. She hates herself, Lisa. Do you think she's back at that office crying over you? *Do you?* She's been cruel to you for as long as I can remember. Even when we were in elementary school, she was evil to you, and it is not at all your fault."

Lisa wiped the tears from her eyes but said nothing.

"I'll bet you any amount of money that she pulled herself together and sat right back at that desk like ain't nothing happened. She's sick, Lisa. She's one sick, backward-ass bitch, and she ain't worth your tears. She ain't worth not one little drop."

Tabitha continued to talk, but Lisa stopped listening. At that point, she could see snatches of the river between the boathouses. She focused on the water and how the sunlight danced upon it. Tabitha meant well but really didn't have one clue what she was talking about. Lisa was glad Tabitha didn't know. No one should feel the heart-wrenching pain of a mother's rejection. She couldn't put her feelings into words, so she didn't even try. She just let Tabitha try to comfort her.

My mother spat in my face, Lisa thought. *Even if Eric whooped Tabitha's ass twice a day every day for a year, it wouldn't compare to the pain I'm feeling right now.*

Her mother's words echoed in her mind. *"You ain't no daughter of mine, you hear me? You ain't nothing to me."* She brought her hand to her face where her mother spat on her and snatched it back as if it burned. A lump rose in her throat, and the incredible pain returned in her belly. Lisa remembered walking on Kelly Drive near the river with her mother when she was young. They would hold hands and feed the ducks. That, of course, was before Carl Lee. That was when hugs, kisses, and kind words flowed freely from her mother. Lisa searched her brain for one such memory—a moment when her mother was actually loving toward her.

"Tabitha, pull over."

"What?"

"Pull the car over right here."

"Lisa, what's wrong?"

"Nothing is wrong, Tab. Just pull the fucking car over."

Tabitha pulled over, and Lisa jumped out before it came to a complete stop. She ran up a grassy knoll and fell to her knees under a willow tree. Tabitha was right behind her.

"Girl, what is *wrong* with you? You got to puke or something?"

"No, I'm okay, Tab. I just need to be by myself for a little while."

"Girl, you trippin' hard if you think I'm gonna leave you out here by yourself."

Lisa sat comfortably under the tree and brought her knees to her chest. She closed her eyes and rocked back and forth until she could see her mom sitting in the grass, holding her in her lap. Clenching her eyes shut, she tried to remember the feel of resting her head on her mother's chest, the feel of her arms around her, and the sound of her soft laughter. Try as she might, she could not remember any other time when this happened when her mother openly showed any tenderness or care concerning her. In fact, the older she became, the less her mother could tolerate even being in her presence.

"Please go, Tab. Just go. I'll be fine. I can walk to my apartment from here. I just need a little time to get my head together. I know my mom is a monster, but I've seen her help people in your situation a thousand times. She is on good terms with every lawyer in that place, and I know she could've helped you. I thought she would. I'm so sorry. I knew she wouldn't help me, but I really thought she would help you and the munchkin."

Tears slid down Lisa's cheeks, and the sight sank Tabitha's heart. Lisa looked like a frightened and unsure little girl. "Look, you never have to apologize to me for the things someone else does. Me and Erica will be fine. You, me, and Shanice will put our heads together like we always do and will figure all this shit out."

Lisa nodded and wiped her eyes. She really couldn't bring herself to say anything else.

Tabitha understood pride and knew Lisa had a lot of it, so she kissed Lisa on the forehead and walked away.

Lisa pulled her legs to her chest, wrapped her arms around them, and laid her head on her knees. "It's fine,

Mom. I don't need you, and you will never have to worry about me again. I'm going to be just fine without you." She buried her face in the crook of her arm. "I'm going to make it without you, and you can put that on everything."

Tabitha started the car and looked at Lisa, who was fingering a bush and staring off into the distance. She wanted to go to her and hold her until it didn't hurt anymore, but she knew that was the last thing Lisa wanted or needed. She knew that Lisa would view her concern as pity, and that would do nothing but hurt her more.

Tabitha looked at her hands, clenching them. *I can't believe I slapped Mrs. Gloria. I know that bitch deserved it, but damn. I don't know what's come over me—first, stabbing Eric, and now this. I must be losing my damn mind. I should be ashamed of myself.* Glancing at Lisa again, all feelings of shame seeped from Tabitha's body. She was proud that she slapped that bitch and would do it again in a heartbeat.

She looked at the clock on the dashboard and started to pull off.

"Please be okay."

Her mind drifted to when they were little, back when Mrs. Gloria was kind to Lisa. She thought about how Mrs. Gloria and her mother used to be tight and how they would always spend the night at their house. Then she thought about how they suddenly stopped speaking, which was right before Tabitha's father died.

Tabitha remembered coming inside from playing in the yard with Lisa. They were making mud pies and were soaking wet from playing with the hose. They found her father's clothes scattered all over the house. Lisa had put on one of the jackets that belonged to Tabitha's father. It had nearly swallowed her whole, sweeping down around her like a fancy gown. They climbed the stairs, searching for something that Tabitha could put on to get dry and warm, and ran into Mrs. Gloria backing out of her parents' bedroom. Her dress was tucked inside her pantyhose. Tabitha giggled and pointed. Mrs. Gloria heard her and swung around with the most horrible look on her face. She swept Lisa into her arms and left, never to return. Tabitha abruptly stopped in the middle of the intersection when it finally dawned on her what had happened.

"That bitch slept with Daddy!"

A car swerved from around her, and the driver yelled, "Learn how to drive, idiot."

Tabitha made a right on Montgomery Avenue and then another on Thirty-Second Street. "I wonder if Mama knew."

Her train of thought derailed. She could have pissed herself when she spotted Eric's car parked in front of their apartment.

Oh shit, shit, shit. Tabitha took a deep breath and stared at her reflection in the rearview mirror. *I can do this. I'll just tell him I was at Lisa's looking after Shanice.* She looked back at her reflection and finished the conversation she knew she would have with Eric. *Well, that's rich, Tab. Why in the hell would you be looking after Shanice?*

She leaned over and braced her head against the steering wheel. She rubbed her hand against her chest. Her heart was beating so fast she thought it might explode.

"That man is going to beat the fuck out of me." A single, salty tear slid down her cheek and into her mouth. Her lip trembled. "No, don't you fucking cry. You can take an ass whooping. What you can't take is not going to school, of not having a future."

Sitting up abruptly, she wiped her tear away. *Pull yourself the fuck together, and get your story straight. If he stops you from going to school, this will be your fucking life forever. Your dreams of having a career and a life free of bullshit will fade the fuck away like every other dream.* She looked at her reflection. "Get your story straight, Tabitha. You didn't come this far just to come this far." She looked up at the house and shuddered. *Come on, Tab,* she thought. *This isn't rocket science. All you need is a simple explanation of where you were and why Erica wasn't with you.* Slumping into the seat, she closed her eyes and sighed. *I was looking after Shanice because she was sick. I left Erica with Mama so she wouldn't catch it.* Satisfied, she took another deep breath before exiting the car and entering the apartment.

However, her mind went blank when she saw Eric sitting on the sofa with Erica in his lap. She stared at him for a full minute before blurting out the truth.

"I was registering for school—"

He put a finger to his lips and nodded toward Erica to indicate she had fallen asleep. He put her down gently and then approached Tabitha.

She dug into her purse to search for the card from the counselor. She wanted to prove she was telling the truth. He took the card, smiled, and studied it.

"I thought you were going to be mad. I had an appointment with Mr. Conner. He helped me register for class."

"Mr. Conner," Eric repeated, flipping over the card.

"Yeah, he even helped me pick a major. I'm going for secondary education."

Eric said nothing. He folded his hands behind his back and continued to smile. Encouraged, she showed him her roster. "I'll be taking English 101, Psych 101, and Algebra 020. Oh, and you're going to love this." She turned to the door.

"Where are you going?"

"Wait right here. You're gonna love this, trust me." She flew outside to retrieve the psychology book Lisa had bought her.

"You can buy books for your classes before they even start. Lisa bought this for me."

"Let me see that."

She handed him the book. She was so happy she thought she might burst. *He's not angry, thank God. Wait until I tell Lisa.*

Eric turned the book over and read the spine. "How much was this?" he asked, opening the book and thumbing through the pages.

"It was eighty-six dollars, but Lisa said I could pay her back when I got my financial aid."

Eric turned around and headed toward the kitchen. *Maybe the price has turned him off. I should have said twenty or something like that.*

Eric unlocked the back door, and she hurried after him, her heart pounding. "We don't have to worry about money or anything. My financial aid will cover everything. You even get a refund check."

She was about to tell him how she could get a part-time job if they needed extra money, but he tossed the textbook in the trash.

"What do you think? I'm stupid or something? Lisa bought you an eighty-six-dollar book? You must think I'm a fucking idiot. How long have you been fucking this Mr. Conner?"

"What?" she whispered. She could not tear her eyes away from the trash can.

"Dude that bought you the book—how long have you been fucking him?"

She couldn't even focus on what he was saying because he had just thrown her future in the trash. The small voice inside of her demanded that she get the book back, but fear silenced her.

"What?"

"Oh, I see. You can't hear me." He tossed the business card in the trash with the book and doused them both with lighter fluid. "Can you hear me now?"

Her dreams were about to go up in flames. She leaped toward the trash can, but Eric blocked and shoved her. She stumbled backward and fell to the ground. Reaching back to break her fall, her hands took the brunt of the impact, and her palms cracked and bled on the cement. But she didn't notice.

"No!" she wailed helplessly, watching in horror as Eric ignited the can.

He smirked. "You better put that shit out before somebody calls the cops," he said smugly as the flames crackled and licked the rim of the trash can.

"Tabitha." He kicked her foot to get her attention. "Tabitha?"

She looked up at him through a sheen of tears. "Why?" she whispered. "Mr. Conner is like 60 years old. Ain't nobody sleeping with him. I just met him. Why would you burn my book?"

The crackle of the flames grabbed her attention. Smoke burned her eyes and stung her throat as she crawled toward the can. "I could've took you to the school. You could have looked at the old man for yourself. You didn't have to do this."

Eric laughed. "I know I didn't have to do it. You really think you're going to go to school and become a teacher or some shit? You think I'm going to sit here with this baby while you're out fucking with college niggas and professors and shit?" He pointed to the trash can. "You think you gonna be coming home with those thick-ass books trying to make me feel stupid and shit? Nah. I'm not about to be disrespected in my own crib. Look, I got to go. Fry up some chicken for dinner. I'm out."

He left, but she just stood there rooted in place, watching the trash can until the fire burned itself out. She wasn't going to get to go to school. She wasn't going to get to go to the prom.

The heat from the trash can caused sweat to mingle with the tears pouring down her face. Erica ran outside with a small glass of water. She tried to run toward the fire.

"No, baby," Tabitha hollered. She snatched Erica's overalls and swooped the toddler into her arms.

"I got water to stop the fire, Mommy."

"It's okay, baby," she said, her voice thick with tears. "The fire will go out by itself." She rubbed her face against Erica's soft, curly hair.

Erica pushed against her mother's hold and craned her neck to get a better look at the flames. She coughed. "The water will help the fire go out faster, Momma."

Her tiny cough motivated Tabitha to take the baby inside finally. They sat on the living room couch. Then Tabitha grabbed the remote, turned on Nickelodeon, and let the Muppet Babies work their magic.

Erica giggled at the TV, and the sound cut through the despair that Tabitha was sinking in. She wiped her eyes and ran her hands over her daughter's hair. *I'm not going to let him stop me, baby,* she thought. *We're not going to live like this forever. We're going to have the life that we deserve.*

Chapter 12

It took a while for Lisa to pull herself together. She sat on the grass at Rock Garden and watched the creek trickle down and pool at the bottom of the stone stairs. The peace helped stabilize her mood and reminded her that she was no longer a helpless little girl. She took care of herself and answered to herself. As she slowly inhaled the scent of freshly cut grass and spring flowers, she emotionally exhaled the image of her mother. *That's not real, Lisa. That woman does not exist anymore. It's past time you got the fuck over it.*

She stood, stretched, and started the long trek home. As the warm breeze stirred, she lifted her thick braids off her neck to reap the calming benefits. Feeling weak and wrung out, Lisa continued her walk with her head down, having no desire to see or speak to anyone. She wound her way through the city blocks numb like a zombie in an old horror movie. Her chest was tight, but there were no more tears. She thought of Tabitha and smiled.

I won't shed one more tear for her, Tab. Not one more.

The smell of weed drifted from her apartment's open window as the bass from her stereo's speakers vibrated the pane.

Tony's here.

The thought of seeing her man brought a smile to her face, and the feeling of despair eased, but it didn't disappear. It may never entirely disappear; however, the thought of curling up in Tony's arms and blocking out the world was precisely what she needed.

As Lisa neared her apartment's open door, the sight of Shanice shaking her half-naked ass on her grandmother's coffee table damn near sent her back over the edge.

"Aww, hell naw. You must have lost your damn mind."

Shanice turned around to make her booty clap for Bunkie and spotted Lisa. Unexpectedly, she lost her balance and slipped. Lisa's beloved antique table collapsed under Shanice's weight.

"What in the hell are you doing?" Lisa screamed.

Shanice scrambled to cover herself with Lisa's robe. "You don't understand." She tried to put the robe on but was so fucked up that she couldn't put her arm through the sleeve.

"I don't understand, my ass! What could I possibly *not* under-fucking-stand?"

"It's not what it looks like, Lisa," Shanice whimpered.

Lisa shoved her hand in Shanice's face to cut her off. She looked at Bunkie, who was doing his best to wake up Nate. Bunkie pulled his T-shirt down over his head and grabbed his keys off the TV.

"Come on, dawg," he said. "Wake the fuck up."

"Why the hell you in a rush now, Bunkie?" Lisa asked in a freakishly calm tone as she walked into the kitchen to get the telephone. "Sit down. Stay awhile. The cops will be here soon."

Bunkie hopped over Shanice and the broken coffee table. He ran into the kitchen and snatched the phone from Lisa. "What you doin', shawty?" He stank of laced weed and malt liquor.

"What does it look like I'm doing?" she yelled, trying to snatch the phone back. "I'm calling the fucking cops. How old are you, Bunkie? Damn near 25 or 26?" She pointed to Shanice. "She's a damn little girl."

Bunkie ripped the phone from the wall and got into Lisa's face. "Yo, I didn't make that bitch do nothing she wasn't willing to do."

"Her name is Shanice, and she is a 14-year-old little girl."

"That bitch is a fucking slut. She was practically begging for this dick."

Lisa slapped Bunkie as hard as she could. "Get the fuck out of my house."

Bunkie jumped at Lisa, but she didn't flinch. "Yo, you lucky you Tony's girl, man."

"Lucky, shit. I don't need Tony to protect me from a fucking pussy. You feeling froggy? Then leap, nigga."

Bunkie stepped back into her face but backed off when Nate called his name. "Aye, yo, dawg. Whatcha doin'? Where's Tony?"

He walked into the living room and snatched his hat off Shanice's head. "I don't know where he's at, man."

Nate stretched and looked around, taking in the broken coffee table and Shanice trying unsuccessfully to get to her feet. "Hey, yo, what happened here?"

He reached out to help Shanice stand, but Lisa ran to block him. "Don't touch her."

"Calm down, shawty. I was tryin'a help her."

"Get the hell out of my house and take your nasty-ass brother with you before I call the cops."

"Yo, what's wrong with you?"

"*Get out.*"

Nate got up to leave, but Bunkie was already down the steps and out the door. Nate paused and yelled, "Tell Tony to call me when he gets in."

"Get the fuck out!"

Lisa waited until she heard the door slam before interrogating Shanice. "What in the hell were you thinking?"

Shanice got to her feet, only to trip over the table and fall back down. Her head hit the floor with a sickening thud.

"Uh-huh, sweetie. It's not bedtime." Lisa grabbed Shanice's shoulders and shook her. "Shanice, get the hell up. What's wrong with you?" She shook her again. "You want to be a ho, fine. You want to be a chickenhead, fine. It's one thing to disrespect yourself, but in *my* house? Girl, you trippin' hard."

Shanice's eyes rolled up into the back of her head.

"Oh my God, Shanice!" Lisa snapped her fingers in front of Shanice's face. "Shanice!" She shook her again and slapped her face as hard as she could, but there was no response. "Aw, hell naw." Lisa grabbed Shanice by the shoulders and dragged her limp body into the bathroom, where she turned on the shower and hauled her unconscious body into the tub.

Shanice screamed when the cold water hit her. She thrashed about, hitting Lisa in the chest and face.

"Shh." Lisa pinned her arms to her side.

Shanice tried to break Lisa's hold but couldn't. Lisa held tightly to Shanice, rocking her back and forth and kissing her forehead.

"Attagirl, sweetie. Wake up. That's it."

Shanice was overwhelmed with sadness, and tears flooded from her core. She stuffed her fist in her mouth to try to stop the wails. Lisa breathed a sigh of relief and eased her hold on Shanice's shoulders.

"I'm sorry, Lisa. I'm so s-s-sorry."

Lisa held her head under the spray and let the water run through her braids. Then she climbed out of the tub, letting the cold water spray on Shanice. Then sitting on the toilet, Lisa leaned over, grabbed a towel, and just stared at her friend.

Shanice returned the stare—eyes brimming with re-morse.

"I can't do this," Lisa said before burying her face in the towel. "I cannot do this. I thought I could, but I can't.

I'm not Jesus, Shanice. I can't save you. Hell, I can't even save myself." Lisa stood. "You have to go."

Shanice tried unsuccessfully to get out of the tub. "What do you mean I have to go? Go where? Where do you expect me to go?"

"I don't know where you will go, but you can't stay here." Lisa pointed toward the living room and her grandmother's coffee table. "That is the only thing my grandma gave me before she died. Do you know that? She brought it to my mother's house and put it directly in my room. She said it was her mother's table and her mother's mother's. It has been in our family for generations, and you danced on it and broke it into fucking pieces. If I didn't come home when I did, God knows what else you would have done on it."

"I said I'm sorry."

"Well, I'm sorry too, but sorry isn't going to fix this. Sorry isn't going to change the fact that my grandmother's table is ruined and that you're taking drugs that almost killed you. I can't do this, Shanice."

"What do you mean, drugs that almost killed me? All I did was smoke a little w-w . . . weed." Her teeth chattered from the cold water. She reached forward to cut it off but couldn't quite get her hands to cooperate. "I am sorry about your table," her voice slurred, and her eyes rolled up into her head briefly before she regained her faculties. "I really am. I will pay you for it, no matter how long it takes. I promise you I will pay you for it." Shanice crawled out of the tub and nearly fell back into it.

Lisa jumped forward to catch her. She wrapped a towel around her and then walked into the bedroom.

Shanice stumbled behind her. "I wasn't doing drugs that could kill me. I was having a bad day, so I smoked a little weed. That's all."

Lisa sucked her teeth. "I've never seen weed make someone's eyes roll up in their head before they passed out. Did you see them roll the weed? Do you know if it was *just* weed?"

"Well, I didn't see them roll it, but it looked like weed and smelled like weed."

"Well, it wasn't *just* weed. You are 14 years old, and I am only 17. *I* cannot do this. *You* have to go."

"Where am I supposed to go, huh?"

"Why don't you go home to your mother?"

"She doesn't want me."

"Why is that, huh? You acting like a chickenhead ho over there? Are you doing stripteases and lap dances for grown-ass men at her house too?" Lisa stripped out of her wet clothes, threw them in the corner, grabbed a nightgown out of her dresser, and slipped it on.

Shanice folded her arms under her chest. "I wouldn't have men at my mom's house."

"Oh, but it's cool for you to have them over here."

"I didn't bring them over here, Lisa. They were here when I got here. I don't hang out with Nate and Bunkie. They are Tony's friends."

Lisa sat on the edge of her bed and pulled thick socks out of her nightstand. "So the fuck what? I don't care whose friends they are and why they were here. It doesn't explain why you were naked and why you were dancing for them like you work at a fucking strip club."

Shanice put her head down, ashamed. "I didn't mean to do all that. I just got caught up."

"You got caught up?" Lisa laughed, but the sound held no humor. "I don't understand how you can get caught up enough to take off your fucking clothes and shake your ass for grown-ass men you barely know. I never got *that* caught up. Do you even understand what could have happened to you? They could have gang-raped your dumb ass—or even worse. I mean, really, *what the fuck were you thinking?*"

"I wasn't thinking. I . . . I made a mistake." She looked up at Lisa pleadingly. "I promise I will never do it again."

"I know you won't do it again because you can't stay here."

Shanice opened her mouth to say something else, but Lisa cut her off.

"No, Shanice. You have to go. You always want to act grown until you fuck up, and then you want to pretend you're a baby. You think you are the only person to have a bad day? You think you are the *only* person who can't get along with your mother? Mrs. Stacy may have hit you, but I bet my last fucking dollar that you deserved it." Lisa got off the bed, walked to the closet, and pulled out dry clothes for Shanice. "Your mom loves you. She didn't let her boyfriend fuck you. She didn't choose another man over you, and she didn't just throw you away like you're garbage." She tossed the clothes at Shanice. "Dry off, get dressed, and get the hell on."

Lisa waited for Shanice to leave her bedroom, and then she slammed the door and collapsed onto her bed. She pulled her bedspread over her head. *This can't be life,* she thought. *Why am I expected to be Hercules in every situation? I just want a little bit of normal. Why can't anyone look after me?*

Chapter 13

Shanice emerged from the bathroom dressed in the outfit Lisa had pulled out for her. Her high had finally bottomed out after puking a month's worth of food into the toilet. She didn't want to leave, but the hurt she saw in Lisa's eyes had burned a hole in her heart.

She walked slowly toward Lisa's bedroom as if she were wading through water with rocks in her pockets. She started to knock on her door but hesitated. She knew seeing that look on Lisa's face again was more than she could bear. There was nothing she could say besides sorry, and sorry wasn't going to accomplish anything.

"I will make it up to you, Lisa," she whispered. "I promise." Afraid to wake her and doubly afraid to face her, Shanice left as quietly as she could.

She walked by a group of dudes standing on the corner store steps. "Aye, yo, Shanice. That ass getting phat, girl."

The heat definitely draws the niggas out, she thought. Shanice rolled her eyes and walked faster. The catcalls were starting to grate on her nerves, which she found odd because she usually loved attention. Not today, though. Today, she felt dirtier and lower with each sexual remark she received. For the first time in her life, Shanice felt deeply ashamed of herself. At the same time, she felt queasy, but she knew that came from the weed, *or did it?* she thought. Her head pounded, and she could not think clearly.

That was definitely not weed. I know weed. It has the triple H effect, and I'm not feeling high, hungry, or horny.

She knew what she was sick of. She was sick and tired of worthless-ass guys and sick of herself.

She stopped in front of her mother's apartment. The electric blue door had the word "welcome" painted in sky blue. Shanice remembered the day her mother painted the word.

"Stand out," her mother said as she continued to paint the letters. "If you want to get noticed in life, you've got to stand out. Don't follow the pack. Be the blue door in a sea of brown."

She was 9 years old then and used to stand there with the paint can, hanging on to every word that came out of her mama's mouth.

Shanice shook her head to clear her thoughts but instantly regretted it. A little dizzy, she leaned on the door and tried to regain her bearings.

Come on, Shanice. Stop being a wussy. She reached for the doorknob. *Where else do you have to go?* She paused. *Well, I can't go here.* She snatched her hand away from the doorknob and rubbed her aching temples. "You don't want me, Mama," she said softly as she looked up at the apartment. "You only want Jesus."

Shanice glanced at the door, turned, and walked away. She passed by a group of guys posted up on the corner.

"Damn, Shanice. What, you shopping at the thrift store now?"

She didn't respond. She just kept walking with her head down.

"Those sweatpants can't hide that phat ass, girl. You got a brotha's dick on rock."

"Shut the hell up," she said without looking back.

"Come back here, Niecy. Let me turn that frown upside down."

Shanice broke into a run. It had occurred to her that she'd slept with that dude before but couldn't remember his name. As a matter of fact, she couldn't remember the name of half the men she'd slept with. She knew she didn't like most of them, but she didn't really care at the time. All she ever wanted was some affection and a little attention, and the quickest way to get that was to give up a little ass.

She stopped, and tears fell. "I'm a fucking ho. The worst part is that I ain't even trickin' for money, food, or drugs. I ho for hugs. Now, what kind of shit is that?"

She sat down on the steps of an abandoned building and stared at the kids running around in the playground across the street. Then she broke off a dandelion from a crack in the pavement and twirled it between her fingers.

There are at least half a dozen dudes I could stay with. Most of them have decent cribs complete with cable, food, and hot water. But I would have to give up some coochie, and after today, I ain't about to do that no time soon.

She knew she didn't have a choice. Nothing left but to carry her ass home. So she threw the flower down, stood, and stretched.

"Oh shit," she said, sitting back down and burying her head in her lap. "Oh great, just great—they didn't see me. Please, God, just let them walk on by."

Finally, she looked up and saw a group of girls headed straight for her.

"Hey, Niecy."

That's not my name, bitch. "What's up, Charlotte?"

"Ain't shit goin' on 'round here. Me and April are 'bout to head up to the park to watch those fools run some ball."

Shanice looked over at April, who quickly turned away. Shanice smiled. *That bitch ain't been able to look me in the face since I whooped that ass last summer.*

"Hello? Earth to Niecy. I asked you if you wanted to come with."

"Huh? Oh no, I don't feel like it. I'm not really feeling well."

"Well, what are you doing way out here?"

Yeah, idiot, why are you out here? "I'm on my way to Tab and Eric's."

"A'ight, yo, I guess we'll check you later. Maybe we could go shopping or something."

"Sure," she said, walking away. *I'll call you as soon as hell freezes over.*

Shanice turned on Thirty-Second Street. She hated to impose on Tabitha, and Eric gave her the willies, but she was out of options. Besides, she would have said she was going to the moon if it would get her away from Charlotte. *Wait a minute. What the hell is Charlotte doing? She don't belong down here. Sis was slumming, for real.* Charlotte lived up in a big-ass house in Mount Airy. Her parents were still together and equipped with money to burn. Little Miss Charlotte had everything and wanted everyone to know it. That's why Shanice couldn't stand her. She hated every inch of her, right down to her Gucci-covered toes.

As she approached Tabitha's house, she saw Lisa's car parked across the street, which caught her off guard until she remembered that Lisa was at her own apartment, in bed. Completely mortified by what she had done, she pushed her humiliation to the back of her mind and painted a bright smile on her face. She took a deep breath, but the dirty feeling was still there, riding just beneath the surface.

Shanice knocked on the door twice. No answer. She leaned over to peek through the windows and spotted Erica playing with her Barbie dolls, so she turned the knob, and the door swung open.

"Hello? Tab? You home?"

Tabitha was in the living room, cleaning. She looked just like Aunt Jemima, dressed in an apron with a red-checkered rag tied around her head. She completed the look with a pair of yellow plastic gloves. Shanice had to cover her mouth to keep from laughing out loud. She didn't know what the hell Tabitha was doing. The place practically sparkled.

Shanice tapped her on the shoulder, and Tabitha let out a scream. She whirled around, brandishing her lemon Pledge like it was a bottle of Mace. Shanice lost it. She laughed so hard she thought she might piss herself.

"Damn it, Shanice. You scared the shit out of me." She threw the dust cloth at Shanice and then began to laugh at herself.

Erica ran into the living room, screaming, "Auntie, Auntie!" Shanice scooped her up and sat down at the table.

Tabitha sobered up and placed her hands on her hips. "What in the hell are you doing here, girl? Have you seen Lisa?"

"She's home."

"Thank God. I was so worried about her."

"What for?" Shanice asked while bouncing Erica on her knee. She kissed her forehead and then put her down on the floor.

"Well, you know we went to see her mom today."

"I forgot about that. How'd it go?"

"Girl, girl, girl. Gloria spat in her face."

"You've *got* to be kidding me. I know Lisa beat her down."

"No, she didn't do anything—just stood there like a deer caught in headlights."

"You mean to tell me that y'all let that gutter whore get away with that?"

"No, I didn't. I slapped the shit out of her."

Shanice stood there with her mouth open. She didn't know if she was more surprised by what Tabitha had done or that she had cursed. "I must be in the Twilight Zone or something. Did I hear you right? You smacked Lisa's mom?"

"I slapped the taste out of her mouth."

"Damn . . ." Shanice stopped as if she lost her train of thought. She stared out the window, looking at the vivid hues of pink and purple cast by the setting sun.

"What's wrong?"

Shanice somberly told Tabitha what had happened at Lisa's apartment. She waited patiently for the lecture she felt was sure to come and was a little surprised when no lecture came.

"Are you okay?" Tabitha asked.

"Girl, please. Yeah, I'm okay."

Tabitha looked at her suspiciously before nodding slowly. "Good. Are you hungry?" she asked, walking into the kitchen.

"Girl, you know a sista is starving." Shanice cleared her throat and quickly painted on a smile. "Hey, do you think I could stay here tonight? I mean, would Eric let me crash here?" Shanice looked down at her hands. "I'm fine," she muttered softly to herself. *At least I think I'm going to be okay.* She thought her forced smile was wilting a little.

Tabitha poked her head back into the dining room. "Shanice, there's pajamas in my room in the top drawer of the dresser. You can sleep in Erica's room tonight. Go run you some bathwater."

The weight of the world lifted off Shanice's shoulders. "Thanks, Tabitha."

"You don't have to thank me, sweetie. Now, hurry up and wash up. I'm frying chicken."

"Hold up, Tab. What is Eric gonna say? I don't want you two fighting over me."

"Girl, Eric don't need much of an excuse to pick a fight. Besides, he hardly ever comes home, and when he does, he never stays for very long. A sista could use the company."

Shanice walked to the kitchen door, hugged Tabitha, and planted a big, wet kiss on her cheek. "Thank you."

"Please stop thanking me, honey. That's what I'm here for."

"Ooh, Tab. You smell like smoke. What? Were you barbecuing or something?"

"No, I wasn't barbecuing anything," Tabitha grunted. "You know I registered for school, right?"

"Yeah, how did that go?"

Erica came skipping into the living room. "Mommy, Mommy, I want to watch Barney." She ran and jumped on the couch. She abandoned her Barbie dolls for the purple dinosaur.

"Okay, baby." Tabitha popped a tape into the VCR and motioned for Shanice to enter the kitchen.

"Erica was so quiet, I almost forgot she was here."

"I know," Tabitha said, checking the flames on her chicken. "God has blessed me with a quiet child. I worry about it sometimes, though. I think it would be better if she made a little noise now and again." Tabitha grew silent, lost in her thoughts.

"Uh, hello? You were telling me about Thornton."

"Oh yeah. It was great. It really was. The campus is big. I had no idea. A sista could get lost." She peeked into the living room to make sure the coast was clear. "And the men. Woo, girl. The men were fine as hell."

Look at Tabitha all lit up like a Christmas tree. "So?"

"So what?"

"What do you mean, so what? When do you start?"

"I'm not going to start." Tabitha reached for the colander from the cabinet, set it in the sink, and filled it with chicken.

"What in the hell do you mean you're not going to start? You just said it was great."

"I know, but Eric wasn't exactly thrilled about the idea."

"Who gives a flying fuck about what thrills Eric? This is *your* dream. You *have* to go."

"No, what I have to do is keep all of my teeth in my mouth. That's what I *have* to do."

"If Eric is still putting his hands on you, why did you come back here?"

"He threatened to take Erica away from me."

"You know Eric ain't even trying to be no full-time daddy. He just told you that shit to keep you here."

Tabitha put more chicken into the pan and watched the cooking oil sizzle and pop. "Yeah, well, that's not a chance I'm willing to take."

"How do you know he doesn't want you to go to school?"

"I know because he burned the damn book that Lisa bought for one of my classes."

"You lyin', girl. No, he did *not*."

"Why in the hell do you think I smell like smoke?"

"Damn."

"Damn is right. I don't have the strength or the energy to fight Eric on this. I thought I did, but I think it would be easier to let it go. Tomorrow is the financial aid deadline, so it's pretty much a done deal."

Shanice got up and began to pace the length of the small kitchen. "Girl, please believe that it's not a done deal. Lisa and I have sat back and watched you give up everything for Eric: your virginity, your graduation, friends, and family. Don't let him take this from you, Tab. Think about Erica and how you always talk about giving her a better life." Shanice spread her arms wide. "This is it? *This* is your life? Is *this* all you get?"

Tabitha started to cry. "You don't understand—"

"Please believe I understand. You look me in the eyes right now and tell me this is it. Tell me you don't want more, and I'll stick a chicken leg in my mouth and shut the fuck up."

Tabitha wiped the tears from her eyes. "You know I want more."

"Good. So, I'll watch the munchkin while you do whatever you have to do with the financial aid people tomorrow." Shanice grabbed a piece of chicken, walked out of the kitchen, and headed for the tub.

"Wait. What are we gonna tell Eric?"

Shanice winked at her. "I'll think of something."

Chapter 14

Tabitha would not call herself paranoid; she preferred the term "watchful."

Paranoia evoked images of shrinks, couches, and medications. The threats that the paranoid person experiences are perceived, but Tabitha's threat was very real, very mean, and would be very pissed if he knew what she was up to.

She tried to put thoughts of Eric out of her head as she got off the subway at Spring Garden Street. *He doesn't need a reason to be mad at you. The nigga will get furious over dust on the lampshade and decide to beat you half to death,* she thought while following the crowd on the platform. *If you're going to get your ass whooped, it might as well be over something you actually want to do.*

Overwhelmed with the excitement of what the day would hold, she sprinted up the steps, tripped over her feet, and fell to her knees.

"Hey, are you all right, shawty?"

"I'm fine." She stood, brushed off her knees, and fingered the hole she ripped in her jeans. *How in the hell am I going to explain this?* She was furious with herself and more than a little embarrassed as she looked around for her purse.

"You know, you look much better when you smile, Tabitha," the voice said while handing the purse to her.

Tabitha looked up, surprised. "Darren? What are you doing here?"

"I'm going to school."

"Well, I know that. I mean on the subway. Don't you drive?"

"My car's in the shop. Where's yours?"

"Well, that's not my car. It's Lisa's. That's my girlfriend. Well, not my girlfriend, girlfriend because I'm not that way. It's nothing wrong with being that way." *Shut up, Tabitha.* "It's just that I'm not . . . She's my best friend."

A student racing for class flew up the stairs and bumped her into Darren's open arms.

"Happy to see me, huh?" he asked Tabitha.

"Yes. No. No!"

"You're not happy to see me?"

"I am, but I'm not. I mean, I'm not supposed to be." Tabitha sighed. "I have to go." Her cheeks flushed as she turned and fled the scene. She weaved through the crowds and tried to avoid running into someone else. Darren called after her, but she ignored him.

This was all his fault. He wasn't supposed to be there. I mean, that was one of the main reasons why I parked the car at Mama's house. I just knew I wouldn't run into him on the subway.

Once she walked inside the Whitaker Building, Tabitha was utterly lost. Nobody was at the help desk, and Tabitha was too timid to stop a random person and ask for help. *I knew this was hopeless.* Frustrated and clueless, she turned to leave but spotted Darren standing at the door.

"What are you looking for?" he asked.

"Financial aid," she replied.

He motioned for her to follow him, and she did so reluctantly. "Come on. I'll show you where everything is. Here is the library," he said, playing tour guide. "You can go on in and get your study on. And over here is the cafeteria. They got some of the best fries you ever tasted in that joint." At that point in the tour, he led her to an escalator and pointed her toward the financial aid offices.

"I'm gonna wait over here for you so you can handle your business. Then, we'll finish our tour."

"Aren't you going to be late for class?"

"Naw, shawty. I came here early to get my workout on and catch up on some research. My classes don't start until two o'clock. I'll be here. You better go and get in that line—it's a beast. It'll be wrapped around the building before too long."

"A'ight."

Tabitha resisted the urge to look back and tried to focus on the matter at hand. After standing in line for a few minutes, she was happy to be in and out within twenty minutes.

She walked over to the seating area where she had left Darren, but he wasn't there. She wandered over to the visiting colleges' information stands, but he wasn't there either. Scanning the crowd, she picked up a few brochures, stuffed them into her purse, and headed for the door.

"Looking for somebody?" he asked, placing a hand on her shoulder.

"No," she lied, smiling brightly.

"*Sure,* you weren't. How did everything go? Are you cool?"

"Everything went great. I'm getting a Pell Grant and a Stafford Loan."

"Sounds like you're cool to me. Let's go celebrate." He took her by the hand and started for the door.

"What? Wait, I can't." She dug in her heels. "I have to get home."

"Come on. It ain't every day you score a Pell Grant *and* a Stafford Loan. This calls for french fries and Pepsi."

"But I really gotta get home."

"Come on, please." He pushed out his bottom lip and batted his eyelashes. Tabitha couldn't help but smile. "You're not gonna make a brotha beg, are you?"

"Well—"

"A'ight," he said, dropping to one knee.

Tabitha's eyes bulged out of their sockets. "What are you doing?"

"I'm preparing to beg."

"Well, stop it. Get up." She tugged on his arms.

"Are you gonna have fries with me?"

"No, now get up."

"Please accompany me to the cafeteria," he shouted.

Tabitha looked around, embarrassed. "Will you stop it? People are staring at us like we're crazy."

"Are you coming?"

"I said no."

He cleared his throat. "All a brotha wants to do is buy you some fries."

"You're embarrassing me."

"Is that a yes, then?"

"Yes, okay, yes, yes. Now get the hell up."

"Okay," he said, straightening and dusting off his knees.

"You're crazy," Tabitha laughed.

"No, I'm hungry."

"You don't need me to eat."

"True, but I like to stare at beautiful women over breakfast."

"I don't think Pepsi and fries qualify as breakfast."

"You've *got* to be joking. It's the breakfast of kings."

Darren was all smiles as they walked to the cafeteria. Tabitha, on the other hand, looked as if she was about to run out of there like an Olympic sprinter. He pulled out a chair at the table for her and then made a mad dash to the buffet line.

Tabitha sat at the table and looked through the brochures, patiently waiting for her fries. She felt good, a little scared, but good. He had opened the door for her and even pulled out her seat. Although it wasn't much, it was much better than what she was used to.

"You're thinking about me, aren't you?"

Tabitha jumped. "Stop sneaking up on me, and, no, I wasn't thinking about you."

"*Sure* you weren't; however, if you were, you better stop, or else I'm gonna get a big head."

"I don't think your head can get any bigger."

"Oh, shawty got jokes. A'ight, you got me. I do think highly of myself, but I'm not conceited."

"You're not?"

"Me? Nah. I'm just a good judge of character." Darren dumped half a bottle of ketchup on his fries. "So, what are you taking?"

"Well, I'm leaning toward secondary education. I want to be a high school history teacher. What about you?"

"I'm a number cruncher."

"Accounting?"

"Yeah, boy. I go where the money goes. Let me see your roster."

Tabitha pulled the folded piece of paper out of her bra and handed it to him.

"Well, ain't that a nifty place for it?" He held the roster up to his cheek. "And it's so warm."

Tabitha tried to snatch it back, but he held it out of reach. Instead, she threw a fry at him.

"Now, that's not nice." He looked over her class list. "I took all of these classes last year. I still have the books if you want them."

"For real?"

"Sure, you can have them. They're probably not the current editions, but all the information should be the same."

Tabitha thought she might burst. "I don't care if they're current. I'll take them. Wait a minute. Can't you, like, sell them back to the bookstore?"

Darren shrugged. "They only give you a couple of dollars for books you spend a grip on. I'd much rather give them to you."

"Thanks," Tabitha said, smiling shyly.

"You are stunning when you smile. I mean, damn. You are already beautiful, but when you smile . . . breathtaking."

As what seemed like genuine compliments poured from Darren, something strange happened to Tabitha. She realized, yet again, that no one had ever said anything like that to her before. She knew in the past that she would have sold her soul to hear Eric say something half as nice. Of course, it wouldn't mean a damn thing if Eric said the same thing now. Every time he put his hands on her, he killed the good feelings she once had for him. Now, fear and contempt were all that was left. She wouldn't care if he wrote her poetry and sang her love songs.

She pushed thoughts of Eric aside and stared Darren in the eyes. A deep yearning grew inside her, and she wanted to know—just this once—what it would be like to have a man like Darren, who was handsome, intelligent, and charming. She wondered what it would be like to lie down with someone she wasn't afraid of.

"Darren?"

He looked up from his plate. "What's up?"

"Would you mind screwing me?"

Lisa's alarm went off. She snatched it from the power outlet and chucked it down the hall. Flicking her bedspread off, she stretched on her bed. Even though she no longer wore the wet clothes, she still felt soggy and musty. A bell sounded, and she reached for her alarm, remembering that she had tossed it away. It sounded again before she realized it was the doorbell. She pulled her pillow over her head and screamed, "Go the hell away."

The bell rang again.

"Whoever this is must be crazy." She shot out of bed and banged her foot on the post. Then she limped over to the window and yanked it open. "Go the fuck away."

Tony stood there, sulking. "Why do you have the double lock on the door?"

"Because, genius, I don't want to be disturbed. What are you doing here anyway? I told you that I'm done. It's over."

"Aw, Lisa. Open the damn door. I told you I didn't have anything to do with that shit."

"You didn't have anything to do with it? Well, who left them here with her, Tony? They don't have keys to my apartment—or do they?"

"No, they don't have keys to your apartment, but I have left them here before, and nothing bad happened. They didn't fuck up any of your shit or take any of your shit. So how would I know that this time would be different?" Tony threw up his hands. "I said I'm sorry. I will never leave anyone in your apartment again. Will you open the door so we can talk?"

"I guess we could talk. I can give you that much. Hold on. Stay right there." Lisa disappeared from the window.

"Thank you. Damn. Got a brotha out here in broad daylight making a fool out of himself." Pulling a cigarette from behind his ear, he patted his pockets in search of his lighter. He did not notice Lisa's return to the window.

"Hey, Tony."

"What?"

Lisa dumped a bucket of mop water on top of his head. "You left Shanice here with two grown-ass perverts. 'I'm sorry, baby' just ain't gonna cut it. It's over."

Tony took the soggy cigarette out of his mouth. He pulled his hat off his head and wiped his face. "All right, Lisa. If that's how you want it, that's how it's gonna be."

Lisa slammed the window down and flung the bucket across the room. "Damn skippy, that's how I want it." She then showered, put on some sweats, and went to school.

When she arrived, she looked for Shanice in the crowd of kids hanging outside. She was nowhere to be found. Soon, Begonia walked up to Lisa with a bright smile plastered across her face.

Lisa returned Begonia's smile, shaking her head at her friend. Begonia and her mom and sisters squatted in a house down the street from Tabitha. Her mom was on crack really bad and had their little family bouncing from place to place, but they always stayed in the neighborhood. Begonia was a thief and a stickup kid, but nobody judged her. She did what she had to do to survive, and nobody could blame her for that.

"Uh-uh, bitch. What you doin' here? I ain't seen yo' ass in a month of Sundays."

"Oh, shut up, Begonia," Lisa said, returning the smile. "It's only been a week. I had some running around to do."

"Yeah, sure ya did."

"I had to get my dress and junk for the prom."

"I know, right? And buying a dress always takes a week or so."

The bell sounded, and they slugged their way into the school. Lisa stood on her tiptoes and looked around again. "Hey, Bee, have you seen Shanice around?"

"Oh, you mean Mike Tyson? Naw, I haven't seen her since she sent Troy's girl Tonya to the hospital."

"She did *what?*"

"She ain't tell you? Well, the way I heard it is that Tonya told everyone that Shanice sucked Troy off in the bathroom. When Shanice came to school yesterday, everyone was clowning her. Girl, Shanice beat the brakes off Tonya's ass."

Once inside the school, Begonia grabbed the security guard Charlie's butt.

"Hey, keep your hands to yourself, little girl."

Begonia licked her upper lip. "Anytime, anywhere, Charlie."

Charlie tried to suppress a smile, and Lisa rolled her eyes. She snapped her fingers in front of Begonia's face.

"Hello? You were telling me about Shanice."

"Oh yeah. I haven't seen her since then. Sorry."

"A'ight, girl. I'll check you later." Lisa bypassed the inspection tables. She kept her books in her locker because she hated when the security guards looked through her stuff.

"Hey, wait up," Begonia called out to Lisa. "I almost forgot. That Charlotte girl said she saw Shanice on Thirty-Third Street yesterday looking smoked out. But you know I don't believe a word that comes out of that bitch's mouth."

Guilt wrapped itself around Lisa's heart. "Did she say where Shanice was going?"

"No." Begonia walked closer to her. "Are you okay? Look, don't stunt Charlotte. She just likes to hear her own voice."

Lisa faked a laugh but was worried sick about Shanice. She didn't want the world to know it, and sometimes telling Begonia something would be just like announcing it on the evening news. "Well, if you don't like Charlotte, why do you hang out with her?"

Begonia shrugged. Lisa was one of the few people who really knew what she was into. She looked around, making sure nobody was in earshot. "Me and Brandon are going to hit her place," Begonia finally said. "I need to be close to her to get the logistics."

"When are you gonna stop that dumb shit, Bee? Your ass is gonna end up in juvie."

"I'll stop soon as my moms stop sucking on the pipe and start putting some food on the table."

Lisa stopped in front of her class. "You could get a job, you know."

"Seriously, Lisa," Begonia said, backing up the hallway, "where's the fun in that?"

Lisa had to laugh. "You're hopeless."

"You love me, though," Begonia said, disappearing into her first-period class.

Shanice watched Erica's chest rise and fall as she slept. She took in her tiny hands, long eyelashes, and mocha-colored skin. "You are truly gorgeous, little girl, but you're busy as a bee." Shanice sighed. "You're a lot of work, kid. I don't know how in the hell Tab does it." Erica stirred a little, and Shanice rubbed her back until she settled down again. Shanice looked around the room at all the beautiful toys and paintings on the wall. Everything was frilly and pink and girly. "You have a great mom, baby girl," Shanice whispered as she soothed Erica. "She really loves you." A lump rose in Shanice's throat. She swallowed hard and looked up at the ceiling. "You getting just as bad as Lisa and Tabitha with this crying shit," she mumbled. "Pull yourself together."

Shanice carefully scooted off the bed so she wouldn't wake the munchkin. She retrieved a brown teddy bear from the dresser and tucked it beside Erica. Then she wound up the ballerina music box on her bedside table. "You are really fun to be around, though. It's nice to just play for the sake of playing. I can't really remember the last time I did that." She looked at the child's tiny face and smiled. "You can hang out with me anytime," she said, walking over and kissing the sleeping toddler on the forehead. "You might just be my favorite person to hang out with. But if there is a God, he will let you sleep for another solid hour or two."

She kissed Erica on the cheek, stood up, and looked around her room. Toys and clothes were everywhere. "You're a little hurricane, child." She put the toys back first, then started picking up and sorting the clothes. She didn't hear the front door open.

Chapter 15

Tabitha didn't know what in the hell had come over her, but she knew she liked it. She was sick and tired of being scared and weak. She wanted to feel powerful. She wanted to decide to have sex instead of just having sex done to her. A few days ago, she wouldn't have dreamed of anybody but Eric touching her. But whatever love she had left for him burned away in that trash can with her psychology book. *Fuck it,* she thought as she followed Darren out of the cafeteria and into a fire exit that led to a stairwell. They went up three flights of stairs and down one hall until he found a suitable place: an open janitor's closet.

Excitement rushed through her entire body until her fingers and toes started to tingle. Then she smiled at Darren, who was nervously fumbling with his belt.

"Are you sure about this?" he asked for the twentieth time.

She didn't respond and didn't feel the need to. She just pushed her jeans down her hips. *I'm gonna screw this brotha cross-eyed, and I don't give a damn that I don't know him. Nope, it don't bother me one bit.*

She slipped out of her shoes, taking in the shelves behind Darren's head. They were adorned with all sorts of disinfectants and various other cleaning supplies. *Nope, it don't bother me at all,* she thought again. She didn't care that they were in a broom closet or that it was nine o'clock in the morning. She didn't even care that the college was bubbling over with students, faculty, and staff who could burst through the door at any moment. All she cared about was that this was a decision that she had made on her own. This wasn't happening *to* her; this was something that *she* was doing. *She* was in control.

Tabitha softly laid her hands on top of Darren's. Easing down on her knees, she gazed up at him and moved his hands off to the side. She slid her thumb over the brick in his pants and delighted in the length of it. He trembled. She smiled. The overwhelming feeling of power aroused her senses and made her wet with anticipation. Slowly, she seductively slipped his pants down his legs in an almost fluidlike motion, snaking her hand between his bare thighs.

She used her fingernails to gently graze the area beneath his testicles, after which he released a deep moan. His moans elevated to a passionate growl when she grabbed the shaft of his penis and slid her tongue across the head. His knees buckled, and he reached for the cleaning supply cabinets above her head to regain his balance.

"I want you to know that I'm doing this for me," she said as she continued to jerk his penis with an expert technique. He could only close his eyes as pleasure gripped him, but she suddenly stopped. She wanted to make sure that she had his full attention. When he opened his eyes, Tabitha tightened her grip, delivering deep, long strokes.

"Whatever pleasure you gain from this is purely coincidental." She leaned up, kissed him softly, and then stood on her feet, turned around, spread her legs, and bent over the counter as a motion for him to enter.

Darren clamped down on her hips like a vice. She braced herself for the pain, but none came. Instead, he moved inside her slowly and deeply until she was utterly consumed with him. He was still for a moment to let her adjust to his size. After that, he went inside her with deep, rhythmic thrusts that were forceful yet gentle. Tabitha arched her back, pushing out to meet each thrust. A moan of passionate madness escaped her lips, so he slid his hand over her mouth. She then took one of his fingers into her mouth and sucked it.

With blinding bliss, Tabitha came hard—harder than she ever had before. That sweet release changed her. It washed over her broken places. It filled her with a peace that she had never known. It was like a part of her that was dying had immediately resurrected.

His hand fell from her mouth, but he stayed inside her. She pressed up against him, savoring the warmth and strength at her back. She didn't know where this was going or if it could even go anywhere. All she knew for sure was that this wouldn't be the last time.

Lisa stood outside of her second-period class and massaged her throbbing temples. The worst part about getting a migraine in school was the lights. Every inch of the school was illuminated by bulbs that seemed to be manufactured with rays from the sun. There was no dark space to get a little rest from the pain, so she focused on the dark specks in the gray floor tiles, looking up at the teacher periodically, trying to gain the courage to enter.

Mrs. Conway eyed Lisa from her desk inside the classroom. She peered over the rim of her outdated frames and motioned for her to come inside.

I don't feel like doing this shit. I don't feel like smiling or talking, and I damn sure don't feel like taking notes. And if I have to explain my whereabouts for the last week again, I just might scream.

Lisa took a deep breath, entered the classroom, and quietly closed the door behind her. She planned to break from her norm and sit in the back of the class. *Come on, Lisa. You only have a couple more weeks of this bullshit.* With a toss of her thick braids, she tucked her notebook under her arm, put on her rubber smile, bypassed her regular front seat, and migrated to the back of the class.

"Aah, Ms. Peirce, so nice of you to honor our class with your presence," Mrs. Conway said as she removed her glasses and rested them on top of her bushy mane. The woman was dressed in a purple muumuu, an ancient black sweater, and sandals that were in style several centuries ago.

She was the type of educator that got off on making fools of her students, so it took all of Lisa's strength, and a little help from Jesus, not to curse her out.

She stood up, walked over to the door, and waved Lisa back out. "It's a shame you can't stay, though. I would love to hear about where you were this past week, but you are wanted in Dean Johnson's office."

Lisa rolled her eyes and put her books down on her desk. "What the hell do I have to go to the dean's office for? I didn't do anything wrong. I wasn't even here to do anything."

"That, my dear, is *precisely* the problem." She returned her glasses to her hawk nose, turned to the blackboard, and grabbed a small piece of chalk. "Wait up here for your escort."

Lisa charged ahead of her escort. She didn't like being treated like a criminal; besides, she knew exactly where she was going. Flying down the stairs, she zipped around the corner and snatched the door to the dean's office open, letting it slam against the cement wall.

"Mr. Jo—" She was unable to finish the statement because the sight of Carl Lee sitting across from the dean froze her words in her throat. He was dressed in his usual flannel shirt, Lee jeans, and construction boots. His distinctive scent of Old Spice, sweat, and mustiness wafted through the air.

Carl Lee's lips curved into a sickening smile, and Lisa's heart sank. Her stomach cramped violently, and she turned on her heels to flee. But instead, she ran into the chest of her escort, who was still standing in the doorway. She stumbled back . . . and fell right at Carl Lee's feet.

"You okay, darlin'?" he asked as he extended his hand to help her off the floor.

Lisa scrambled away. "Don't touch me."

She backed herself into the corner. Her eyes wildly darted back and forth, looking for an exit. Seeing the fear in Lisa's eyes caused Dean Johnson some alarm, which relieved some of her panic. She realized that Carl Lee couldn't hurt her here.

The little girl inside of Lisa was freaking the fuck out—crying and screaming desperately to go. She just wanted to get out of there.

Carl Lee smirked at her, delighting in her fear.

Lisa mustered up every ounce of courage she had and forced that frightened little girl back into the dark, quiet, safe place in her mind. She silently counted to ten and returned to her feet. Then, operating on sheer willpower, she sat next to Carl Lee.

Breathe, Lisa; just be.

"Are you okay?" the dean asked.

"I'm fine," she replied between clenched teeth. "What is *he* doing here?" She pointed at Carl Lee, then snatched her hand back as if afraid he might touch it. Lisa gripped the arms of her chair and pushed her feet into the floor to keep herself centered.

Dean Johnson cleared his throat and said, "Well, Ms. Peirce, you have had a lot of unexcused absences in the last couple of weeks. Unfortunately, due to this behavior, we will have to place you on in-school suspension."

"You can't be serious. Graduation is just a few weeks away. I may not be in class all the time, but I turn in my work, and I never miss a test. My grades aren't slipping. I don't see why everyone is making a big deal out of this. I know tons of seniors who often skip.

Carl Lee sat up in his chair. "Don't you think you should drop the attitude and show some respect?"

Lisa closed her eyes and gripped the arms of the chair with such force that her knuckles turned white. "Why is he here?"

"I'm here because you need help."

"I don't need anything from you."

Carl Lee turned to the dean and said, "You see? *This* is what I have to put up with."

"Lisa, your stepfather has come here to report your problem."

"Problem?" Lisa sat up indignant. "What problem? I don't have a problem."

"I told you," he said with a fake air of care and concern. "She's in denial."

"Lisa, your stepfather suspects that you may be using drugs. He says you may have a drug problem, which is why you've missed school."

"*What?* Are you *kidding* me? You've *got* to be fucking kidding me. First of all, he is not my stepfather. He is *nothing* to me. And second, I don't do drugs. The hardest thing I've ever done is weed, and that was over two years ago."

Carl Lee leaned over and patted Lisa's arm. "You don't have to lie, darlin'. They have programs here that can help you."

Lisa bolted out of her chair, sending it skidding across the floor. "Don't you fucking touch me! Don't you *ever* touch me again."

He held both hands up to indicate that he wouldn't do anything to her. "You see what I mean, Dean Johnson? There is clearly something wrong with her."

The dean wasn't paying any attention to him. Instead, he was focusing on Lisa's eyes, which troubled him. But he didn't feel qualified to address it.

He knows, Lisa thought. *If he doesn't know, he's thinking it.* Lisa tore her eyes away from the dean's penetrating stare. She fastened her eyes to the floor in front of her. *I can't deal with this. Why is he here? Why can't he just leave me alone?* Despair rose in her chest, but she swallowed it hard and blinked away the tears that threatened to fall.

The dean cleared his throat and started scribbling on the notepad on his desk. "Lisa, I want you to go and speak with your counselor—*now.*"

Lisa meekly nodded and kept her eyes focused on the floor, hoping to escape her hidden shame. Carl Lee sighed triumphantly and sat back in his chair.

"Thank you, sir. Thank you. You don't know how much her mother and I have worried."

Johnson shot Carl Lee a murderous look of distrust, which immediately put Carl Lee on edge.

"Charlie, please escort Ms. Peirce to Mrs. Fowler's office," the dean told the security guard.

What little bit of strength she had was gone. She felt powerless. The last grip she had on her control loosened, and her stomach began to ache. The little girl inside of her, now free from her ties, rejoiced that she no longer had to remain in the room with Carl Lee. Lisa followed the security guard out of the office and closed the door.

Her head pounded as she walked down the hall. She chuckled as tears fell down her face freely. *I don't know what made me believe that I would catch a break here,* she thought. *Silly of me to think I could have a normal day anywhere.*

Shanice wanted to make sure everything was perfect before Tab got home. This was her first time watching Erica, and although it was tiring, she did not want it to be the last. She walked over to the miniblinds and ran her hand over them to close them since the wands were missing.

"Where's Tab, and what the fuck are you doing here?"

Shanice nearly jumped out of her skin. Her hand went through the miniblind, and when she tried to free it, she ripped the entire blind which fell from the window.

Eric walked over, chuckled, and untangled her from the blinds.

Shanice then raced over to Erica to make sure the commotion didn't wake her, but the baby was actually snoring.

She smiled up at Eric. "She slept right through it," Her smile quickly faded when she saw the look in Eric's eyes. She knew that look. She was notorious for causing that look. Eric ogled her flannel pajamas like they were nothing more than a flimsy nightie from Victoria's Secret. Feeling awkward, Shanice grabbed Tab's robe off the door and walked back into the living room.

"Tabitha took her mom to the doctor," she said casually, attempting to shift the uncomfortable atmosphere. "She said I could stay here for a few days while my mom is out of town. She says I'm too young to be by myself." Then nervously, she picked up the remote and switched on the TV.

"Is that right? Well, I don't have a problem with you staying here. Although you *definitely* look old enough to take care of yourself." Eric walked to the couch and sat right beside Shanice, which was a little too close for her comfort.

"I just turned 14, so I think she may be right." She told many grown men her age, and they never seemed to care, but she was hoping it would make Eric pause, seeing as how he had a little girl of his own. She scooted toward the opposite end of the couch and started flipping through the channels.

Eric moved in closer and rubbed his fingers over the robe's lapel. "So, how long has Tabitha been gone, and when did she say she was coming back?"

Her skin began to crawl, and she hopped off the couch. "Oh, I don't know. I think she's been gone for about a half hour, and she didn't really say when she was coming back, but I think it's soon." *He can't be serious. Nah, I know he ain't serious. If he thinks he's getting some this way, then buddy is trippin' hard for real.* "I'm hungry. Are you hungry?" She put the TV remote down and headed for the kitchen.

Without fail, Eric got up and followed her. "I sure am hungry."

Shanice got some eggs from the refrigerator and pulled a pan from the cabinet. "So, what's up? I hope you like scrambled eggs because that's really all I know how to make."

"Same shit, different day. You know how that is," he said while he pulled out a wad of money, leaned against the table, and started to count it.

Shanice looked at the stack of cash and shook her head. *Now, Tabitha and Erica are one step up from tore up. So, if this nigga has money, how come they always look so bad? I mean, they're always clean, but it's not like he keeps them laced in the flyest shit.* She was relieved when he finally put his money away. It didn't make him look like a big-time drug dealer. It just made him look like a big-time asshole.

Eric pulled a bottle of orange juice out of the fridge and poured himself a glass. "You know me, Rich, and Peanut is heading up to AC this weekend. So you should go with us."

"Is Tab going?"

"Naw, she has to stay here with the baby."

"Why don't you stay here with the baby?"

"Girl, stop trippin'. What do I look like, sittin' around here babysitting?"

"I don't think they call it babysitting when it's your baby. I think they call it being a man."

Eric's face turned evil for a split second before he got it under control. "So, what you tryin'a say, huh? I ain't no man? Girl, you lucky you so damn cute 'cause any other ho talking to me like that would find themselves laid out."

"I ain't no ho."

He doubled over in laughter. "Sure, you're *not* a ho."

"Whatever." Her appetite was gone. She put the eggs back in the refrigerator and tried to leave the kitchen, but Eric blocked her.

"Excuse me. Damn."

"Hold up, shawty. You didn't answer my question."

"What question?"

"Do you wanna go up to Atlantic City with us?"

"Eric, please. I'm not going up to no AC with three dudes. Come on now. Get real. I'm not even old enough to do anything in Atlantic City."

"Whatcha mean, get real?" He reached out to stroke her hair, but she pulled back. "Why you actin' all innocent, ma? I know your steelo. And trust me, there are plenty of things you're old enough to do."

"You don't know shit about me."

"I know you fucked Steve in his backyard for a dub."

Shanice cringed inside at the memory. Her mom had lost her job, and they hadn't eaten anything in two days, and she was hungry.

"Aha. You didn't know I knew about that, did you?"

She pushed past him. *Fuck this shit. I love Tab, but I don't have to put up with this. I'd rather face my mom than put up with this shit.*

Eric grabbed Shanice's robe and pulled her back into the kitchen. She tried to yank the robe from his hand but was too weak. He just pulled harder.

"Come on, man. What are you doing?"

"Stop frontin', girl. You know you want this."

"Want what? Want *you?* You must be smoking, boy. I *don't* want you."

Shanice slipped out of the robe, but Eric grabbed the collar of her pajama top and pulled her into him. He had an erection, and his breath reeked of vodka.

"You know you want this, bitch. I don't even know why you frontin'." He slid his hand up her shirt and ripped off her bra. "Plus, I can give you way more than twenty funky dollars."

She elbowed Eric as hard as she could, which caused him to loosen his grip and allowed her to run to the door. Her mind was scattered. She couldn't think, could barely breathe, and began to fumble clumsily with the lock. She jerked on the doorknob with all her might, trying and failing to undo the latch in her haste.

Eric came up behind her and knocked her head against the door. Momentarily dazed, she turned around and violently started swinging. He blocked each of her wild punches, grabbed her wrists, and twisted each until she dropped to her knees in mind-numbing pain.

"You *like* this, don't you?"

Tears streaked her face. "Stop, Eric, please."

"That's right, bitch. Beg for it." He slapped her hard and started to unfasten his belt buckle.

Shanice screamed and clawed at him. She was no longer trying to free herself; all she wanted to do was inflict pain. Then she saw Erica looking terrified in her bedroom doorway, crying, clutching her teddy bear, and watching the scene unfold.

"Your daughter," Shanice said between clenched teeth. "How can you do this in front of your daughter?"

Eric looked at Erica. "Get back in your room and close the door," he shouted.

When her door closed, he turned his attention back to Shanice. He let one of her hands go and then punched her in her temple.

Shanice slumped to the floor.

Chapter 16

Although the floor of the janitor's closet was hard and cold, Tabitha was having difficulty letting this moment end as she stretched and snuggled into Darren's neck.

Being with a man because she chose to instead of being forced to was simply wonderful, and when this man was a patient and generous lover, it was spectacular. Tabitha's body still tingled from head to toe from the earth-shattering orgasm he gave her. She had never before experienced a climax that powerful.

"Mmm," she whispered, "I could stay like this forever."

He tightened his arms around her and said, "I wouldn't have a problem with that." He wiggled and tried to find a comfortable position, which was nearly impossible, but like Tabitha, he didn't want to break the spell of the moment.

She smiled. "You might not, but my daughter would. Oh no . . . my daughter. I gotta go. What am I doing? Shanice is going to kill me." *And Eric might actually kill me,* she thought.

She jumped up, suddenly terrified, and reached for her jeans. She hit a mop bucket in the corner, which caused the mop to fall out and hit Darren on the head.

He winced, set the mop upright, and resisted the urge to rub his forehead. "I didn't know you had a daughter."

Tabitha laughed. "Of course not. You don't know anything about me."

"That's true, but I would love to get to know you," he said, standing up and slowly inching into the corner to give her some extra space.

Tabitha tugged on her jeans and got down on all fours to get her shoe from under the sink. She pulled her shirt over her head before realizing, after the fact, that she didn't have her bra on. She ripped the shirt back off and looked around frantically for her bra. "Believe me; you don't want to know me," she said after spotting it on top of the fire extinguisher in the corner. "You do *not* want to know *anything* about me."

Darren chuckled. "You buggin', girl. After what we just did, I want to know your grandmother's maiden name and what your great-uncle did for a living. I want to know what you do on Tuesday evenings and Saturday mornings. I want to know the name of your favorite teacher." He buckled his pants and tried to smooth down her hair. It was all spiky from him repeatedly running his fingers through it.

Tabitha put on her shirt again, picked up her purse, and tried to give herself the best look-over she could without a mirror. She tried not to watch Darren put on his clothes because she would be tempted to take them right back off him. She did her best to avoid his eyes because she was sure he would be able to read her thoughts through them.

Uh, I don't know what to say, she thought. *Thanks a million?* The thought made her smile, which intrigued Darren. He hopped on the counter and pulled Tabitha into him, nuzzling her neck.

"When am I going to see you again?" he asked.

Tabitha frowned. "What time is it?"

He looked at his watch—a little hurt by her rejection but too macho to show it. "It's half past ten." He rested his head on the cabinet and just stared at her.

Tabitha glanced at him but was not able to look into his eyes. She wanted to thank him and tell him how wonderful her experience was. She wanted to tell him that she had never done anything this wild in her life and how it had forever changed and healed her. But she settled with a simple "I got to go" and headed for the door.

He slid off the counter and grabbed her wrist. "Hold up, shawty. You ain't gonna give me your number or nothing?"

Tabitha stood stark still. Cold, rigid fear gripped her, which showed painfully in her eyes. She just knew he would hit her, and she braced herself for the blow.

Darren recognized her reaction. He knew she was scared shitless, but he had no idea what caused it. He dropped her wrist and asked, "Yo, what's wrong with you, shawty? Did I hurt you or something?"

She shook her head slightly, and he leaned in to kiss her cheek. *He's not Eric, Tabitha,* she thought. *All men don't hit women.*

"A'ight, look. I know you got to get with your little girl, so I'm not gonna press you. You have my number, right?"

Tabitha gave him a small smile and nodded in acknowledgment.

"A'ight, bet. When you get some time, give me a call." He opened the closet door and watched Tabitha as she walked out. When she entered the hall, there were a few I-know-what-you-did stares from a couple of passersby. However, their amused looks didn't faze her at all. Despite the emotions churning inside of her, she tried to keep her mind focused on getting home before Eric did.

Nothing good can come out of going to school these days.

Lisa stared out the window in the counselor's office, wringing her fingers. She longed to be outside and away from these fucking people with all their fucking questions. *Breathe, Lisa. Just be cool. All you need to do is tell them what they want to hear, whatever they want to hear, and this will be over.*

Lisa inhaled, exhaled, and opened her eyes, only to see Mrs. Fowler staring blankly at her face. She pretended not to hear Mrs. Fowler's question, which only made her more determined to break down Lisa's walls. So, she tried a different approach.

"What type of relationship do you have with your stepfather?" she asked.

Oh no, she didn't. "I don't have *any* relationship with my stepfather."

"Really? Dean Johnson said you seemed quite terrified of him."

Fuck being cool. They don't want me to be cool. They just want to be up in my business. Lisa shrugged. "The dean doesn't know what he's talking about. I wasn't afraid. I was pissed. I didn't know why he would be here. I take care of myself. I am my own damn guardian, and you guys already know that." Lisa pointed her finger at Mrs. Fowler accusingly. "Tell me this, why in the hell would you guys give a flying fuck about my attendance?" she continued. "I know people who come to school twice a month, and I don't see anybody hassling them."

Mrs. Fowler folded her arms across her chest. "Are you finished?"

Lisa was silent, and the counselor took that as assent. "First of all," she began, then paused, waving Lisa toward the chair, "do not raise your voice inside my office. Second, we are *not* hassling you. We are concerned about your attendance because it is not your usual behavior. And yes, we do realize that you are emancipated; however, when a parent—"

"He's not my parent."

Mrs. Fowler shot her a look, and Lisa snapped her mouth shut. "When a parent—step or otherwise—comes to us with concerns about our students and drug abuse, we take those concerns seriously."

"I do not use drugs," Lisa said between clenched teeth. "I don't believe this shit." She flopped down in a chair, folded her arms against her chest, and began to shake her leg impatiently. *I'm not going to cry. I'm not going to cry.* She felt her eyes start to fill. Lisa held her head high and bit her bottom lip. *I'm not going to cry.* However, the tears came anyway. *What the fuck,* Lisa thought. Her shoulders fell, and she let her arms follow suit. A light knock on the door brought her back as she quickly sat up and wiped her face.

The dean came in, and Lisa sighed.

"Good morning, Mr. Johnson," Mrs. Fowler said.

He nodded to her in response and then turned toward Lisa.

Lisa stood and defiantly marched up to the dean. "If you want me to take a drug test, I'll take the damn drug test. Whatever you want, whenever you want. I just don't give a shit anymore."

"I'm not here to talk about that." He turned to Mrs. Fowler. "If you could excuse us for a few minutes?"

"Of course," she said, rising smoothly from her chair. She left without sparing Lisa a glance.

Dean Johnson sat on the corner of the desk and motioned for Lisa to take a seat. "I did not come here to talk about drug tests. I know you and have known you for four years. I do not believe that you use drugs."

Lisa felt she should have been relieved by the news, but she wasn't. Instead, she just wanted to go home. "What are you here to talk about then, Dean Johnson, because I'm tired."

"I came here to talk about your stepfather." He raised a hand to stop her before she could speak. "Now, I'm not going to ask you anything. I'm here to *tell* you something." He breathed deeply. He found the hurt in her eyes almost too much to bear. "I told Carl Lee he was no longer welcome at this school."

Surprised, relieved, and struck silent, Lisa listened intently as the dean continued.

"I could not do anything to him officially. I know you can't have a man locked up on suspicion." He leaned toward Lisa and lowered his voice. His features had become vicious, his eyes piercing hers with their ferociousness. "But I would personally break his legs if I heard that he was within fifty feet of you."

Relief washed over Lisa's face. She did not know what to say. It was the first time—outside of Shanice and Tabitha—that she felt someone truly had her best interest at heart.

Dean Johnson cleared his throat. "Now, take a few minutes, get yourself together, and then return to class. I'll deal with Mrs. Fowler."

Shanice's head pounded. She opened her eyes, but everything was blurry and out of focus. She tried to move, but her body was pinned to the floor. Eric was on top of her. His arm felt like a boulder against her chest, and his free hand was frantically tugging at her pajama bottoms.

Fury blazed through her, clearing the fog from her head. She screamed and dug her nails into Eric's skin.

"You fucking bitch," he grunted. "Stay the fuck still."

"Get off of me," she screamed. "Get the fuck off me!"

"Shut the fuck up," he hollered, placing his hand over her mouth.

She bit into his flesh and jerked her head back, now even more determined to tear into his skin.

"You little bitch," he yelled. He drew his hand back and swung at her head, but Shanice moved to the side. Eric's hand struck the floor, and he screamed as his knuckle split against the hardwood. The force of the missed blow threw him forward.

Shanice scrambled to her feet, grabbed the VCR off the coffee table, and cracked it over his head. Unfazed, Eric turned and rammed her into the wall. He punched her in the gut, knocking the wind out of her. She crumbled back to the floor in a huff.

Outside at the corner, Tabitha hopped off the bus, still tingling from her sexual encounter, but as she walked toward the house, fear of Eric's wrath overwhelmed her. When she turned the corner, Erica's wails pierced through the air and hit her like a punch to the gut. Her daughter's sounds of anguish caused her to break into a run.

"Erica! Are you OK? Mommy's coming," she yelled.

She nearly ripped out the lining of her purse, trying to find her house keys. Then in a near panic, she dumped the purse's contents onto the doorstep and dropped to her knees, trying to pick out her keys amidst all the junk. Next, she heard Shanice scream, "Get the fuck off of me!"

Fighting off several knees to the gut, Eric had her pinned on the floor again.

Shanice could wiggle enough to raise her elbow and give him a double whack to the chin. The blows left Eric stunned, and he stumbled. Shanice ran into the dining room to grab one of the chairs, but she wasn't quick enough. Eric grabbed her and punched her in the temple again.

Erica watched from behind her bedroom door. She wanted to do what her grandma had taught her, but she was too scared after she saw Shanice fall.

Suddenly, Tabitha burst through the door and jumped on top of Eric, but she was no match for the demon she knew too well. Eric slammed her on the floor and ferociously began to beat her. When she fell to the floor nearly unconscious, he continued to hit and kick her.

"Stop, Daddy! Get off Mommy!" Erica screamed, but he wouldn't. Erica ran to the phone and dialed 911—just like her grandmother had taught her.

"Come help! Daddy's hurting Mommy."

Eric snatched the phone from Erica and asked, "What are you doing?" He put the phone receiver to his ear and heard the police dispatcher ask for an address. He panicked and slammed down the receiver.

Erica was shaking Tabitha and screaming, "Wake up, Mommy, wake up! Help is coming. Please, Mommy, wake up, please."

The scene was brutal, and Eric didn't know what to do next. Looking around the apartment, he saw that Shanice was starting to wake up, and Tabitha was lying still on the floor, covered in blood.

He did the only thing a man like him would do.

He ran.

Chapter 17

"No, oh my God, Eric. Get off of her! Shaniceeee!"

Shanice hopped out of the chair and rushed to Tabitha's side. "Shhh, it's okay. I'm here." She smoothed Tabitha's hair. "I'm right here. It's okay, Tab. I'm here."

Shanice looked over her shoulder to see Erica still curled in a ball in the chair by the window. She was fast asleep.

"Open your eyes, Tab. Look at me. I'm okay."

Tabitha slowly opened her eyes. Disoriented and unsettled from reliving the horrible scenes within her home, she sat up and looked around the hospital room. Then moving too quickly, she grabbed at her aching side and throbbing head.

"Where's Erica?"

"She's here. You don't have anything to worry about. We're both here, and we're both all right."

"Where are we?"

"University Hospital."

"What? What happened? Where's Eric?"

"Long story short, Munchkin called the cops, and who gives a fuck where Eric is? He's not here, and that's all that counts. I called your mom. She wasn't home, but I left a message on her machine. I left a message on Lisa's pager too. She's in school, so I don't know when she'll get it."

Tabitha winced from the pain as she tried to reposition herself in the bed. "Erica called the police?"

"I know, right? How cool is that? She said your mom taught her how."

Tabitha looked over at her little girl, full of pride, and held her hands out for Shanice to hand her over. Tabitha scooted over to make room in the bed. Shanice picked up Erica and laid her down next to Tabitha.

Tabitha's breath caught. She brought her trembling hand up to the younger girl's chin. Shanice's face was covered with black and blue bruises. "I'm so sorry," Tabitha whispered. Her heart broke, and the tears began to flow.

Shanice grabbed Tabitha's hand and held it against her cheek.

"Aw, baby," Tabitha said. "I'm sorry. I'm so sorry he hurt you."

Shanice sat on the edge of Tabitha's bed and wiped away her tears. "What are you sorry for? You didn't do this. Shit, girl. I still look good. I may be a little banged up, but it takes more than a few whacks to hide this kind of beauty."

Shanice's right cheek was various shades of green and purple, her bottom lip was split and swollen, and deep purplish marks ringed her left eye. Despite her attempts at humor, she was fucked up.

"I may look bad," Shanice continued, staring down at their linked fingers, "but I can cover this shit up with some Maybelline. You, on the other hand . . . He really hurt you," she said, her voice shaking. A lump rose in her throat, and tears welled up in her eyes. "He really, really hurt you." Sobs tore through Shanice's body, and Tabitha grabbed her shirt and pulled her close. She wrapped her arms around her and smoothed down her hair.

"I'm so sorry," Tabitha repeated. "I'm used to him hurting me, but I never in a million years thought he would try to do something like this to you."

"It's not your fault, Tabitha. This shit is all on Eric. That dude is a fucking monster. Something's seriously wrong with him. He ain't right in the head, Tabitha. Don't apologize for him. This ain't on you."

"I know, but I'm still very sorry. I should have never left you there alone." Tabitha moved over a little more so that Shanice could also lie down.

Shanice kicked off her sneakers and swung her legs over the guardrail. She pushed the IV pole up to the head of the bed and then lay down, careful not to disturb Erica. "Don't be sorry, Tab. Be angry. You don't deserve this shit. None of us do." She squeezed Tabitha's hand. "This ain't on you. This is on *him*." She looked at the IV running from Tabitha's arm and the bandage wrapped around her head. "This is *all* on him."

The two lay there as Erica slept soundly between them.

I just can't take any more of this bullshit.

Lisa stared at her reflection in the warped mirror of the stinky girls' bathroom. She washed her face for the third time but still couldn't erase the fact that she'd been crying all morning. The thought of going to class and explaining her swollen, bloodshot eyes to anyone made her cringe.

"To hell with this. I ain't staying here." *If I'm gonna be suspended, fuck it. I can just go home. Hell, I don't care if they keep me on in-school suspension until I graduate.*

With that thought, she walked out of the bathroom and didn't stop walking until she had made it to her apartment complex.

When she approached her apartment, she spotted Tony sitting on the steps reading the paper, and she paused. *This nigga won't give up,* she thought. A small part of her wanted to run and jump into his arms; instead, she rolled her eyes in absolute disgust.

I'm not my mother, and I don't need a man to feel better. I'd be damned if I let a man do anything he wanted to somebody I love and then act like it didn't happen. What Tony did to Shanice was unforgivable.

These thoughts ran through her mind, but deep inside, she knew that Tony really had nothing to do with what had happened. Nonetheless, her outside anger was not ready to let Tony back in.

"I ain't in the mood for this shit, Tony," she said as she walked around him and began digging in her purse for her keys. The scent of his Gucci cologne hung in the air above him. Lisa breathed in deeply. *Damn, he smells good,* she thought. *Why does he always smell so good?*

"Well, I ain't leaving until you talk to me."

"You're gonna be sitting here for a long damn time."

"That's fine with me. I don't have shit to do."

Lisa went into the house and slammed the door. She walked to the kitchen to check her voicemail and then remembered that Bunky had ripped the phone from the wall. She swore softly and quickly walked to use the portable phone in her bedroom. She had to listen to Shanice's message a couple of times to make any sense out of what she was saying. "Ain't no way," Lisa said as ice slid through her veins. "*Ain't no fucking way.*" She dropped the phone, picked up her purse, and ran out the door and down the street.

"What the fuck, yo?" Tony asked. He dropped the paper and took off after her. It only took a few moments for him to overtake Lisa. Tony was tall, lanky, and lightning fast. "What's wrong with you, yo?"

Lisa looked up at Tony, panting. "I need you to take me to the hospital."

"Why?" Tony asked, looking her up and down with concern wrinkling his brow. "What's wrong with you?"

"It's not me. There's nothing wrong with me. It's Tabitha. Her evil-ass baby daddy kicked her in the head. Shanice says she has a concussion."

Tony's jaw hardened, and his nostrils flared. "Come on," he said roughly. "My car's around the corner."

Shanice eased out of bed, trying not to wake Tabitha or Erica. She stretched, yawned, and walked to the door to get some air.

"Where are you going?" Tabitha asked.

"I didn't mean to wake you. I just need to stretch my legs for a bit."

"Okay." Tabitha turned over and quickly fell back asleep. Shanice walked into the hallway and looked around in disgust. Hospitals had always made her feel uneasy. Everything was too bright, and they were always full of sick people. Who in their right mind wanted to be surrounded by sick people? She spotted a nurse down the hall writing something in somebody's chart. Shanice eyed a little box in the nurse's spotless white pants pocket. The fabric was transparent enough for her to make out the writing on the box. Newport. She walked over to the nurse and tapped her on her shoulder.

"Excuse me. Can you spare a cigarette?"

The nurse reached into her pocket without hesitation but then took a moment to look at Shanice. "Uh, how old are you?"

"I'm 18."

"Yeah, and I'm Miss America."

"You sure are pretty enough to be Miss America."

"Thanks, but beat it, kid. Smoking is bad for your health." The nurse turned and walked away to finish her rounds.

Shanice watched in agony as the nurse carried her cigarettes around the corner. It was worth a shot, she thought. Then sighing, she made her way down to the lobby.

Moments later, she came across a janitor sitting outside the hospital on his break. Unlike the nurse, he didn't mind sharing his cigarettes with a minor. She sat down on the edge of the sidewalk, took a long drag, and blew several smoke rings. Inhaling slowly, she let the nicotine smooth over her jagged nerves.

A flurry of activity was taking place in the valet parking circle. She watched a flock of pigeons fight over some scattered pretzel crumbs. Cars zoomed past, horns blared, people rushed by, and snatches of random conversations hummed through the air. A little boy suddenly ran into the circle of birds and chased them off, and Shanice looked into the afternoon sun as she watched the birds' flight.

She wondered what it would be like to fly. The closest she had ever been to it was when she was high. She would close her eyes, spin around, and enjoy the light airiness of the movement. She figured that's why she loved to swim. Her mother used to take her swimming all the time. She closed her eyes and remembered her mother gently guiding her into the middle of the pool and teaching her how to float. They would play ring-around-the-rosy and Marco Polo for hours. Being in the water was the next best thing to flying, and Shanice absolutely loved it. Thoughts of her mother made her heart sink into her stomach. She really missed how things used to be.

I need a drink. She lifted her arm and took a sniff. *Hell, make that a bath* and *a drink.*

Shanice took one last drag and flicked the burning butt into the street. *I hope Ms. Mabel will get here soon because I can't stand the thought of going back into*

Tab's room. Shanice's eyes misted. *None of this would have happened had I stayed my black ass home.*

Shanice hung her head down as guilt mingled with shame. *Trying to be grown broke Lisa's heart and almost got Tabitha killed,* she thought. She hoped Lisa got there before Ms. Mabel.

She stood, brushed off her behind, and decided to wait in the lobby to see everybody before she was spotted.

I'm not being a coward, she thought over and over. *I'm just being practical. As soon as somebody gets here, I'm leaving—not because I am afraid to face anybody, but because I've got loads of shit to do.*

While watching the traffic outside and waiting to see who would show up, Shanice fell asleep.

Chapter 18

Tabitha smoothed Erica's hair out of her face and wondered what was taking Shanice so long. She figured Shanice had probably left, and she wasn't upset that she might have left. She just worried about where she might go. Although she knew that Shanice wasn't as tough as she pretended to be, there was nothing she could do to help her at the moment.

How can I help her when I'm such a mess? The television was on, but the sound was muted. Erica was still asleep, and Tabitha wanted her to stay that way for as long as possible. She grabbed the remote and started surfing through the channels. *How did I get here?* She reached for her cup of ice and dropped the remote on the floor. The cup was empty, and the call bell was on the remote. "Shit," she said, softly wiping the tears from her eyes. "I'm tired of being here."

Tabitha still didn't know the whole story of how she got hospitalized, but she knew she was ready to go. She picked at the tape covering the IV in her arm and looked up—only to see Eric at the door.

Tabitha stiffened. Scenes of him trying to force himsel on her friend flashed through her mind. Rage swelled her chest. "What do you want?" she demanded.

"Are you okay?"

Tabitha cackled. "Are you *serious? Am I okay?* Eric, I'm *not* okay. Do I *look* okay? You kicked me in fucking head." She pointed to the bandages. "I'm okay, and I haven't been okay for a long time."

Eric sniffed and shifted his weight from one foot to the other. He wiped away the tears streaming down his face and stepped inside the room, but he stopped midway when he saw the expression on Tabitha's face.

"You step one more foot inside this room, and I will scream for security. How did you even get in here?" Tabitha tried to sit up, but pain sliced through her side. She winced and rested her head back against the pillow. *Where the hell is security?* she thought. *This isn't nothing like the TV shows that had cops posted at your door when somebody beats the hell out of you.*

Eric looked around nervously and promptly pulled the brim of his hat down low enough to hide his eyes. "Do you hate me?"

"I don't hate you, Eric. I don't feel *anything* for you at all. You killed everything inside of me that could feel anything for you. I don't love you. I don't hate you. I don't pity you. I *nothing* you, Eric."

He looked longingly at his daughter sleeping on Tabitha's legs. "Can I hold her?"

"You touch her, and I'll kill you."

The statement was devoid of emotion, which gave him pause. He looked into Tabitha's eyes and saw a woman sitting there—not the little girl he was accustomed to. He swallowed hard and took an involuntary step back.

"I think you should go, Eric. The cops are looking for you, and even though I could care less if they catch you, I don't think my daughter should see them lock up your ass. Thanks to you, she's seen enough already."

"Whoa . . . Hold up. Pump your brakes. What do you mean the cops are looking for me?"

Tabitha laughed at the ignorance he portrayed. "Eric, you beat me bloody and tried to rape a 14-year-old girl. So you think the cops *won't* be out looking for you?"

"Aye, yo. I didn't try to rape that girl. Did she tell the cops that?"

"No, she didn't tell them that. *I* did. I saw what you did with my own eyes, *remember?* I came home, and you were on top of my friend. She's 14, Eric. You lost your entire mind if you think I'm going to let you around *my* daughter after seeing what *you* did. I will put a bullet in you myself before I let that happen." Erica stirred, so Tabitha pulled her closer to her side. "Shhhh, baby, go back to sleep. Mommy's here. Go back to sleep."

She looked up at Eric with murder in her eyes. "Get out of here, Eric. Ain't shit here for you. You need to worry about avoiding the cops." She gave him a cold smile. "I can't wait until they find your ass, but I don't want them to find you here. Erica has been through enough."

Lisa was uncomfortable during the entire drive to the hospital. Her stomach churned the whole way, and her mind played out all the worst-case scenarios.

Oh my God. Oh my God. "I'ma kill him. I'm going to fucking kill him."

"It's gonna be OK," Tony said, but she wasn't trying to hear that. She appreciated his efforts, but she needed to see for herself.

When they pulled into the parking lot, Tony turned off the car and grabbed Lisa's hand. "Look, shawty, I'm not going inside because hospitals freak me out, but I ain't going nowhere. I'm going to be right here." He squeezed her hand. "Look, I hate hospitals, but if you need me, call me. I will wreck this whole place if you need me to."

Lisa didn't respond. She squeezed his hand quickly and then hopped out of the car.

When she entered the lobby, she spotted Ms. Mabel and ran to catch up with her. The two entered the elevator hand in hand, praying all the way to Tabitha's room.

"Hey, Munchkin."

"Auntie! Grandma!" Erica jumped out of the hospital bed and ran into her grandmother's arms. "I did what you told me to do, Grandma," she continued. "I was too scared to do it when Daddy hurt Auntie Shanice. So I let Daddy hurt her 'cause I was too scared."

"Hush and wipe those tears up now. You did well, baby. You did just fine," Ms. Mabel said. She held her granddaughter close, rubbing her hair and rocking her back and forth.

Lisa fought back her tears and reached out for Erica. "It's all right, Munchkin."

Ms. Mabel sat next to Tabitha's bed, grabbed her hand, and brought it to her cheek. "I'm so sorry, baby. I should have never let you leave with that man."

"How are you?" Lisa asked. Then her eyes widened as Erica's words hit home. Lisa walked over to the bed and stared at the munchkin. "What is she talking about? What does she mean by he 'hurt Shanice'? What's wrong with Shanice?"

Tabitha forced herself to meet Lisa's gaze. "He beat her and tried to rape her."

"Jesus," Ms. Mabel said.

"Where is she?"

"She said she needed some air. I thought she was waiting downstairs for you," Tabitha said before the tears started to flow. "I should have never left her there. I went to the school to sign up for my financial aid. I wasn't gone that long, and . . . a-an-and when I came home, he was—oh, Mom, Erica was screaming, and he was beating the hell out of Shanice and trying to rip her pants off. I think she was fighting back for a while because Eric looked tore up, but she was unconscious when I got in the house, and he was *still* hitting her. I shouldn't have left her there, Mom. I should have known better."

"Aw, baby, when will you stop taking the blame for his sins? You are *not* responsible for what Eric does—not to you or anybody else. Ain't no way you could have known he would do something like that."

As Lisa and Ms. Mabel sat in disbelief, Erica fell back asleep. Lisa got up and laid her down on the bed. "Is Shanice all right?"

"Hell, she's doing a lot better than I am," Tabitha joked. "You should have seen what she did to Eric's face. I don't know where that little girl learned how to fight like that, but she gave Eric a run for his money. His face was tore up from the floor up."

Ms. Mabel leaned over and hugged Tabitha, admiring her daughter's strength and ability to smile still.

Seeing the love between Tabitha and her mother made Lisa long for the same thing with her mother and brought Shanice back to the forefront of her mind.

"This is it, right?" Lisa asked. "You *can't* be thinking about going back to Eric after this."

"I can't go back. I mean, it's a shame that it took him to hurt somebody else for me to see that he's not any good for me. Eric has killed any kind of feelings that I had for him."

Lisa looked into Tabitha's eyes and saw something she had never seen before: affirmation. "Okay. Well, I'm going to see about Shanice. After that, I will get Erica's and your stuff."

Tabitha pulled Lisa down and hugged her. She kissed her on the cheek and whispered, "Keep Shanice with you. Don't let her run."

Lisa nodded and left.

Shanice woke up to the sounds of a baby screaming. She jumped and looked around, but the stark white of the hospital's walls left her disoriented. Unfolding herself from the chair, she stretched, spun around, and found herself face-to-face with Lisa, then stumbled back.

"Damn," Lisa said smiling, "I know I don't look *that* bad."

Shanice smiled, a bit uncomfortable. "You don't look as bad as I do."

"I know," Lisa said sadly. She stretched out her arms, and Shanice hesitated a moment before walking into them. The flood of tears came, and Shanice did nothing to stop them. Instead, she clung to Lisa and buried her face in Lisa's neck. Shanice let out all the fears and pain she had hidden from Tabitha.

"It's okay," Lisa crooned. "Let it all out." She rubbed Shanice's back. "It's all right. You're all right now. I'm sorry for the things I said—"

"It's nothing. Don't worry about it," Shanice sniffed.

Lisa pulled out of the embrace, squeezed Shanice's hands, and looked into her teary eyes. "It *is* something, and I am *so* sorry. I shouldn't have put you out, but I had a very bad fucking day. When I came home and saw you like that . . . I just went off."

Shanice looked away in shame, but Lisa gently grabbed her chin and turned her head. "Shanice, when you passed out, I was so scared. I've never ever been afraid like that before, and you know the type of shit I've been through. Seeing you like that freaked me out, and I'm still a bit freaked, but I'm here. I will *always* be here, and you are *always* welcome in my house. You *do* know that I love you, and I'll always be here for you, right?"

Shanice nodded and pulled her in for another hug. "I really am sorry, Lisa."

Lisa laughed. "Bitch, please. You know we like family." Lisa held up her hands to high-five Shanice like she used to when they were younger. She smiled. "I got the peanut butter."

"And I got the jelly," Shanice giggled.

Lisa tugged Shanice toward the door. "Come on. Tony's outside. He's going to take us to my car, and then you and I will get Tabitha's shit out of that house."

As they approached the car, Shanice could tell Tony was pissed, but he didn't say anything. After he got a closer look at her and the bruises on her face, his anger melted into sympathy.

"Yo, shawty, you all right?"

"Puh-lease, you should have seen what *I* did to *him*."

His emotions went from sympathy to pity, which made Shanice's heart drop into her stomach. She could take anything in this world but pity. She forced out a laugh, hoping that would conceal her hurt.

Lisa grabbed the passenger-side door. "Tony, can you take me to my car? It's at Tabitha's mom's house."

He nodded. "Anything you need, shawty. I got you."

The traffic outside of the hospital was bumper to bumper. It took them a full ten minutes just to get out of the parking lot. Shanice did her best to appear invisible. She pressed herself into the corner and kept her eyes pasted to the window. The tension between Lisa and Tony was so thick you could touch it, and Shanice knew it was all her fault. She rested her head on the window and tried to fight the guilt. Soon, lightning flashed, and rain began to fall, creating diagonal tracks across the windshield.

God's tears. That's what my mom called it. Mom, she sighed as a yearning so deep filled her and left her breathless. . . . *I want my mommy!* Shanice closed her eyes as the lump welled up in her throat. She wiped away her tears. *But she doesn't want me.* She was relieved when Tony turned on the radio—any form of distraction was good. She leaned her head into the headrest and let the music flow through her. With each downbeat of the music, she pushed out another thought of her mother.

Chapter 19

Tabitha watched the heart monitor on the screen as her mother sat in the chair next to her with Erica sprawled across her lap.

They shouldn't be here, she thought.

She had spent nearly an hour trying to convince her mother to take Erica home and get some rest, but that was useless. Ms. Mabel adamantly repeated that she wasn't going anywhere until she was sure that Tabitha would be OK, which meant the nearly impossible: talking to a doctor. An army of nurses, aides, and housekeepers trooped in and out of that door, but still no doctors.

Tabitha watched as her mother fought fatigue between her head nods and soft snores. Finally, she lowered the volume on the television and flipped through the channels. Still, Ms. Mabel's snores became louder and louder by the second until they grew into a deafening crescendo.

I wish she would go home. She needs to lie down, stretch out, and get some rest. I wonder if one of the nurses would take Mama's blood pressure and check her sugar.

She repositioned herself in the bed, and pain sliced through her rib cage. She had to bite her lip and grip the bed rails to keep from screaming out, but the pain would not let up.

Fuck being brave. Where's a nurse? She groped around the bed for the call bell. Finally, she spied it down around her feet and reached for it, whimpering in pain.

"May I help you?" the nurse asked over the intercom.

"Yes, I need something for pain." Tabitha's distressed voice awakened Ms. Mabel, and she jumped to her daughter's bedside.

"Where does it hurt, baby? What can I do for you?"

"Nothing, Mama. I'm fine," she lied.

"Someone will be right in to help you," the nurse responded.

"Are you OK, Mommy?" asked a sleepy Erica from the window before she rubbed her eyes and stuck her thumb in her mouth.

"I'm fine, sweetheart."

"Then can we go home, Mommy?"

"Not just yet, baby. I still need to see the doctor. So we'll see after that, okay?"

"Okay, Mommy."

Tabitha switched the TV channel to Cartoon Network, and Erica was quickly lost in the land of Scooby-Doo. Soon, the nurse came in with a very tall, young-looking doctor. He grabbed Tabitha's chart off the end of the bed while the nurse administered the pain medication.

"I am Dr. Oswald."

"Oh, excuse me. Hello, Doctor. I'm Mabel Williams, Tabitha's mother."

"Nice to meet you. Now, I have some good news and some not-so-good news. How about I start with the good news first?" He looked through Tabitha's chart, then placed the chart behind his back before he continued. "I just finished reviewing your X-rays. We didn't find any broken bones, but your ribs are quite bruised. Your blood pressure is normal, and we didn't see any signs of internal bleeding. However, as I told you earlier, your CT Scan revealed a slight concussion, and although it's not severe, we would like to keep you overnight for observation."

"Excuse me, but if it's not severe, why can't I take her home now?" Tabitha's mother asked. "I can take care of her."

"Normally, we would discharge her, ma'am, but Tabitha was unconscious when she arrived, so I would like to keep an eye on her a little while longer just to ensure everything is good."

The doctor returned the chart to the foot of the bed and left the room.

"Oh, baby, I am so sorry," Tabitha's mother whispered.

"Oh, Mama, stop it. You didn't do this to me. You didn't even know that Eric was doing this to me."

"I didn't want to know—"

"But Mom—"

"I know what it's like to have somebody you share your heart with, that you share your bed with, put their hands on you. It just doesn't hurt physically or mentally. Instead, it crushes your spirit and attacks your very soul."

Tabitha swallowed hard. "Did Daddy hit you?"

Mabel frowned at her daughter. "He beat me mercilessly."

The terrible revelation brought Tabitha to tears.

"So you see . . . All the signs were there that the same thing was being done to you, but I didn't want to know." Ms. Mabel walked over to Tabitha's bed, bent over, and kissed her forehead. "I'm going to take this baby to get something to eat. Let me know if anything changes." She turned and picked up Erica. "Are you hungry, little girl?"

"Yes, Grandma."

"Well then, let's go take care of that."

"I'll be back, Mommy. I love you."

"I love you too, baby," Tabitha said as she watched them leave the room. She closed her eyes and tried to remember her father beating her mother, but nothing came to mind. She couldn't recall ever hearing her father raise his voice at her mother.

Tabitha cut off the TV and stared out of the hospital window. The view offered nothing but more hospital windows across the courtyard, but the image and sound of the rain were soothing.

She did nothing but watch the rain for a few moments, and then memories started flowing. She remembered seeing her mother limp down the hall and crying on the kitchen floor. She remembered her mother sitting in the corner of her room with a black eye. She remembered calling out to her and not getting a response. Then dozens of images started coming to mind. Although she couldn't remember the actual fights, she remembered the aftermath.

How young was I? she thought, struggling to place an age to the images. She shook her head in disbelief and put a trembling hand to her mouth. "I was the same age as Erica." *I'm going to be sick,* she thought. She looked for her hospital basin, which was just out of reach. She frantically pressed the call bell and clamped her hands over her mouth. *This has to stop with me.*

Lisa's mind raced with everything she wanted to say to Tony, but she kept silent. The rain had stopped when they pulled in front of Ms. Mabel's house. Lisa reached over the backseat and patted Shanice's leg.

"Wake up, hon. We're here."

"I wasn't sleeping."

Lisa saw Shanice's tear-soaked face and bloodshot eyes and gave her leg a reassuring squeeze before Shanice got out of the car. Then just as she reached for the door handle, Tony grabbed Lisa's hand, and she resisted the urge to snatch her hand away.

Weak. So fucking weak, she thought. She wanted to thank him for being there. She wanted to slide into his arms and block the rest of the world out, but she wasn't ready to forgive him. Lisa looked into his eyes and saw love there, but she wasn't her mother. She refused to let a man do anything to her or those she loved and act as if nothing had happened. She dropped his hand and exited the car. She stood on the curb and watched him drive away. She was conflicted. She wanted him but hated herself for it.

She turned and found Shanice sitting on the steps. "Come on, girl. Get up. I want you to tell me everything that happened. Ms. Mabel was in with Tab, so I didn't ask her for details."

By the time Lisa and Shanice got into Lisa's car and drove to Tabitha's house, Shanice had revealed all the details. Lisa was beyond pissed, hoping they would find Eric at Tabitha's house so she could finish off his ass.

The house was empty when they arrived to pick up a few things for Tabitha and Erica. Although Lisa wanted to kick Eric's ass, she didn't want Shanice to go through any more shit.

"Shanice, go and get the munchkin's stuff, and I'll get Tab's clothes. She said there were some trash bags under the kitchen sink."

As Shanice went for the bags, Lisa walked into Tabitha's bedroom and stared at the bed, wondering what it must have been like for her friend. "Why do people have to be so evil?"

"Huh?"

"Oh, nothing. Just talking to myself."

Shanice handed her three trash bags. "Here ya go."

Lisa took the bags and flung open the closet door. She snatched Tabitha's clothes off the hangers and stuffed them into bags.

"Damn, look at this. Just a bunch of cheap shit from the Seven Dollar Store. His shit ain't cheap. Fucking Gucci, Louis Vuitton . . . fucking pussy."

She ripped his outfits from the hangers and threw them on the floor. She spat on the clothes and kicked them into the corner. It took her a minute to get herself together before she moved to the dresser. Tabitha had nothing else; everything else was his. "You've *got* to be fucking kidding me."

Lisa went through the nightstand drawers and paused when she found a picture of the three of them when they were little. She remembered that day. They were on the monkey bars, and they were happy, so damn happy. Ms. Mabel had taken them to the park and McDonald's.

The happy memories overwhelmed Lisa with tears that began to fill the picture frame. She sat on the bed and continued to stare at the three of them. Tabitha was posing under the monkey bars with her hands on hips, and she and Shanice were hanging upside down with pigtails dangling like antennas. *We were so innocent. We had no idea how bad a heartache could be or how cold the world could be.*

What gave him the motherfucking right to hurt her? "Huh, Eric? Who gave you the motherfucking right?"

Lisa ran over to the TV stand and kicked the TV to the floor.

"What in the hell—" Shanice mumbled.

"Let's trash this motherfucker."

Shanice ran into the living room, grabbed Eric's beloved Sega, and gave it to Lisa, who threw it out the window. From that point on, *everything* was free game as the pair went throughout the house, breaking and smashing nearly everything in sight.

"Hello, hello?"

The girls froze after the door opened, and the booming voice resonated throughout the house. Shanice turned around and brandished a boot like it was a weapon, and Lisa swung a broom as if it were a Louisville slugger.

"Hello? Does Tabitha Williams live here?"

"Who wants to know?" Shanice asked.

"A friend."

"I know all of Tabitha's friends," Lisa said, "and you definitely *aren't* one of them."

"Yo, what in the hell are you doing here?"

"Are you one of Eric's boys?" Shanice asked.

"Listen, youngin', pump your brakes. I don't know any Eric. I just came by to see Tabitha. Name's Darren. We go to school together."

Lisa squinted at him. "I know you. You're that ignorant-ass boy from the parking lot," she said as she released her grip on the broom.

"Oh yeah. You're that feisty chick. How you doin', ma?"

"You know this fool?" Shanice asked, pointing her finger in the guy's direction.

"No, I don't *know* him, but I have seen him up at Thornton College." Lisa walked over and leaned against the table, ready to interrogate Darren. "How you know where Tabitha lives? Because I know she didn't give you her address."

"Yeah, you following her or something?" Shanice chimed in.

"Ain't nobody following her, and no, she didn't give me this address," he said. "She left her roster at school, and I wanted to make sure she had it."

"That's a bunch of bullshit, and you know it," Lisa said as she sneered up at Darren.

He stuck his hands in the air and looked at them with wide-eyed innocence. "Rosters are not easy to come by."

Lisa snorted. "Hold up; wait a minute. I could be wrong. Let me see. Rosters, rosters. How does somebody replace a roster? That's right. You can just log on to any computer at the college and print one the fuck out." She picked up the broom again.

"OK, you got me. It's a lame excuse, I know. I was chilling with Tabitha at the school earlier, and I wanted to see her again."

"What do you mean by 'chilling'?"

"You know, kicking it. We had lunch together and shit."

Shanice's eyes lit up. "Go ahead, Tab!"

"Look, just tell Tab that I stopped by." He looked around at the mess they had created in the apartment, shook his head, and turned to leave. "I knew this wasn't a good idea."

"Tabitha's in the hospital," Shanice blurted out.

"Shanice," Lisa hollered, dropping the broom again.

"Her baby daddy beat her up." Shanice defiantly stuck her chin in the air and refused to look at Lisa.

"What? When did this happen? I was just with her this morning. What hospital is she in?"

"University Hospital."

"Shanice, you've got a big-ass mouth," Lisa said, staring at the younger girl like she'd just lost her mind.

"Thanks, shawty," Darren hollered over his shoulder as he bolted out the door.

Shanice nodded and closed the door behind him, but she had to duck Lisa's swing. "What?"

"What do you mean what? Why did you tell him that, girl? You don't even know him."

"I know he's not Eric, so he can't be all that bad."

"You can be so stupid sometimes."

"That's true. Look, Lisa, what's done is done. Do you want to finish breaking shit?"

"I don't think there's anything left to break."

"Then let's get the fuck out of here." Shanice lifted her hand. "Give me the keys, and I'll meet you in the car."

Lisa handed her the keys and stood in the center of the room, staring off into space. Then as Shanice lugged the bags to the door, she turned to Lisa and said, "When you get to the car, you can tell me what else is bothering you."

Lisa nodded absently, then shook off the mood that was consuming her. *I'm not about to tell you that I am missing the man who let you get hurt,* she thought as longing and guilt churned inside of her. *I am* not *my mother.*

Chapter 20

Twenty ceiling tiles, twenty-four if you count the half tiles in the corner. Six tiles with lights, two with vents, and one discolored.

Tabitha was restless as she switched the television on and off. The phone rang. *Thank God,* she thought. She picked it up before it got a chance to ring a second time. "Hello?" she said breathlessly.

"Hi, can I speak to Jenna?" an older woman asked.

Tabitha sighed. "I think you have the wrong number, ma'am."

"Oh no, I'm sorry."

"It's okay," Tabitha said softly and hung up the phone.

She picked up the receiver five seconds later and dialed the first number that came to her head. "Mama—"

"Baby, is everything OK? What's wrong? Do you need me to come back up there?"

"No, Mama, I'm fine." *Now I wish I hadn't called. I don't want her to worry any more than she already is.* "I just called to check on you and Erica and make sure y'all got home all right."

"Oh, I thought something was wrong. Honey, Erica is fine. The poor thing is still sleeping. All this excitement has worn her out. Do you need anything? Has anyone been in to see you? What did the doctor say?"

"Nobody's been in to see me yet, Mama. And I don't need anything. I'm fine. I'll call you back as soon as I hear anything; don't worry."

"Okay, baby. Try to get some rest."

"I will, Mama. I love you."

"I love you too, baby."

Tabitha hung up the phone and looked at the ceiling to start a new count of the tiny holes in the tile above her head.

This is crazy. I can't take this anymore.

She turned back the covers and swung her feet out of bed. The sudden movement caused her ribs to ache, but she ignored the pain. Instead, she walked over to the window seat and picked up the fresh linen the housekeeper left earlier that morning for the empty bed beside her. She took a pair of gloves out of the box hanging on the wall and began to strip the linen from the bed. The sounds of Erica and Shanice screaming replayed repeatedly in her head. She shuddered at the memory of seeing Eric on top of Shanice, trying to assault her.

For the first time, Tabitha saw Eric as the monster he truly was. She couldn't explain or reason his actions away this time. The tears fell as she smoothed the wrinkles out of the sheets. She fought off the pain as she limped around the bed to unfold the blanket and spread it across the sheets.

"Miss, what are you doing?" the housekeeper asked as she came to empty Tabitha's trash. "You should be lying down. I'll do this."

"No, I need to do this."

"You do *not* need to do this. What you need to do is rest. You're in no condition to be up trying to clean. Hell, you look like—"

Tabitha chuckled. "I look like what? Huh? Like somebody walked all up and down my ass? You don't have to be afraid to say it. My daughter's father did this to me. He beat my ass like I stole something after I stopped him from trying to rape my 14-year-old friend." Tabitha tugged on the blanket to give it some slack over the edge. "He's been whooping my ass for years, but this is the first time he's put me in the hospital. I don't know if that means he's getting better or worse at it. But what I *do* know is that cleaning clears my head and keeps me sane. So, could you please just let me do this? Please?"

The housekeeper turned and left the room without saying a word. She returned moments later with some disinfectant spray, disposable cloths, and trash bags. "I understand, sweetie. You do what you need to do, and I won't say a word. You do whatever it is you need to do." The housekeeper left the room and partially closed the door behind her.

Tabitha flopped down on the bed, clutched the spray can to her chest, and cried. She tried to regain her composure and began to clean everything in sight. After she had tackled nearly every possible surface in the room, she went to the bathroom to wash up, which left her feeling much better. By the time she made it back to the window seat, Lisa and Shanice had called to check on her. She felt even better after hearing a more upbeat Shanice. She hung up the phone and leaned over to peer through the window and look down at the courtyard below.

"I hope you're not planning to jump."

Tabitha yelped and lost her balance. Darren rushed to her side and grabbed her arm to keep her from falling onto the floor.

"What in the hell are you doing here?" she asked, confused and delighted at the same time. "How in the hell did you even know I was in here?"

He just smiled.

Lisa decided to go to work early. She needed something to do to take her mind off everything that was going on. She told Shanice everything while they put Tab's stuff up in her room. She felt better after talking about it, but the memories left her nerves frazzled, and she needed the chaos of McDonald's to distract herself.

Lisa remembered the look on Shanice's face when she unloaded on her. *The girl looked like she could chew through nails when I told her what Carl Lee did to me.* Most times, Shanice had something to say about everything, be it right or wrong. But as Lisa poured out her darkest secret, Shanice didn't utter a word. Instead, she listened attentively and had nothing to add, and Lisa was thankful for that silence.

Even though it was still early, Lisa had already had a long-ass day and wasn't in the mood for an actual conversation. She just needed to vent, and somehow, Shanice understood that.

Finally, Lisa walked into her job and ignored the curious looks from her coworkers as she headed to the back of the store to clock in. She felt like she didn't have to explain to them why she was there. She just was. *Hell, if I don't make up that day I missed from work last week, my paycheck will look like stir-fried shit.*

Carla hopped up on the counter beside her. "Girl, did you hear what happened to Wanda?"

"No, what happened? Is she okay?"

"If you call servin' five to ten okay, then yes, girl, she's fine."

"No, she ain't! You lyin'. When did this happen?"

"Last night, the cops kicked in her door looking for her old man. He wasn't anywhere to be found, but she was there, and so was two kilos of coke."

"Damn."

"Damn is right," Carla said, "so I guess you gonna get promoted, huh?"

"Girl, please. They ain't gonna promote me. I'm 17 years old. Everybody in here is older than me. Most days, I can't even get anybody to listen to me."

"Well, girl, you never know. Nobody thought they would make you assistant manager, but they did. So who's to say they won't promote your ass to the top dog?"

"I know you trippin' now. Get the hell off the counter and get back to that window. You've got people waiting."

"Yes, sir, top dog, sir," Carla said as she gave Lisa a mock salute.

Lisa tied an apron on so she could help the line workers when Mike called her name from the back office.

"Aye, yo, Lisa. The phone."

"Who is it?"

"Do I look like a secretary? I'm assistant manager just like you, shawty."

"Whatever, Mike. Tell them to hold on. I'm coming." Lisa finished her Egg McMuffin and headed to the phone. "Hello."

"You know I don't like to be kept waiting," Carl Lee said in his trademark country drawl.

"Leave me the fuck alone." She slammed down the receiver several times before letting it drop to the floor.

"Damn, shawty. You all right?"

"I'm fine, Mike, but the next time I ask you who the fuck it is, you better damn well find out."

"OK, shawty. Sheesh."

"My name is Lisa. I am not nor have I ever been anybody's shawty. Now, get the hell out of the office and get back to work."

Lisa walked out into the restaurant and the employee bathroom. She locked the door and leaned up against it. "Why can't that man leave me the fuck alone?" She pushed off the door and started pacing the length of the small room. *You took everything from me,* she thought.

I don't have anything left for you to take. Finally, she sat down on the toilet and burst into tears. "Please, God, make him leave me alone."

Shanice waited across the street from the school for Begonia. It was early in the afternoon. The rain stopped, but the sky was still dark and cloudy. She'd called Begonia from Lisa's apartment and told her she had a job for her. Shanice stared at a little old lady shuffling down the street and frowned. *It isn't exactly the kind of job Begonia is used to,* she thought, looking back at the school, *but I'm sure she can get it done.*

Shanice leaned up against the stoop she was standing next to. *Damn it. I'm going to kill that girl. She's fifteen minutes late. I know she told me to meet her ass at noon. If she couldn't make it, she should have fuckin' let me know.*

As soon as Shanice turned to walk away, Begonia ran through the side exit of the school.

"Bitch, you better run!"

"What's wrong—"

Before Shanice could finish her question, Mrs. Butt-gut came running through the door after Begonia. Shanice didn't know what to do except to take off running. After the two cleared a city block, they slowed to a walk. Shanice turned around and saw Butt-gut way down the street. She was out of breath and bent over with her hands on her knees.

"That's OK," Butt-gut screamed. "I'll catch your ass when you least expect it."

"You can't even catch your breath, Butt-gut!" Begonia yelled. "How in the hell you gonna catch me? Come on, Shanice. That shit she talking ain't fazing me."

"Why is she chasing you, girl?"

"Because she's hungry."

"Bee, that don't make no kind of sense," Shanice said, panting.

"It does when I have her lunch in my book bag."

"What the hell? Why do you have her lunch?"

"Because I overheard her tell Charlie that my mom is a crackhead and that I'm a thief."

"Hell, your mom *is* a crackhead, and you *are* a thief."

"I know, but she ain't have to tell him that."

"So, hold up. Why did you take her lunch?"

"Shit, I had to hit that bitch where it would hurt the most."

"You must be slipping if she caught you."

"Slipping, my ass. That ho didn't catch me."

"So, how does she know that you stole her lunch, and why is she chasing you?"

"'Cause I told her on my way out the door." Begonia went into her book bag and pulled out a turkey hoagie. She offered Shanice some, and Shanice took it without hesitation.

"A'ight, Shanice. First off, tell me what the hell happened to your fucking face. Did you get hit by a Mack truck? And, second, what was so important that I had to leave school before my art class? You know art is my shit."

"Well, the answer to your first question is simple. I got my ass whooped. The answer to your second question . . . It's a little more complicated. I know this is short notice, but I need to break into Lisa's parents' house. You're the only real criminal I know."

"You see, *that's* what I'm talking about. 'Criminal' sounds much classier than 'thief.' Anyway, why in the hell do you want to break into their place? I thought Lisa was your girl."

"She *is* my girl, and she don't live with them anymore. She lives in the projects. So trust me, I'm doing this for her."

"Damn, that's right. I forgot she was doing her own thang."

"Well, can you help me?"

"Is there some serious cash involved?"

"No."

"Then I can't help you," Begonia said, turning to walk away.

"Wait," Shanice sighed. "Lisa told me this in confidence, and if you say anything, I'm going to whoop your ass."

Begonia laughed. "You couldn't whoop my ass on a good day, but now, I'm interested. Why should I help you if there's no money involved?"

"You should help me 'cause you have little sisters, and Lisa's stepfather has a thing for little girls. I think it would benefit the hood if more people knew about it."

Begonia sighed. "Yo, that's fucked up. A'ight, I'll help you. What do you need me to do?"

"It's simple. Just get me inside."

"Shanice, ain't shit simple about breaking into somebody's house in the middle of the damn day."

"Come on, Bee. Damn. It's the only time I know the house will be empty, for sure. Carl Lee's drunk ass is down at the 31st Street Bar and Mrs. Gloria's at work. Are you gonna help me? We only have a couple of hours."

"I said I was going to help you, didn't I? But we've got to stop at my house first so I can get my tools."

Shanice started to object, but Begonia cut her off. "Look, Shanice, unless you want me to break into their house with a brick through the window, I suggest you let me go and get what I need."

Shanice nodded, took a bite of the hoagie, and followed Begonia to her home. *Nobody gets to hurt us in secret anymore. Whatever y'all do to us in the dark is finna shine bright as fuck in the light.*

Chapter 21

Tabitha sat in the chair beside her hospital bed, looking like a decrepit old woman dressed in two blue-speckled hospital gowns with a blanket stretched across her lap. Darren sat on the foot of her bed while they waited for the housekeeper to bring in another chair. She reached up to touch the bandages on her head, then snatched her hand back down as if someone had popped her fingers. She grabbed the edge of the blanket and started rolling it between her fingers.

Darren frowned at her. "Look, if I'm making you uncomfortable, I can leave. I just came by to make sure you were all right."

"No, you don't have to leave. I just wasn't expecting you, that's all." Tabitha ran her hands across the bandages. "I know I look crazy," she mumbled, fumbling with the IV on the back of her hand.

He was trying to tell her how he found out she was in the hospital, but she couldn't focus. *How in the hell are you supposed to act around your one-night stand after you were placed in the hospital by your crazy-ass baby daddy? You know what? I should write a book. When this is all over, I will write a book so that other women can benefit from my stupidity.*

". . . so that's when your girl Shanice told me you were here."

Tabitha rolled her eyes. *Shanice. I should have known. I will wring that girl's neck as soon as I get out of here.*

"Aye, yo, you all right?"

"Oh, I'm fine." *I'm just trying to figure out where I will bury that little girl's body after I kill her.*

The nurse came in with Tabitha's discharge papers, and she was relieved by the distraction.

"All right, Ms. Williams," the nurse said. "All you have to do is sign here that you are leaving the hospital AMA, which means against medical advice, and I explained the consequences to you and all of your rights."

Tabitha signed where the nurse indicated.

The nurse washed her hands, put on gloves, and took the IV out of Tabitha's hand. "I just need to go over a few things with you, and then you are free to go."

Tabitha listened as the nurse carefully and intently went through her instructions and gave her the prescriptions.

"Very good," said the nurse, who gave Darren leery looks. "Remember, if any of those symptoms worsen, you must return to the ER immediately."

"You know my car is outside," Darren said. "I'll take you anywhere you need to go."

The nurse gave Darren a murderous look. "Oh, Ms. Williams, I almost forgot. We can call you a cab to take you directly to your mother's house if you like."

Darren gave the nurse a "what the hell" look, and Tabitha arched her eyebrow.

"Do you think this is the guy that hurt me?" she asked.

"No, I just wanted you to know we could do that for you if you need it."

"It's okay. I understand, but please don't think I would leave here calmly with the man who hurt me. This is a friend from school. The father of my child did this to me. I wouldn't follow him to heaven."

"I'm sorry. I didn't mean to insinuate that—"

"There is no need to explain, and you don't have to be sorry. On the contrary, I am actually glad that you're concerned."

"I truly am sorry, Ms. Williams. Seeing you like this has, I don't know, brought back a lot of bad memories." Before she turned to leave, she squeezed Tabitha's hand and said, "You take care."

"So, do you want me to give you a ride?" Darren asked once the door was shut.

"Sure would. Oh, wait. I need to call my mom and tell her that I've been discharged and everything's okay."

"Cool. I'm going to go pull the car up front."

"All right." Tabitha felt light and airy. She felt free for the first time in a long time. Limping to the closet, she pulled out the plastic hospital bag that held her clothes. Her shirt was bloody, but nothing was wrong with her jeans, so she slipped them on and tucked the hospital gown inside them. Then she sat down on the edge of the bed, stuffed her feet inside her sneakers, and thought about Darren.

He didn't question my decision or even ask if I wanted to leave. I mean, I don't know much about the dude, but I know for a fact that Eric wouldn't have done that. Eric still treats me like I'm the little girl he met six years ago, but that ain't going to fly anymore. If he comes around me and my daughter again, he's going to see how grown I am.

Lisa walked to the back office to call Tabitha for the fourth time. She let the phone ring over ten times before hanging up. *Where are you?* she thought. *I hope you're resting. I hope you're doing better than me.* Ever since Carl Lee called, she was in a funk that she just couldn't shake. Lisa walked back to the line to help them with the late-lunch rush.

Why doesn't he just leave me alone?

"Damn, you all right?" Mike asked after he saw her put a fish filet on top of a cheeseburger.

"Yeah, I'm fine."

"Sure," he said, taking the fish burger out of her hand. "Why don't you go help up front? They're okay back here."

Lisa looked at him, confused. "You sure you guys don't need my help?"

Mike scooted her out of the kitchen. "Yeah, we're sure."

She drifted toward Carla's cash register as her thoughts scattered all over the place.

Damn, what is really going on? A guy walked into the lobby with the same coloring, build, and height as Tony. *God, I miss him,* she thought sadly.

"Can you repeat that, sir?" Carla stared blankly at the squat little man at the counter.

He pushed up his glasses, folded his hands in front of him, sighed heavily, and repeated his order as if talking to a small child.

"I . . . would . . . like . . . a . . . Big . . . Mac on a regular bun with just one patty. Hold the special sauce. Hold the lettuce, tomatoes, pickles, and onions."

"That's a burger," Lisa blurted out.

"No, it is not a burger. It's a Big Mac."

"Noooo . . . a Big Mac is a Big Mac, and a burger is a burger. So what you just described is a burger—a dry-ass one at that."

The man looked at Lisa with narrowed eyes and pursed lips. "May I speak to your manager?"

"I *am* the damn manager. So what would you like to speak about, huh? That dry-ass burger?"

Mike ran from the back office and stood in front of Lisa. "Whoa. Sir, I apologize for my coworker."

Lisa gave Mike a startled look. "You don't have to apologize for me. Dude is the one trippin'."

"Will you shut the fuck up?" Mike muttered. He pointed to the back office. "Go to the back and let me handle this," he said between clenched teeth. Then he returned his focus to the insulted customer. "Carla, make sure this gentleman gets whatever he needs—free of charge."

Carla rolled her eyes and filled the man's order.

Mike shook the customer's hand. "Again, I'm sorry for the inconvenience and the rude treatment. She will be dealt with accordingly." He walked to the office, where Lisa was pacing like a caged tiger.

As soon as he approached the doorway, she pounced. "You don't have the authority to treat me that way, Michael. You *don't* outrank me. I am an assistant manager like you, and I have more seniority than you. That man wasn't making any sense. Ask Carla. He was standing out there with a straight face ordering a Big Mac that wasn't a Big Mac. It's a burger, ya idiot. A fucking burger."

"Are you finished?"

Lisa plopped down in the chair and gave a nonchalant sigh.

"You know, I questioned whether a 17-year-old girl should work as an assistant manager when I first started here. Then I met you. At times, you can be more mature than me, and I'm 27. You are an extremely intelligent young woman that usually runs this place with poise and grace. You're not the best authoritarian, but you're quick on your feet, and I've seen that sharp wit of yours smooth out the worst situations. On the other hand, today was the first time I've seen your age, and I don't like it. What you did out there was childish and uncalled for. I'm not going to make a big deal out of it because I know whoever called you this morning upset you. But if it happens again, I will make sure that you are permanently placed on fry duty. Am I understood?"

Lisa nodded.

"Good. Now take a few minutes to get yourself together and then go back out front."

Lisa looked up to the ceiling and tried to fight off the tears. She missed Tony so badly that her head was all messed up. *I am not my mother. I don't need a man to complete me. I won't give a man anything so that he will stay with me. I am not my mother.*

After she returned to the floor, Lisa floated around McDonald's. Her outburst landed her with cleanup duties, but she wasn't doing much cleaning. She tried to push Tony out of her mind and repeatedly failed. She glided from table to table, simply going through the motions. Finally, she grabbed a napkin and picked up a couple of fries off the floor. When Lisa looked up . . . Tony was standing in front of her.

He looked as miserable as she felt. He took a step toward her and then a quick step back. He took off his fitted hat and started knocking it against his thigh. "Look. I'm sorry. I couldn't sleep last night and can't stop thinking about you and Shanice. I fucked up leaving her there with those dudes. I fucked up by even having them in your place. I am supposed to protect you and the people you care about, and I didn't do that." His voice cracked, and his eyes watered. "I never meant to hurt you, and I understand why we can't be together . . . I'm just here . . . Yo, I came here to see if you could still be my friend. Because I really fucking miss my friend."

Lisa stared at him for a few moments before opening her arms.

Tony rushed to her and swept her off her feet.

"I miss my friend too," she said against his chest. "I miss my friend so badly."

"So, how are we gonna do this?" Shanice asked as she and Begonia walked up to Mrs. Gloria's house.

"We are going to walk right up to the front door and walk right in."

"The front door?"

"Yes, the front door."

"But what if it's locked?"

"That's why I stopped for my tools, dumb ass. A locked door ain't nothing but a five-second barrier for somebody with skills. Now, don't start looking around and acting all nervous and shit. The key is to be cool. Act like you're supposed to be there. People don't question that kind of confidence."

The girls walked up the steps, Begonia picked the lock, and they were in. Shanice knew exactly what she wanted as she scanned the mantle and entertainment center for pictures.

Damn, where are all the pictures? Ain't shit here but some knickknacks and weird-ass artwork. "Bee, where the hell you going?"

"To find you some pictures," she said as she headed up the stairs.

"Pictures and nothing else. Bee—"

"I heard you the first time, Shani."

Shanice was starting to think that this was not one of her better ideas. She glanced down at her watch and then walked into the dining room. She spotted a couple of photo albums in the china closet.

"Shani! Get the hell up here and look at this shit."

"What is it?"

"Girl, just come look."

Shanice jumped when she looked into Lisa's old bedroom. "What the hell?" The walls were painted black, and dozens of dildos and other sex toys were positioned on the walls. A reclining chair sat in the middle of the room in front of a big-screen TV. A collection of kiddie porn was scattered on the floor. Two sex swings hung in the back of the room, facing a wall plastered with pictures of small children in sexual positions. The sight left Shanice sick to her stomach, and she ran downstairs.

"That is some sick and twisted shit," Begonia said. "I got half a mind to set that shit ablaze. I don't even want to steal nothing. I can see why Lisa doesn't live here. These people are fucking wrong."

Finally, Begonia came down the stairs. She didn't want to be there any longer.

Shanice tucked a photo album under her arm and walked toward the phone.

"What in the hell are you doing, Shani? This ain't the time to reach out and touch nobody."

"We have to call the cops."

Begonia walked over and snatched the phone from her. "I agree with you wholeheartedly, but you do *not* call the cops from the house you just broke into. Did you find what you needed?"

"Yeah, I think so."

"Good. We're out of here. We can call the cops from a pay phone somewhere else."

Begonia yanked Shanice out of the house and ensured everything was back in place before closing and locking the door.

Shanice found a suitable picture of Carl Lee, threw the rest in the trash, and went to Maple Market to make copies. She didn't have any money but usually didn't need any there. Ever since she caught the store's owner in bed with her mom, he pretty much let Shanice do whatever she wanted, especially since he didn't want his wife privy to that little bit of private information. So she made 300 copies of Carl Lee's picture with the caption that read, *"Hi, my name is Carl Lee, and I have a thing for little girls. Have I hurt your daughter?"*

Shanice and Begonia walked out of the store and posted the flyers throughout the neighborhood.

Finally, Shanice stapled the last flyer to the telephone pole across the street from Strawberry Mansion. She smiled at Carl Lee's demonic face. "You don't get to hurt my friend anymore, you sick motherfucker. *No one* gets to hurt us ever again."

Chapter 22

Tabitha wondered why it took her so long to realize that all she had to do was choose not to be with Eric. She had wanted Eric, and that was the simple truth of it. She'd wanted him more than she'd wanted herself or anything for herself.

I got the shit knocked out of me so much that I started to think it was normal. It warped my thinking. We were both sick—him for hitting me, and me for accepting it.

She rolled down the car window to let the cool breeze blow across her. She thought about all the times Eric hurt her and decided she needed a therapist to help her sort through things. However, that was for later. For now, she was going to enjoy herself at this moment. She looked over at Darren and smiled.

"I was thinking," she said in a breathy voice, "I don't have to go home just this minute."

"Oh, is that right?"

Tabitha reclined her car seat and put her feet up on the dash. "That's exactly right."

"I guess so. Where do you wanna go?"

"I don't know. Surprise me."

"A'ight, shawty."

Darren lowered the top on his convertible and headed toward the river. He had a smooth jazz CD playing, which Tabitha found appropriate. The music's erratic notes seemed to fit her mood perfectly. Darren turned on Kelly Drive, and Tabitha felt giddy as the distant view of the river slowly came into view. To be fair, she didn't know if the giddiness came from the Darvocet she had been given before discharge or from the moment itself, but she couldn't care less either way.

Darren pulled into the parking lot at Rock Garden. He cut off the car and got out to open the door for her. Tabitha floated out of the car and walked down to the river. She sat down at the edge of the dock and let her feet hang over the side.

"This is my favorite place in the world," she said, smiling.

"I see."

"It's that obvious, huh?" Tabitha spotted a few ducks in the water, and her mind returned to a happier place. "You know, one day when I was young, me and my girls played hooky from school to come here and feed the ducks our lunch. We were convinced that the ducks would starve if we didn't. Lisa and Shanice stood on these docks and threw their food into the water. I would go off by myself to feed some of them. They tore up my tuna fish sandwich. But when I ran out of food, they chased my little butt all the way down to the end of Boathouse Row."

"Didn't anyone ever tell y'all not to feed the ducks?" He laughed. "I mean, I'm sure there are signs and shit posted around here."

"We read the signs but thought the park officials were just being cruel."

Darren laughed even harder. "You're special, you know that?"

Tabitha's demeanor quickly changed as the smile fell from her face.

"Yo, what's the matter? Did I say something wrong?"

"No, you didn't say anything wrong. It's me. I'm trying to process all of this. It's hard, you know? Someone calling you special shouldn't bring you to tears. That ain't normal."

"How long have you been with him?"

"Since I was 12."

"Jesus, how old are you now?"

"I'm 19."

"So you've been going through this for seven years?"

"No, not exactly. He never hit me when we were really young. We were more like friends. We spent a lot of time at the park and the arcade. You know, just kid stuff. I was 14 the first time he hit me. It was a week after he took my virginity. He got really mad after seeing me talk to a guy from school. He slapped the taste out of my mouth."

Darren scooted closer to Tabitha and placed his arm around her shoulders. Her tears just flowed freely.

"He apologized, and I forgave him. It was a whole year before he hit me again. It wasn't an everyday thing, but it got worse every time it happened. Then I woke up one day, and that was my life. I was one of *those* women. He beat, raped, and humiliated me on a whim, on the regular, until it *was* regular, and I couldn't remember when the pain wasn't normal. Five years of pain, and I could have stopped it with a choice. Yesterday, I chose not to go through this shit no more, and now, I'm free."

Darren grabbed Tabitha's hand and laced his fingers through hers. "I'm sorry you had to go through that, shawty, for real. If you were my girl, I'd never hurt you. You can believe that. I'll show you how a woman is supposed to be treated. I would never, ever hurt you."

Tabitha slid her hand away from Darren's and dropped her head. "I'm sorry, Darren, but I can't be with you. Not now. I lost myself through all of this, and it's going to take some time to figure out who I really am."

"I have time."

"You're sweet. Thanks for bringing me here, but I should get home to my daughter."

"All right, come on."

Tabitha stood and headed toward the car. Darren pulled his keys out from his pocket, followed her, and tried to act like the rejection didn't sting.

"I'm good, Darren. I can walk home from here."

"Look, shawty, I said I was going to take you home, so come on. I ain't leaving you out here."

"I said I was walking. I appreciate you bringing me here, but I'd like to walk home and clear my head. This is where the change starts, right here—today. And the only way that's going to happen is if I start doing what I want to do. I'm not trying to hurt your feelings or be difficult. I'm just trying to be me. I'm sorry if you can't see that."

"And I'm sorry you can't see that I'm not your baby's father. I'm not trying to control you, Tabitha." He walked to his car and opened the passenger-side door. "I just don't want to leave you at the river. Now, can you please choose to get in the car and let me take you home?"

Tabitha smiled and walked to the car. "As long as you understand that it's my choice."

"Oh, believe me, I understand the fuck out of that, ma."

Lisa kissed Tony softly on the neck. He hugged her tighter and apologized for disrespecting her house and Shanice again. His arms felt like heaven, and she savored the feeling as she buried her face into his chest.

So what if this means I'm just like my mother? I don't even care about that anymore. I'm tired of being strong, tired of being responsible.

She just needed to be loved, and as much as it shamed her to admit it, at that moment, she would forgive Tony of anything as long as he kept holding her. He kissed her slowly, which drew a rowdy response from her coworkers. Lisa forgot she was at work, she was so lost in the moment.

"So, babe, does this mean I can still take you to the prom?" he asked. "I saw your dress hanging in the closet. I think I can find something fly to go with it."

Shit, I forgot to tell him I was taking Tab to the prom. Lisa bit her lip and tried to think of a gentle way to break it to him but was distracted when Shanice swished through the door in one of her Massimo T-shirts.

It will be impossible to keep that girl out of my clothes.

"Hi, stud. I need to borrow your wife for a minute." She tugged Lisa behind the counter and grabbed a cheeseburger from the counter. Lisa snatched the burger away from her. "But I'm hungry."

"OK, here, take it. Now, what is it, huh? What's got your panties in a bunch?"

Shanice pulled out one of the flyers from her back pocket and handed it to Lisa.

"What in the blazes?" She snatched it and stared. "But . . . How did you get this?"

"I broke into your mom's house and took one of her photo albums."

"You *broke* into my mother's house?"

"Sure did. Look, I was tired of him fucking with you. So I decided to fuck with him a little bit."

"Shanice, this is way more than a *little* bit. How many of these did you make?"

Maybe this wasn't such a great idea after all. "Just a few hundred."

"Jesus, girl. Well, where are they?"

"I posted them around the neighborhood."

"You did *what?*" Lisa's mouth dropped open. She looked up at Shanice like she was crazy.

Damn, now I feel like dog shit. I thought this would make her feel better. "I'm sorry. I was just trying to get back at them for hurting you."

Lisa took a step toward Shanice, who braced herself for some type of blow. Instead, Lisa wrapped her arms around Shanice and hugged her. "Thank you."

"You're not mad at me?"

"Are you kidding me? I wish I had the balls to do this. Unfortunately, I would have been way too chickenshit."

"Girl, please. You are the strongest person I know."

"I'm not as strong as you think I am, Shanice." Lisa clutched the flyer to her breast and started to cry. "I'm not strong when it comes to this."

"Sheesh, what is up with you and Tab crying all the time? You guys should be all cried out by now."

Mrs. Gloria banged through McDonald's double doors with an armful of Shanice's vigilante flyers. "Lisa! Lisa! Where the fuck are you?"

Lisa hid behind the wall leading to the back offices. "Looks like my mom found your flyers."

Shanice watched Mrs. Gloria tear up the restaurant and head toward Carla's register.

"Where in the hell is Lisa?"

"Lisa? Uh, I don't think she's working today."

"You don't *think* she's working today? Why don't I go back there and see for myself?"

"Excuse me, but you can't come back here."

"Hell, if I can't."

Tony jumped into Mrs. Gloria's face and demanded, "What do you want with Lisa?"

"Boy, you better get out of my face. I'm her mother. Lisa! Lisa! I know you're back there. If you're woman enough to post those lies about my husband, you should be woman enough to face me."

Shanice looked over at Lisa, who was still ducking behind the wall. Then she took a deep breath and stepped out into the hall to face Lisa's mother.

"Hi, Mrs. Gloria. I see you've found some of my flyers."

"What do you mean by *your* flyers?"

"I mean my flyers. I copied them. I posted them. Hell, I was the one that broke into your house to get the picture. Do you like them?"

"Why, you little bitch." Mrs. Gloria went to slap Shanice, but Mike grabbed her. "Get the hell off me. I'm not going to hit the little whore."

Mike released her hands and stepped between Mrs. Gloria and Shanice. "Ma'am, I don't know what the problem is, but I'll call the cops if you don't get from behind this counter immediately."

"I think I'll just call the cops on her for breaking into my home."

"Go ahead and call the cops, Mom," Lisa said, stepping out of the shadows. "I would like to tell them about your husband. He won't leave me the hell alone, so I need to get a restraining order."

"That's a damn lie, and you know it."

"Don't worry, Lisa," Shanice said, anger radiating from her. "I already called the cops. I sure did. I told them all about the little pleasure room y'all got upstairs. You know, the one with the sex swing and the kiddie porn."

Mrs. Gloria turned and looked at Lisa. "Why are you doing this to me?"

"I'm not doing anything to you. It's Carl Lee, Mom. He's sick."

"Stop it. You just stop. *You* are the one who's sick. It's bad enough you slept with him, you fucking little slut. Wasn't it enough that I paid for your abortion? What else do you want from me, huh? What more can I possibly give you? That evidently wasn't enough."

Lisa's eyes widened in disbelief. "You—" she began but paused. It took all her energy to finish that question. "You *knew*, Mama?"

"Of course, I knew. Who do you think paid for it?"

Lisa thought her heart would burst from the pain. She gripped the wall to keep from collapsing. Shanice looked at Lisa and her mom . . . and then punched Ms. Gloria in the face.

"That's it!" Mike shouted. "You need to get the fuck out of here before I throw you out myself."

"She assaulted me. Why don't you throw *her* the hell out? All of you are my witnesses."

Mrs. Gloria backed up to the main door and ran out. Shanice started to go after her, but Lisa held her back.

"You better go see about your husband, bitch," Shanice said. "I'm sure they've locked his ass up by now." She turned and looked back at a still-shaken Lisa. "Are you all right, girl?"

"No," Lisa replied sadly, "but I will be." She pulled Shanice into a tight hug. "Thank you, Shani. Thank you so fucking much. I hope they lock up both of them." She pulled away from their embrace. "Can you believe she knew? What type of person can do that to their own child?"

"A really evil person, Lisa." Shanice grabbed Lisa's hand. "But we're not letting people do evil shit to us anymore. We're going to have each other's back *always*."

"Always," Lisa said, pulling Shanice into another hug. "Always and forever."

Chapter 23

Tabitha stood in the doorway of her old bedroom and watched Erica sleep. Her mother quietly approached behind her and placed her hand on her shoulder.

"Don't you even think about waking up that little girl, you hear me? I put her down for a nap not too long ago."

Tabitha patted her mother's hand. "I'm not going to wake her, Mama."

"You sure aren't. Come on down here and get some of this coffee."

"I'll be down in a minute."

"All right, honey, but I can't guarantee that this peach cobbler will still be there when you finally make it down."

"You didn't tell me you made peach cobbler."

"Now, don't knock me down, child. I was just playing with you. That doggone cobbler ain't gonna grow feet and leave."

Tabitha sat at the kitchen table, pulled the whole pan of cobbler in front of her, and inhaled the sweet aroma of cinnamon, vanilla, and peaches. "Aww, Mama, it smells so good."

Her mother removed the pan and replaced it with a plate and fork. Then she scooped out a big piece and placed it on Tabitha's plate.

"Now, baby, you know we need to talk."

Tabitha sat up straight in the chair and mashed her fork into her cobbler.

"Not that, honey," her mother said. "We'll talk about that when you're ready. I mean, we need to talk about this prom business. It is tomorrow, right?"

"Yes," she said as she stuffed a piece of cobbler into her mouth.

"Well, I think that dress is just beautiful. I have just the thing to go with it too."

Ms. Mabel pulled a velvet box out of the kitchen drawer. The box contained a pearl and diamond necklace and matching earrings.

"My goodness, Mama. Where did you get this?"

"They were your grandmother's. I wore them on my wedding day and saved them for your wedding day. Come on; let's try them on."

Tabitha turned in her chair so her mother could place the necklace around her neck. Suddenly, a loud knock on the door made them both jump. Tabitha got up to answer the door, and her mother grabbed her hand.

"You should let me get it. Baby, what if it's Eric?"

"Mom, I ain't wasting no more time being afraid of Eric. If it's him, just get the police on the phone and tell them where they can pick up his ass."

"Tabitha, watch your mouth."

"I'm sorry, Mama."

Tabitha opened the door and found Shanice's mother on the other side.

"Ms. Stacy, what are you doing here? I mean, is everything okay?"

"Hello, Tabitha, Ms. Mabel. I'm sorry to bother you, but I can't find my daughter. I've searched everywhere I could think of before coming here." She looked at Ms. Mabel, and her voice cracked. "You've got to believe me. I'm not trying to disrespect you or anything. It's just that we fought, and I haven't seen her since. I am scared for her."

Ms. Mabel gestured for her to come inside. When Ms. Stacy entered the living room, Ms. Mabel greeted her with a big hug.

"Tabitha, do you know where little Shanice is?"

"Yes, Ma. She's staying with Lisa."

"That's perfect. Call them and get them over here. We need to tell you girls something. It's way overdue."

"Oh no," Ms. Stacy pleaded. "We can't. *I* can't."

"Yes, we can. Yes, we will. This should have been done a long time ago, Stacy, and we ain't gonna put it off any longer. So now, Tabitha, you get those girls to come over here right now, and then you go on upstairs to check on that baby while I talk with Ms. Stacy."

Tabitha went up the stairs slowly. She looked over her shoulder and saw Ms. Stacy clinging to her mom. *What the hell is going on?* she thought as goose bumps rose on her arm. She raced to her mother's room to page Lisa.

After all the drama at work, Lisa had been given the go-ahead to go home. Shanice watched as Lisa changed out of her uniform in the women's bathroom.

"Are you sure you're all right?"

"I'm fine, Shanice, really. Just drop it."

"Shit if you're fine. You still look like a fucking ghost."

"I just can't believe she knew, Shani. All that time, I thought that if there was some way for her to see for herself—catch him in the act or something—it would be different. She would believe me, and everything would be different. But that bitch knew all along and *just didn't care.*"

Lisa laughed hysterically, and Shanice didn't know what to do. She silently prayed that her friend wasn't losing her mind and just continued to listen. At this point, that's all she knew how to do.

"What kind of person is that, Shanice, huh? What kind of woman knows that her husband is raping her daughter and does nothing? What kind of woman pays for her daughter's abortion like she's paying the electric bill? I'm done with her, Shanice. I don't want her love. I don't think she's capable of love. I think she's one sick bitch."

Lisa pulled on her T-shirt and stuffed her uniform in a bag, which she handed to Shanice. "You know, I thought I would die when she said that. My heart felt like it was going to explode, and I would drop dead right there in front of everybody. She probably would have liked that, huh?"

She walked over to the sink and splashed water on her face. She then wiped her face on her T-shirt and looked at her reflection in the wall mirror.

"You didn't kill me with your little secret, Mom. All you did was kill any feelings I had left for you. Shanice, that woman just burned away all the longing I had in my heart for her, all the hopes I had that she would come to her senses and kick Carl Lee's ass out. As far as I'm concerned, they are made for each other, and I hope both of them burn in hell."

Her bag started to vibrate, which startled Shanice. "What in the hell?"

"That's just my pager. Damn." She laughed, took out her pager from the bag, and checked the message. Dread washed over Lisa—cold, hard fear that turned her veins to ice. Her hands trembled as she dropped the pager into the bag and looked at Shanice.

"Come on, girl. I just got a 911 page from Tab's house."

Gloria drove down Kensington and Allegheny Avenue, looking for her pusher. She needed a hit badly but didn't recognize these dope boys. Then turning on Front Street, she saw a crackhead she recognized as one of his loyal customers. Rolling down the window, she hollered to her.

"Angie, aye, yo, Angie, come here." The woman looked to be on death's door. Her baggy jeans and T-shirt were filthy and tattered. Her hair was matted to her scalp on one side and dreaded to her shoulder on the other. She walked toward the car, and Gloria resisted the urge to roll up her window again. The woman smelled like a sewer system.

She smiled at Gloria, displaying several rotted and missing teeth. "Heyyyy, I know you. You're that rich woman who buys from Caleb. What are you doing down these parts so early?"

"I'm not rich."

Angie took a step back to admire Gloria's truck. "Nah, you look rich to me."

"Well, I'm not," Gloria snapped. "I'm here looking for Caleb. Have you seen him?"

"Nah, it's too early for Caleb to be out here." She looked up at the sky and then back at Gloria. "He ain't never out this early." She squinted her eyes at Gloria's hands that trembled on the steering wheel. "What's the matter? You getting sick? You need to cop something?"

Gloria dropped her hands self-consciously and sighed. "Yes, I'm getting sick. Do you know where I can get something?"

Angie laughed and waved her arms up and down the street. "You don't see all these dope boys out here? You can find anything you want, whenever you want."

"Well, I would prefer someone discreet like Caleb."

"Welp, you should hit up Rodney. That dude is all business, all the time. Why don't you park your ride in a better spot, and I walk you down the street where Rodney does business?"

They walked a couple of blocks up to Banzil Street and stopped in front of an abandoned lot next to a wide alley.

"Hey, Drew," Angie called out to an older Puerto Rican man, "you seen Rodney?"

The old man smiled at Angie. "Yes, mami, he went to the store to get something to eat. He'll be right back."

"Thank youuu, papi," Angie said in a singsong voice. She turned to Gloria and pointed to the steps of the neighboring house. "Yo, have a seat. He should be coming down the block in a few seconds."

Gloria looked at the dirty steps and shook her head. "I'm good. I don't mind standing."

Angie took a look at her high heel shoes and snorted. "Yeah, okay."

A car pulled up with a portly man inside. "Angie, baby, been looking for you all day."

"Well, you found me, baby."

"Can you hook me up? I had a long day and need to relieve some stress."

"You know I got you."

"Where you want to go? The usual spot?"

Angie looked over her shoulder at Gloria and shook her head. "Nah, I can't go that far. I'm helping a friend out with some business." She looked around and then smiled. "There's an alley right here. Give me twenty dollars, and I'll fix you up real nice."

"I know you not about to leave me out here to turn a trick?" Gloria asked between clenched teeth.

Angie sighed. "Go park up and head to the alley. I'll be right there." She turned to Gloria and smiled. "Looky here, ma'am. You took me off my corner to help you. This man right here is one of my regulars. I'm trying to help you do business, and you are trying to stop me from handling mine. That ain't fair. Just relax. Rodney will be right back, and my man papi will look out for you. Now, this old dude finna cum quicker than you can say fast, and I'll be right back."

Gloria sighed as the portly man came out of the alley, fixing his pants. *She's right,* Gloria thought. *That didn't take long at all.* She stared across the street, waiting for Angie to appear, but she didn't come out. Impatient, she looked down the street for the mysterious Rodney, who hadn't yet returned, and even the little Puerto Rican man was gone. Gloria rolled her eyes when she watched another man go into the alley. "Now, I know she ain't about to serve another john. I need to get home to Carl Lee and figure out our next move." Gloria crossed the street and followed the man into the dark alley.

"I don't have any money, Earl."

"Don't play with me, bitch. I saw that nigga give you the money as soon as you finished gobbling down his nut."

"All he gave me was twenty dollars, and I need that to buy my kids food."

"How is that my fucking problem? If you came out here every day like I told you to do, maybe you would have some milk money."

"I don't want any trouble, Earl. I'll come right back to the strip after I feed my babies," Angie said as she walked toward the dumpster.

Earl grabbed her by her hair. "Any money you make on *this* strip belongs to *me.*"

"Get off of me," she screamed as she turned around and slapped Earl across his pockmarked face.

Earl grinned viciously. He yanked her head down until she bent at the waist. Angie grabbed his hand tangled in her hair with one arm and extended her other arm in front of her so her face wouldn't smack the pavement. Earl kneed her in the face, and she flew backward. Angie screamed as blood spurted from her nose. She caught her balance before falling into the filthy, muddy water.

Earl closed the distance between him and Angie with two quick steps. Then he punched her in the face so hard that blood and teeth splatted across the alley wall. Angie hit the ground with a sickening thud. Gloria's heartbeat sped up as time seemed to slow down. Earl kicked Angie in the side so hard that her ribs snapped like twigs. Angie grunted and rolled over. Her eyes fastened on a loose brick near the wall, and she wrapped her hands around it.

Earl stood over her and snarled. "What you gonna do with that?" he said while reaching down and snatching the brick from her.

Angie looked over at Gloria and opened her mouth to tell her to run, but no sound would come out of her swollen lips.

Earl followed Angie's gaze to Gloria's small frame frozen with terror by the dumpster. She looked more like a statue than a grown woman. He smiled at Gloria . . . before ramming the brick into the side of Angie's skull.

Gloria screamed and then slapped her hand over her mouth to muffle the sound. Her eyes widened as she watched Angie's eyes glaze over as the life quickly drained from her body. *Oh my God,* she thought as she watched a stream of blood oozing from the wound.

Earl walked over to Gloria, grabbed her by the throat, and started bashing her head with the brick.

Pain exploded in Gloria's head. She choked, sputtered, and clawed at Earl's hand, but she could not free herself.

"This is taking too long," he murmured, dropping the brick. He pulled Gloria close . . . and then violently snapped her neck. "Talk about being in the wrong place at the wrong time, baby."

Carl Lee burst through the front door of his house, covered in sweat. "Gloria," he shouted, racing back to the kitchen. His shirt was ripped and splattered with blood from his cut lip and busted nose. Andrew had attacked him in the bar. His niece saw one of these flyers and told her uncle about their "little secret." Carl Lee clutched a handful of Shanice's flyers in his hand. They were posted all over the place.

The kitchen was empty.

He slammed his hands against the refrigerator door. "Gloria, where are you?" he screamed while running back into the living room and up the stairs. "Gloria, I'm in trouble, baby." Their playroom was empty, and she wasn't in the bathroom. He walked into the bedroom, frantic. "I got to get out of here."

He grabbed one of Gloria's suitcases and placed it on the bed. Then he quickly opened the closet, grabbed a line of his shirts, and tossed them inside. He ripped the top drawer open and dumped that inside the suitcase. Then stooping low under the bed, he grabbed the shoe box where Gloria kept emergency money and threw that into the suitcase as well. He needed to get far away from that place. Whoever posted those flyers opened the floodgates. Lisa wasn't the only girl in this neighborhood he fucked with. She was just the most convenient.

As he stood up to close the suitcase, he heard the police sirens. "Shit," he screamed. Grabbing the suitcase, he ran down the stairs to the back of the house. He was about to go out the back door when police flooded in from the front.

"Freeze," shouted one of the officers. *"Drop the case and put your hands in the air."*

So close, Carl Lee thought. He looked at the doorknob. *They can't be fast enough to stop me.*

"Try it," an officer yelled as he walked up behind him. "My little sister recognized your picture on the flyer. Please give me a reason to fill you up with holes."

Carl Lee dropped to his knees, sobbing.

Shanice acted silly all the way to Ms. Mabel's house. Although Shanice wasn't really in the mood to play, she sensed that Lisa needed to keep things light and airy. So Shanice did silly dances, mimicked, and made fun of the people standing at the bus stop—whatever she needed to do to keep a smile on Lisa's face. Because whenever there was silence—even the slightest pause in the conversation—Lisa's face drooped, and Shanice couldn't handle that.

Her mind flooded with thoughts of Mrs. Gloria and how badly she had treated Lisa. *She is just foul. How could anyone be so messed up? I'm glad she's not my mom.* Her eyes moistened. *I miss my mom.* When they pulled up to Mrs. Mabel's house, a dull ache covered Shanice's chest. She then realized that she might have missed her mom more than she cared to admit.

Lisa jumped out of the car, ran up the stairs, and banged on the front door like she was the police.

"Girl, what's wrong with you?" Ms. Mabel asked when she opened the door.

"I'm sorry, Ms. Mabel. Is Tabitha here? Is she okay?"

"Honey, she's fine. She's upstairs bathing Erica. Shanice, come on in here, girl. What you standing there for?"

Mabel gasped when she pulled Shanice into the light and saw the bruises on the child's face. "Oh, baby, look what that devil did to you. I'm *so* sorry." She pulled Shanice in for a hug.

Shanice returned the hug fiercely and kissed Ms. Mabel on the cheek. "I'm sorry."

"Oh, baby, don't be sorry for that. That sin belongs to Eric and Eric alone. I'll tell you what you *should* be sorry for. You should be sorry for almost giving your mom a heart attack by running away and actin' all simple and stuff."

"I wasn't tryin'a hurt my mom. I just needed to clear my head for a little bit. I knew I was wrong. I just needed some space. I thought my mom didn't love me anymore."

Shanice's eyes widened when her mother appeared behind Ms. Mabel.

"How could you ever think that?" she asked.

"Mama? What are you doing here?"

Shanice briefly hesitated before she flew into her mother's arms. The two just stood and held each other. There were no words said—and no need for any. Stacy kissed Shanice on the forehead as she rocked her.

"How could you ever think I don't love you, girl?"

"Because you started going to church and acting all different."

"Different doesn't mean bad, Shanice. It just means different. You are why I started attending church in the first place."

"Me?"

"Yes, you. I needed to get my life together so you could get yours together. I needed help, Shanice. Help to be a better person, a better woman, and a better mother."

Tabitha came down the stairs, and Shanice and Lisa both smiled.

"You look better than you did before, chick," Shanice said.

"That's funny, Shanice, 'cause you sure as heck don't."

"Is that right?"

Lisa walked over to Tabitha and gently poked her in the side. "That sure is right, Shanice. You look like warmed-over crud. I ain't say nothing earlier 'cause I didn't wanna hurt your feelings."

"Hush that nonsense, you two. Now, come on in the kitchen. There is something I want to talk to y'all about. Let's give Shanice and her mother some privacy."

Tabitha and Lisa looked at Shanice before following Ms. Mabel into the kitchen.

Chapter 24

Tabitha and Lisa sat at the kitchen table while Ms. Mabel got plates and napkins from the cabinet.

"What's going on?" Lisa mouthed to Tabitha, who didn't know and turned her focus back to her mother. Her stomach rumbled with negative energy.

Ms. Mabel poured three cups of steaming coffee and cut two heaping servings of peach cobbler before sitting across from the girls. She sighed and stared down at her hands.

"Now, what I have to say to you girls ain't gonna be easy," she began.

Tabitha reached across the table and grabbed her mother's hand. "Mama, are you all right?"

"What's wrong?" Lisa asked, nervous.

"I'm okay, girls. Really. Now, just hush and let me get through this 'cause this is hard for me."

She squeezed Tabitha's hand and reached out for Lisa's. Then she took a shuddering breath, and a single tear trailed down her face.

"What I have to tell you involves me, but it don't concern me, not the way it concerns you girls." She looked at Tabitha and smiled sadly. "I ain't done right by you, little girl."

"Aww, Mama, don't cry. What happened to me ain't your fault. It's not even my fault."

"Go on and let me finish telling you what I got to tell you. You know your father was something else: tall, smart, and too damn handsome for his own good. Yes, indeed, Arthur Williams II was sex walkin' and honey talkin', with eyes that could convince you of anything." She closed her eyes and smiled at the memory. "That man had me convinced from the word go. He swept me right off my feet.

"My cousin Janet used to say that we met on a Monday, kissed on a Tuesday, and was married on a Wednesday. Now, it took a little bit longer than that, but not much. I was what you call green—fresh off the bus from Norfolk, Virginia—and I didn't know nothing about nothing, which suited your father just fine. We were married for eight years before we had you. Did you know that?"

Tabitha shook her head.

"I didn't think you did. Well, anyway, after you came, your father got a job at the state, and we were one little happy family . . . for a short while. I was finally blessed with the baby girl I'd always wanted, and your father had his dream job."

Ms. Mabel turned to Lisa. "That's where Arthur met your mother. She was his coworker's secretary. He introduced us and encouraged us to hang out together. He said it would be good for me. So we hung out, just like that. Back then, I did whatever Arthur said without question. He ruled our house with an iron fist, and I learned early on to do what I was told . . . or else."

Lisa felt a slight twinge in her stomach at the mention of her mother, and Tabitha pushed her cobbler around on her plate with the fork. Tears began to flow from Ms. Mabel's eyes, but her focus remained on Lisa.

"You see, me and your mother became real tight. She was my closest friend in Philly besides Janet, and Arthur didn't like Janet—wouldn't let her come around. So Gloria and I did everything together—two peas in a pod. We were like sisters, and for the first time in a long time,

I was happy, real happy. I didn't pay no mind when the whispering started. I was used to it."

She returned her focus to Tabitha, who was looking more concerned by the minute. "As I said, your daddy looked and talked like silk, and people was always whispering about him being with this woman or that woman. So, when they started whispering about him and Gloria, I just ignored it. I didn't want to believe it. I couldn't believe it. They would never do no stuff like that to me. They loved me."

Mrs. Mabel got up from the table, walked to the sink, and placed her hands on the counter. The girls watched as her shoulders shook from the silent sobbing. Tabitha slid over closer to Lisa. She did not look at her but just extended her hand. Their grips were firm as they sat and listened, terrified by what they might hear.

"I did my best to ignore the gossip until one day at church, I went to the bathroom and overheard the pastor's wife talking about it. She hadn't said anything different than anyone else, so I can't tell you why I took it to heart that day. Maybe it was because of the source; perhaps it was because of the location. I went to church to escape the whispers and hear a little good news, the gospel. So, when I heard her say how stupid she thought I was and how if she were to catch the pastor runnin' around with one of her friends, how she would tear fire to him and Jesus himself wouldn't be able to save him, I was done.

"I had had enough. I left the church that instant and went home to confront Arthur. He denied it, of course, and because I didn't want to believe it no way, I pushed it out of my mind. Shortly after that, your mother became pregnant with you. I was so excited. She told me that Lisa's father wanted nothing to do with it, so I vowed to help her."

Mrs. Mabel walked back to the table and flopped down in the chair.

"Lisa, you were born three months after Tabitha's second birthday. So much hair, my God. You were born with a head full of curly brown hair and the brightest little eyes. Then just about two and a half years after you arrived, your mother finally told me that you were Arthur's baby. We have barely spoken since." Mabel sighed. "I put all the blame on your mother, but the truth was, she was too young for Arthur to be messing around with. She was barely 17 years old. She had lied on her application to get that job, and both me and Arthur knew that." Tears rolled down Mabel's face. "I was wrong to blame her." She walked over to Lisa and cupped her chin. "However, it doesn't excuse what she has done to you, child. *Nothing* excuses that."

"Mama," Tabitha said, tears rolling down her face. "I'm so sorry he did that to you. You didn't deserve that either."

Lisa looked from Tabitha to Ms. Mabel in disbelief. "You mean to tell me that me and Tab are sisters?"

"When I confronted Arthur about it, he didn't deny it. He was furious, but he did not deny it. He beat me bloody that night, but I didn't care about that. I don't think I even hollered out loud. No pain could match the heartache."

"But she told me that my father was killed."

"He was killed. He was killed in a car accident in 1983. I believe you were about four."

"Mama," Tabitha said, "why didn't you tell me?"

"Baby, I didn't know how. The mere thought of your father and my best friend together—"

"But you could have told me."

"How could I have told you something that I didn't even want to believe, huh? After I confronted your father about the affair, he beat the living crap out of me. He openly did what he used to keep in the dark, running around after anything in a skirt and leaving you and me alone for weeks at a time. Janet was gone. Gloria was gone. All I had was you and the pain of their betrayal. So, I shut it out and kept on keeping on. And when it was clear that you and Lisa was gonna be friends, I encouraged it. Despite your mother's protests, Lisa, I encouraged it."

Mrs. Mabel brushed the tears from Lisa's cheek. "I didn't want no parts of your mother, but you, I fell in love with you the moment I laid eyes on you. The evil that your mother has done, both then and now, has *nothing* to do with you. You hear me? Your mama is one sick and twisted woman, and she always has been, but it has nothing to do with you. I love you. Do you hear me, little girl? I love you, and I always will."

"Thirteen years. Tabitha, your father has been dead and cold for thirteen years, and I'm just now finding my voice. He stole something from me every time he hit me. He stole my ability to see what was around me, and 'cause I got so used to ignoring the bad, I failed you."

"Oh, Mama—"

"I failed you. I saw only what I wanted to see until it was almost too late." She then turned to Lisa and said, "He stole my ability to protect you, but that's done. I am here, I am whole, and I am willing to be your mother, if you will have me."

Lisa flew into Ms. Mabel's arms.

"Well, I'm gonna take that as a yes. Now, after the prom, I want you to close up that apartment and move in here with us. *We're* your family now. Tabitha's your sister, and I am your mother, and we're stronger if we stay together. You girls will start Community College in the fall, and I mean to see you through it. Now, I promised myself that I would tell you girls everything, but I haven't done that yet. This last part isn't really my story to tell, but Stacy asked me to do so because she didn't want to tell it twice."

She reached out for both girls' hands. Tabitha took her mother's hand to offer what little support she could. Ms. Mabel smiled at her daughter and continued to divulge more secrets.

"Right before your father was killed . . ." Ms. Mabel paused briefly, and in that short time, the girls could see a flurry of dark, sad emotions run across her face. "Before he was killed, he did a horrible thing. He followed Stacy home from school one day and raped her in an alley two blocks from her house. She told anyone who would listen, but no one would believe her 'cause her shorts were too short, her shirts were too tight, or she was too fast or too fresh. Whatever the reason, they didn't believe her. But I did. I knew Shanice was Arthur's baby the minute I laid eyes on her, even though I was too weak and scared to do anything about it."

Tabitha and Lisa moved in to embrace Ms. Mabel, who welcomed them into her arms. She felt naked but knew that revealing the truth sometimes had that effect. She rocked both girls in her arms and felt as though the weight of the world had suddenly been lifted from her shoulders.

Shanice burst through the kitchen doors, ran into Ms. Mabel, and wrapped her hands around Tabitha and Lisa.

"I have sisters!" she screamed with tears of joy pouring from her eyes.

Ms. Stacy stood in the doorway and watched all the love in the room.

"Come on, Stacy," Ms. Mabel said. "We are all family now, honey, and that means you too."

Chapter 25

Tabitha, Lisa, Shanice, Ms. Stacy, and Ms. Mabel all spent the night huddled in Ms. Mabel's room, talking, laughing, and crying. No one slept because no one wanted the night to end. The next thing they knew, the sun was rising through the clouds.

Ms. Stacy made breakfast and started dinner, and Mabel was determined to send all three girls to the prom with a bang. She even invited half the neighborhood to the house to see them off. Lisa left to run some errands and pick up her prom dress, and Stacy had brought Shanice's dress over at dawn.

Everything was perfect, and Tabitha could not describe her joy whenever she looked at Shanice.

"Hand me some more tape, Shanice," Tabitha asked as she hung black streamers from the ceiling.

"How many of these things are you gonna hang up, Tab? You can barely see the ceiling."

"Shut up and hand me the tape."

"I think it looks pretty, Mommy," Erica said.

"You're only saying that because you don't know any better," Shanice replied.

"I do so know better, don't I, Mommy?"

"Sure you do, baby. Aunt Shanice is a butthead."

Ms. Stacy came out of the kitchen with a pan of steaming sweet potatoes slathered in melted marshmallows.

"Mm, Mama, that smells good," Shanice said, practically drooling over the pan.

"I will break every bone in your body if you touch one thing on this table."

"Mama, I'm starving."

"You'll live."

Ms. Stacy kept a close eye on Shanice, who took another step toward the table with her lips poked out.

"Try me if you want to."

Shanice turned and stomped back into the living room.

Ms. Stacy shook her head and walked back into the kitchen.

"Tabitha, turn that radio on. We need some music in this house," Ms. Mabel said.

Tabitha turned the radio to her mother's favorite station. The Isley Brothers' "Between the Sheets" came pumping through the speakers.

"Now, *that's* what I'm talking about," Ms. Mabel screamed from the kitchen. "Ohhh, baby, baby. I feel your lovvvve surrounding me. You girls don't know *nothing* about this."

Lisa walked in the front door with her prom dress draped over her arm. "Your mother is tearing that song up. What did the Isley Brothers ever do to her?"

Tabitha swooped Erica into her arms and twirled her around the room. "She's your mother too."

Lisa's entire face brightened up. "I know, right? Well, I guess her singing isn't that bad, then."

Lisa playfully hit Shanice on the arm before heading upstairs to hang up her dress.

"Why are you guys always abusing me?" Shanice asked.

"Because you deserve it," Lisa said halfway up the stairs. "Come on up here, Shanice. I have something for you."

"I hope it's food."

"Come on, Tab. Give the munchkin to Mama for a while. You need to hear this too."

Tabitha walked into the kitchen amidst the smells of fried chicken, collard greens, and bread pudding. "Mama, can you look after Erica for a while? Lisa just came back, and we're going upstairs to start getting ready."

Ms. Mabel took Erica out of Tabitha's arms and sat down at the kitchen table.

"You wanna help Grandma cook?"

"Uh-huh."

"All right, then, baby. Go over there and get the footstool out of the corner so you can wash your hands."

"Okay."

Aunt Stacy looked at the clock on the wall that read two o'clock. "Don't you guys think it's a little early to start getting dressed?"

"Aunt Stacy, perfection takes time," Tabitha said.

"Oh, well, excuse me. I didn't know that you guys were aiming for perfection."

Stacy and her mother's laughter warmed Tabitha all the way up the stairs.

"OK, I'm here," Tabitha said. "What's got your panties in a bunch?"

Lisa searched in her purse and pulled out a prom ticket. "Begonia stopped me on the way here and gave me this to give to Shanice."

Shanice snatched the ticket from Lisa. "*That's* what I'm talking about. I knew my girl would come through."

"Ya girl needs to stop stealing before she gets in serious trouble," Tabitha said.

"She ain't gonna get in no trouble. She's an artist."

"What she is, is a crook."

"Will you two be quiet? I'm trying to tell you guys something," Lisa said in a last-ditch effort to reclaim the conversation. "Begonia said she saw the cops raid my mom's . . . I mean Gloria's house. They dragged Carl Lee off in handcuffs."

"*That's* what I'm talking about," Shanice shouted. "It's about time the boys in blue start doing their jobs around this muthafucka."

"Shut up, Shanice," Tabitha said. "Are you all right, Lisa?"

"I'm fine. I mean, I'm glad he's going to jail. I hope they lock up my mom too. They could spend the rest of their lives there if I had anything to say about it. I'm just glad it's all over with. As far as I'm concerned, Gloria and Carl Lee Richardson can rot under the jail. My family is here with my sisters, mom, aunt, and niece. To hell with everybody else."

Tabitha walked over and wrapped Lisa in her arms. "I know exactly how you feel. You guys are all the family I need."

"Please don't tell me you two are about to cry again," Shanice said. "Lisa, aren't your damn eyes dried out by now? Sheesh. I thought you was supposed to be tough. You ain't nothing but a li'l punk."

"Oh, I got your sissy. Come here. I'm going to decorate your face some more. You gonna look real pretty for the prom."

Shanice squealed with laughter and ran from the room.

Tabitha smiled at the thought of having sisters, seeing them enjoy each other, and finally having everyone feel the love they deserved. She never believed that she could be so happy. Tonight, she was going to the prom, and soon, she would go to college.

God is good.

A few days ago, she thought she was losing her mind when, in reality, she was reclaiming her spirit. She went to the closet, pulled out her dress, and held it close to her chest. Then she turned to the mirror and finally loved the reflection that was staring back at her.

"Now that I have you, I'll never let you go."

~Prom Night~

Ms. Stacy put Erica on her hip and rushed to the front door. "I'm coming, I'm coming," she hollered. The small house was filling up with neighbors and members of the church. Everybody was coming to see the girls off to prom and fill their bellies with some of Mabel's southern cooking.

"Excuse me, pardon me," she said, swerving around the line forming from the living room to the kitchen. She put the baby down and took her by the hand as soon as they got outside. She looked around at the people milling about in front of the house. "Now, baby, show Aunt Stacy the fellas you said wanted to speak to us."

"Them over there," Erica said, pointing to the two young men across the street.

Ms. Stacy smiled, recognizing Tony. She waved them over. "Hey, you made it just in time. The girls are about to come down and take their pictures."

"Oh, I know, Ms. Stacy. I just got off the phone with Lisa."

Ms. Stacy smiled up at the young man standing next to Tony. "Are you going to introduce me to your friend?"

Tony nudged Darren, and Darren cleared his throat and extended his hand. "I'm sorry, Ms. Stacy. My name is Darren. I'm Tabitha's friend. We'll be going to school together."

Ms. Stacy shook his hand. "Well, it's nice to meet you." She looked at them. "What can I help you fellas with?"

Tony smiled. "When we came over last night, the girls told us we weren't invited to the prom because it was a sister event now. No guys allowed."

"And even though we are not invited," Darren chimed in, "we decided they shouldn't have to go in the hunk of junk that Lisa calls a car."

Tony laughed. "Aye, man, I told you to stop clowning my girl's ride. She loves that little scoot bug." He put his arm around Ms. Stacy's shoulder. "No, but seriously. We rented them a limousine. I need Lisa's keys to move her car off the corner so the stretch can make it up the block."

Ms. Stacy's smile threatened to split her face in two. Instead, she grabbed both men up in a bear hug. "Oh, that's just wonderful. Glory to God. You two are a blessing. Erica, run and get your aunt Lisa's car keys." She turned back to the guys. "Thank you so much. They are going to love this."

Butterflies fluttered in Tabitha's stomach as she followed her younger sisters out the front door.

"Oh my God," Shanice said over her shoulder. "Mom, Mabel brought the entire hood out to see us off." Lisa and Shanice stepped onto the pavement and immediately started posing for the cameras.

"Yessss," someone screamed from the crowd. "Y'all look beautiful."

Overwhelmed, Tabitha stopped at the last step and placed her hand on her stomach. A part of her wanted to turn around and dart back into the house.

Lisa took her hand and gave her a reassuring smile. "Don't be shy now, bighead. Come over here and Vogue with your sisters."

Tabitha's nerves faded away. She returned the smile and joined them in the impromptu photo shoot. A car horn sounded on the corner, and the crowd parted and moved out of the street for a shiny black stretch limousine.

"Oh shit," Shanice screamed, jumping up and down.

The door opened, and Sister Sledge's "We Are Family" blared from the speakers. Tony got out carrying an ivory and black corsage. Darren followed with a blue corsage for Tabitha and a yellow one for Shanice.

Lisa shook her head. "I can't believe you did this." She looked at the limo. "Sister Sledge, though?" she laughed. "You are so corny."

Tony grinned. "What, you said this was a sisters' event, and you love corny, though, don't you?"

"Yes, I do," she answered, leaning in to kiss him.

Darren put on Shanice's corsage first and then slipped Tabitha's on her wrist. "You are stunning. Can a brother get a hug?"

Tabitha opened her arms, and Darren swooped her up off her feet. "I hope you choose to see me tonight."

She winked at him. "Hope is a good thing."

Ms. Mabel cut through the crowd. "All right, come here, girls. Give me a hug and get on in that fancy ride. It's time for y'all to go have some fun. The good Lord knows y'all deserve it."

"Oh, wow," Tabitha said as she stepped into the hotel reception room. The DJ was playing Brandy's "I Wanna Be Down," and some of her favorite teachers were mixing and mingling amongst the students. "This is soooo cool," she said, staring at the elegant decorations and everyone dressed in ball gowns and tuxedos.

"I can't believe we made it," Shanice remarked. Her eyes looked like they were going to pop out of her head.

"I know, right?" Lisa said, taking both of their hands. "I didn't think this would happen a few days ago."

Shanice pulled them over to a table nestled in a corner far away from the faculty. She pulled out a seat for Tabitha and Lisa. "You ladies sit your beautiful selves down here. I'll be right back. I'm finna take somebody's man." She turned toward the dance floor, and Tabitha caught the back of her dress and spun her around.

"No, you will not. I'm not trying to get kicked out before the DJ plays the Electric Slide."

Lisa burst out laughing. "Is that the *only* dance you know how to do?"

Tabitha smiled. "Yup, and I'm going to slide my ass off."

Shanice gasped. "Such naughty language." She pried Tabitha's hand off her gown. "Calm down. I'm not going to steal anyone's dude. I'm going to get something to drink. I'll be right back." She turned and made a beeline to the buffet tables.

"I'm watching you," Lisa called after her.

Shanice flipped her the bird.

Lisa shook her head. "What are we going to do with that girl?"

Tabitha laughed. "I don't know why you keep asking me that. I have no clue what to do with either one of you."

Lisa snorted. "Some big sister you are."

Tabitha placed her arm around Lisa's shoulder. "I promise to be the *best* big sister I can be."

Lisa kissed her cheek. "You always have been."

Dear Readers,

The following is a brief history of the journey this book has become. I wanted to give you a peek into my world. I've come a long way from the streets of Strawberry Mansion, and that is all due to my God, family, and readers. Thank you.

The Beginning
1992 (North Philadelphia)

At 15 years old, I fell in love with a young man who stole my innocence and pushed me to the brink of insanity. At 16, I was a young mother who was effectively cut off from her family. At 17, I started to write my story. He found it, beat me bloody, and burned it in the backyard. However, you cannot erase words from the soul of a writer, nor can you erase the bonds of friendship between young women who have nothing but each other to cling to.

2007 (Harrisburg, Pennsylvania)

I was having a really fucked-up day. I made it to the clinical portion of the nursing program at Harrisburg Area Community College. I forgot the name of the nursing home I was assigned to, but I remember being completely overwhelmed while there. We were given green sheets to do nursing assessments on select patients. Most of my classmates completed their sheets at the facility, but I was thinking about getting home in time to make dinner and not be late for work.

That evening, I had two jobs. I worked at Bethany Village in Mechanicsville in the mornings and at Spring Creek in the evenings. Long story short, I went to the wrong job and had to hightail it to the other side of town. I was late, we were short-staffed, and I was given the worst assignment. I brought my green sheets to work, thinking I could complete them during my breaks. However, I received no breaks. I came home exhausted.

The house was a wreck, and I was on the verge of a mini breakdown. I ignored the mess, sat at my computer, and pulled out the green sheets. It looked like Swahili. I couldn't remember my patients, their diagnoses, or my professor's instructions. The sheets were due in the morning, and I had no idea how to complete them. I started to cry. I mean . . . ugly cry.

My son woke up at that moment. He sat beside me, took the green sheets out of my hands, and wiped my eyes.

"Mom, why are you going to school for nursing when all you do is write? I never see you cry like this when you're writing." One little question rocked my world. I dropped out of college the following week.

2008 (Harrisburg, Pennsylvania)

I never stopped writing my story. I just never wrote it in a single book. *Strawberry Mansion* was written on stray pieces of paper napkins and receipts tucked in hidden spots around my tiny apartment. I pulled out my shoe box with all of the story notes from *Strawberry Mansion* and spread them out on the table. Fifteen minutes into organizing the notes chronologically, my hands began to shake. My eyes misted, and my stomach did a sickening flop. I stood up, confused. How could I be afraid of someone I was no longer associated with? My son's father and I had been divorced for years, and we lived over 100 miles from each other. I wiped my eyes and took a deep breath.

I picked up another note. It was a paper bag with brown stains in the corner. I touched the stain gently. It was blood. I remembered writing that snippet in the kitchen after he busted my lip for forgetting to fold the laundry. My stomach churned again. I dropped the paper bag and ran into the bathroom to be violently ill. I couldn't make myself go back to the dining room. I was in a very dark space, trapped by fear I hadn't felt in years.

I lay across the bed, defeated. I was a wreck by the time my ex-husband came home. He held me in his arms and made me tell him what was wrong. It was hard, but I told him. I told him everything. After many tears and a lot of cuddles, he walked me into the dining room, sat beside me, and told me to write. He assured me that no one would hurt me again.

A month later, I could write on my own. I wrote everywhere . . . at work, at the bookstore, at church, on the steps. Sometimes, I wrote while driving. (However, I don't recommend that.) I wrote my heart out and read my writings to anyone who would listen. These days were the happiest of my young life. Writing the book was therapy. This might sound a little cheesy, but I could feel the deep scars of my soul begin to heal with each chapter.

I was elated when my manuscript was complete. I bought a bunch of books on writing and getting your book published. I joined writing groups online and in person. I just knew that this book would change my life for the better. Finally, a poor chick from North Philly was about to release a masterpiece to the world, bringing her friends and family fame and fortune . . .

Boy, was I wrong. There was no fame. There was no fortune. There was, however, a great adventure, and I will detail it as much as possible here.

2008 January

I received my first and only rejection letter for *Strawberry Mansion*. So, I purchased Dan Poynter's

Self-Publishing Manual and started Queen Midas Books. *Strawberry Mansion* was published on June 21st.

2009–

It took me a year to come to grips with how truly ignorant I was about the book industry. Self-publishing was growing but was really frowned upon, and it was almost impossible to garner distribution and shelf space. African World Books in Baltimore and Black and Nobel in Philadelphia distributed my books to street vendors and independent bookstores up and down the East Coast. Still, major bookstores refused to carry my titles. My dreams of fame and fortune were slowly dissipating, and my life was quickly falling apart. My marriage was ending, and I moved back home with my parents. I released my second book, *Begonia Brown,* in a fog of heartache and pain. You can read all about that at Behind Begonia . . . (jpsimmons.com).

2010–

I was single again, working as a CNA at the VA and struggling with depression, obesity, and complications of diabetes. I no longer thought fame and fortune were my future, but writing was my lifeline. I wrote *Violet,* my third book, and tore up the expressway on bootstrap book tours. I loved interacting with readers. You guys are my dream come true, and every interaction made my writing journey worthwhile.

2011–

My father was diagnosed with prostate cancer. I was named his power of attorney and took on the weight of the household. In a couple of short weeks, I was up to my eyeballs in soul-crushing debt. I watched my mother nurse my father back to health—only to be abandoned when his cancer went into remission. Throughout all this turmoil, I continued to write. Then, of course, I couldn't afford to print books anymore, but I did start to publish on Kindle and other eBook platforms.

2012–My Great Depression

My hours were cut at the VA, and things started to spin out of control one by one. My truck was repoed. My cell phone was cut off, then the cable, gas, water, and finally, the electricity. I struggled to keep food on the table, and my father sold the house while my mother and I still lived there. I was at the end of my rope and didn't know what to do. I checked my bank account to see if I had enough money for a hotel room. Astounded, I noticed that my balance was $2,067. What the actual fuck? How in the hell did I get that money? I went online and found out *Strawberry Mansion* was selling about 500 eBooks a day, and I was due to get a $3,000 payment in a couple of weeks. With divine intervention, I moved my mom into a four-bedroom, four-bathroom house with a storefront in a month. I was beyond happy.

2013–

I quit my job at the VA and published *Fornication*. I started a Blog Talk Radio show, and I had three bestselling titles and was making more money than I ever saw in my life. People began to reach out to me on social media. They wanted me to publish their work, and—*bam*—I was a small press overnight. My responsibilities were starting to triple. But my writing took a backseat to publishing, my royalties began to suffer, and there was turmoil in my small company. Then without warning, my father's cancer metastasized. He passed away in May, and I found out about it on Facebook. I couldn't function. I let go of the authors I signed. My health took a turn for the worse.

I couldn't keep my fancy new house, and my second truck was repoed.

2014 to present

I attempted to revive my publishing company without resolving all my underlying issues. On the surface, I was fine. I was dieting, working out, and finally, under a doctor's care for my thyroid disease. I was thriving, losing weight, and making moves. However, beneath the surface, I was a wreck. My emotions were out of control. I found it hard to focus. And when I did focus, it was on the wrong shit. As a result, my business and my writing suffered. My entire life started spinning out of control.

I wrote several other books but put no heart into their promotion, so they did not do well. I closed my social media accounts and decided to walk away from the industry for good . . . but my readers wouldn't let that stand. I started receiving emails and handwritten notes from my readers and texts and phone calls from my peers. I returned to social media and went on tour to meet the people who pulled me out of the dark. Meeting my readers around the country was the medicine that I needed. It was soul food. My readers reminded me of why I write. They blew life back into my dream, and I am forever grateful. Now that Urban Books has picked up my work, I get to meet more readers, which is a dream come true.

I am back, baby. I write drama, and thanks to my readers, my partners Braheim and Charlotte, my writing coach Shonell, my agent K'wan, and the good folks at Urban Books, I will continue to do so.

With Love,
Julia